Con ACJ5722

810.8035 Gay travels.
GAY

DATE			

BAKER & TAYLOR

Gay
Travels

A Literary Companion

—

EDITED BY
Lucy Jane Bledsoe

WHEREABOUTS PRESS   SAN FRANCISCO

Permissions continued on page 242.

Published in the United States by Whereabouts Press
2219 Clement Street, Suite 18
San Francisco, California 94121
www.whereaboutspress.com

Distributed to the trade by
Consortium Book Sales & Distribution

Designed and produced by BookMatters.

Manufactured in the United States of America.

Library of Congress Cataloging-in-Publication Data
Gay travels : a literary companion / edited by Lucy Jane Bledsoe.
p.   cm.
ISBN 1-883513-06-5
1. Gay men—Travel—Literary collections.
2. Americans—Travel—Literary collections.
3. Voyages and travels—Literary collections.
4. American prose literature—20th century.
5. Gay men's writings, American.
I. Bledsoe, Lucy Jane
PS647.G39G39   1998
810.8'0355—dc21   98–19303
CIP

10 9 8 7 6 5 4 3 2 1

Contents

A character in an Oscar Wilde comedy remarks that having her diary by her side while traveling is a great comfort because she is therefore always assured of having something scandalous to read on the train.

Wilde being droll was Wilde at his most authentic. In addition, he appears to have augured an impending century of homosexual writers who would go on to keep diaries, pen travel books, write memoirs, and somehow commix them all, creating a new form: not unequivocally fact, not demonstrably fiction, yet with the advantages and usefulness of both, and with a bit extra, that immeasurably attractive property that subatomic physicists have come to refer to as "charm."

I think immediately of that most disreputable volume of revelations, *The Diaries of Roger Casement,* by an Irish diplomat who traveled extensively, had gay sex several times daily, and kept detailed notes of each encounter, including exact penis size and the precise amount of semen discharged. By some unforeseen algebra indicative of what would often later recur, Casement's sex—and his writing about it—improved the more distant from home he traveled. And while those scalding diaries would end up destroying Casement once they were used as evidence at his trial for treason, it is difficult for us to read them without marveling at his sexual appetite, his daring at initiating encounters in any language—and his long run of luck!

Far more sexually circumspect—and successful, once his works reached publication—was Norman Douglas, lover for decades to the husband of the American heiress and lesbian painter Romaine Brooks. Douglas's pre–World War I books about southern Italy—*Siren Land, Old Calabria, Fountains in the Sun,* et al.—seamlessly integrate history, landscape, and portraiture. And what portraits he paints! Each Italian boy, youth, and young man glitters and glows and glowers in Douglas's supple prose, attracting new travelers to Reggio and Anacapri, Messina and Taormina, decades after he and those lads are long gone. Almost simultaneously and in the very same locales, Baron von Gloeden was photographing Sicilian and Sardinian boys, scantily clad in his own renditions of chitons and togas *avec* laurel wreaths, as he went about creating his own unique, pseudo-Greco-Roman visual travel diary. Apparently these were the same photos Henry James grumbled were being handed around by Hugh Walpole and the younger gay set in Westminster Cathedral to enliven Poet Laureate Robert Browning's otherwise cheerless memorial service. The Miss Manners in James thought this inappropriate behavior, although given Browning's broad love of all things Italian, many might differ.

Appropriateness becomes a most debatable issue not twenty years later in what is one of my desert island books, J. R. Ackerly's *Hindoo Holiday.* The opening says it all: "He wanted someone to love him—His Highness, I mean: that was his real need, I think." And so he hired Ackerly as an English tutor and dragged him across the world to a small kingdom in the heart of colonial India, a true "fairy" realm, in that the maharajah who summoned Ackerly was openly gay and surrounded himself with gay boys and men. "The Greeks are born again in Chhrokrapur," the maharajah assured Ackerly, as, melancholically and mock-tragically, he pursued a life of gay romance—to his eventual disillusionment and to our endless delight, thanks to Ackerly's book.

Since the 1930s the flood sluices have flown open, and today one can find travel writing by good homosexual writers (albeit mostly closeted) on every library shelf. E. M. Forster and Somerset Maugham spring to mind most prominently, although later another closeted Brit, Bruce Chatwin, made a substantial run at their eminence. But if I had to choose my own circa-Stonewall favorites, rather than anything by Chatwin, I would opt for Truman Capote's delicious, malicious *The Muses Are Heard,* an account of a U.S. State Department–sponsored African-American touring company that brought Gershwin's opera *Porgy and Bess* to mystified audiences across the Soviet Union; and Tobias Schneebaum's amazing ethnography *Keep the River on the Right,* an account of his year living in the males-only long hut of a group of New Guinea cannibals, sleeping and having sex with them, hunting alongside them, and even joining to war against their enemies.

What sets this book apart, what makes it so absorbing, is that every author here is an openly gay man writing from that perspective. Only the pieces by James Baldwin and Joe Orton predate that defining moment in gay history, the Stonewall Riot. Of the other authors, a handful are from the founding generation of overtly gay writers, others are just becoming established, and still others are up-and-coming writers. As a result we are able to read about places and people, adventures and misadventures, as if we were there ourselves. No need to ask, "What if I were there with my lover?" or "Will I be looked down on if alone? Out of place? Culturally shocked?" These men will tell you.

This volume makes no attempt to rival those gay travel guides that already exist. It is something different, far more intriguing: a collection of stories that aim at being what Herman Melville deemed "an inside narrative." That is, what being a gay man in a foreign land really feels like, smells like, tastes like, and hurts like. The voices here might be likened to those of friends sitting around a dinner table the night before your journey who provide you with insights and warnings that only later do you discover add infinitely to your excursion.

But it is the book's diversity that is its greatest asset. As one delves further and deeper into the unexplored—whether in travel or in life—the very best companion may end up being the one who is the most multifaceted.

Felice Picano
JANUARY 1998

For me, literature and travel are inextricably linked. Opening a book is much like entering a new country. I read for the same reasons that I travel: to pry open my limited world view. Of course it is possible to read only those books that reflect one's own ideas and lifestyle, to travel in a manner that bolsters one's concept of oneself and one's place in the world. But a true traveler, like a true reader, enjoys stretching his or her limits, crossing borders, even scary ones.

Because border-crossings are about change, new territory, and anticipation, they make great stories. And because gay people have special expertise in crossing borders, we have access to a special kind of travel story. All gay men and lesbians who come out cross a border of sexuality, which for many of us contributes to our feeling like outsiders (often gladly) within the dominant culture. With varying degrees of success, we learn to cope. This outsider status at home can have a profound effect on our experiences traveling in other countries, or even within this country. It is possible, though certainly not always the case, that our experience of difference increases our sensitivity to difference abroad, allowing us to look more deeply into the place we are visiting, to see beyond cultural constructs—particularly our own. Our strategies for negotiating as queer people in a straight world, strategies that work in some parts of the United States, may not work abroad or in other parts of this country. Yet for the lover of travel, these are exactly the reasons we do it: to place ourselves in contexts that challenge our assumptions, help us to see more clearly our individual and cultural characteristics. For the gay traveler, this opportunity is multidimensional. The essays in this book reveal the adventures of seventeen gay men as they discover more about themselves and others through travel.

Twenty years ago, a trip to northern Africa presented me with an experience of gender separatism unrivaled by anything in the United States of any decade, including that one—the 1970s. I traveled with my girlfriend to Tangier where she was making a film. One night, the mixed-gender film crew was invited to a private party in a Moroccan home. We dressed as appropriately as we knew how, meaning that, in spite of the heat, I covered everything but my face. The moment we arrived, my girlfriend and I were whisked upstairs to the awaiting women's party, but on the way I peeked into the westernized living room where the Moroccan men stood stiffly, holding what looked like bourbon on the rocks, in gray business suits and conservative ties.

Upstairs was another story. The women were traditionally decked in layers of brightly colored cloth laced with glittering gold lamé threads. They delighted in teaching us how to eat properly and in forcing us to eat much more than we wanted. Then the real party began. Someone put on a record and the oldest, fattest woman began dancing slowly, removing first her *dfina*, a shimmering, transparent outer layer, and then even her kaftan, revealing a great expanse of simultaneously undulating and jiggling flesh. Our yips, clapping, and raucous laughter drifted down the stairway to the men's party below, which, we later learned from our male American cohorts, consisted of endless discussion about the newest technology, no food, and definitely no belly-dancing.

This perfect travel experience illuminated both the Moroccan culture and my own. The Arabic approach to separatism, although brutally exclusive in many ways, allowed women a wild kind of freedom within their own realm, even the freedom to dance erotically for one another. I realized that the system did have some advantages, advantages that might even apply in the United States. Yet, in the end, I understood the disappointment of the American men from the film crew who chafed at being excluded from the happening party. As a traveler, as a border-crosser, I couldn't imagine a lifetime of separate parties.

Therefore, my initial vision for the book you now hold was a co-gender world tour: an anthology of lesbian and gay travel stories. I wanted our communities to celebrate culture and travel together. However, there were just too many good stories! The opportunity to present twice as many essays convinced me to divide the project. *Gay Travels* and *Lesbian Travels* are setting out as traveling companions under separate titles.

Searching and soliciting pieces for this book was a wild journey in itself, giving me an excuse to sit down and read, or reread, such classics as James Baldwin's *The Price of the Ticket* and Christopher Isherwood's *Condor and the Cow*, as well the travel diaries of Stephen Spender, Joe Orton, André Gides, Paul Bowles, and many, many others. In the end, I chose to use only pieces that were contemporary (which I defined as those whose authors' lives overlapped mine). I had a strong preference for writing that told a story, nonfiction narratives rather than philosophical musings. I also chose to use pieces in which the author's gayness was explicit because, after all, that is what is unique about our generation of writers. Most important, I looked for fine writing. My greatest interest lay in writing that explored the deeper meaning of boundaries—not just geographical, but cultural, sexual, intellectual, and even temporal.

The selection process for an anthology is tricky at best, and I have intentionally included a wide diversity of material. Because this is the first anthology of openly gay travel writing, I wanted to provide a spectrum of styles and stories. Here are sto-

ries about sex, stories about grief, funny stories, and serious stories. All are true. All are gay. All are about travel.

I am truly grateful for the help I have received from many
sources. First of all, a big thank you to Mary Bisbee-Beek, whose
early interest in the book made an enormous difference. Besides
the sheer fun and excitement of receiving e-mails from eastern
Europe and faxes from the Netherlands, I was deeply moved by
the generosity and charm of so many of the contributors. For
sharing their Rolodexes and reading knowledge, and in some
cases much-needed encouragement and enthusiasm, I am grateful to Brian Bouldrey, Michael Bronksi, Katherine Forrest, Ed
Hermance, Andrew Holleran, Richard Labonte, Michael Lowenthal, Michael Nava, Felice Picano, Susan Fox Rogers, Sarah
Schulman, and Jerry Thompson. For love, travel companion-
ship, endless listening, and amazingly on-the-mark advice about
all matters, but especially concerning this book, I thank Patricia
Mullan.

I have been very lucky with publishers, and Whereabouts
Press is no exception. After all, if you're going to do a book, it
had better be fun. Thank you to David Peattie and Ellen Towell
for their good humor, insistence on making beautiful books,
and accessibility.

This book has been like all journeys, sometimes joyous and
sometimes a struggle, but what a wonderful bunch of traveling
companions! *Gay Travels* has widened my sense of community.
I hope it does yours as well.

Lucy Jane Bledsoe
FEBRUARY 1998

Brian Bouldrey

Pilgrim's Regress

After the apostle James the Greater was martyred in Jerusalem, his followers took his decapitated body in a rudderless stone boat and, praying to God for guidance, sailed for many weeks until they landed on the northwestern coast of what is now Spain. They placed his body on a boulder that immediately softened like wax and shaped itself into a sarcophagus. Beginning in the eleventh century, pilgrims have come to this shrine, Santiago de Compostela, on foot, on horseback, and, in these days, on bicycle.

Louk, the Dutchman I'd walked with for the first two days out of St. Jean Pied-de-Port, must have thought I was the dopey naive American incarnate: I'd come without a sleeping bag (several guidebooks suggested that they were a good idea but not required), my pack was too heavy, and now this—THIS!—I'd walked into Spain without a single peseta.

I don't know what I was thinking, except that perhaps Roncesvalles was a town, not just a monastery. I had visions of the way tourist towns go: restaurants that honor Visa, Coca-Cola machines, and a convenient ATM installed in the side of a church. After all, at the monastery in Samos there's a gas station; in one of my most beloved photos, a shrine of the Virgin rises above an overloaded dumpster. Somehow, to my dismay, Roncesvalles has remained pure.

We'd crossed into Spain on a Saturday. Even if the villages we passed had banks, it was now Sunday, and everything was closed.

At lunchtime in Linzoain, a weensy village that venerated St. Saturnine, Louk said, "Good thing I'm taking care of you," and bought our *bocadillos* with the pesetas he'd had the foresight to change back in St. Jean Pied-de-Port. I let him chide me, though I would have liked to point out that he wouldn't have gotten his sandwich exactly the way he wanted it if I hadn't ordered for him. Louk knew a lot of languages, but not a word of Spanish.

From around the corner came a *romero*, a gypsy, with a rucksack. He sat down next to us on the picnic table. I'd dealt a little with gypsies in Seville the year before. If they managed to get their sprig of rosemary into your hands, you were doomed until you gave them money. Of course, I knew all about the practice of mistrusting gypsies, but for *americanos*, gypsies were more theoretical than the nuisance Europeans made them out to be. I watched Louk shut down as I fearlessly made conversation with the stranger, practicing my Spanish and asking questions.

He was a curiosity. First of all, he was wall-eyed. Second of all, he was traveling alone, something I don't think of gypsies as doing. Most important, he was a pilgrim, but traveling in the opposite direction, away from Santiago. The perversity thrilled me.

"I'm going to Rome," he explained. "I hope to be there by Christmas." He'd left Santiago on July 25, St. James Day. He showed me his *compostela,* something I looked forward to getting myself. He had a pilgrim's passport, he was for real; he was going to all the places we had already been to, and he was eager to tell me about all the places I'd be going.

He pulled out a folded, tattered list of *refugios* he had stayed in and began to rate them for me. He told me a tantalizing story about the hostel in Ribadixo, hundreds of miles away in Galicia. Next to it he wrote "Dream of Peregrino." He said something about rowing out to an island in a river, where the refuge was beneath—what? I was struggling with my Spanish—a trap door? I imaged a wide lake, a castle in the middle, a boatman transporting Christians to safety for a coin. *Arzúa, muy mal. Puente la*

Reina, muchos gentes. All the way down his ratty sheet he'd write *sí* or *no.* He handed me his list as a gift.

I kept talking to him, while Louk looked on askance. He didn't like my encouraging the gypsy and kept studying his own little guidebook.

The gypsy, whose name was Jesús, wanted to know about the *refugios* in the other direction. What could he expect? Did he have to pay? Would they understand his Spanish? He asked me, "How do I say this in French?" and wrote on a slip of paper, "Could you please give a pilgrim some money?"

In English, sounding as naive as I could, I asked Louk, "How do you say this in French?" Louk narrowed his eyes, then slipped on his backpack.

"I'm going to get a head start," he said. "Since you're so fast, you'll catch up to me soon."

The barkeep came out, perhaps out of concern for me, left alone with the gypsy. I wondered whether Jesús could see it, was he used to it, did he get this wherever he went?

In the Middle Ages, gypsies surged into Spain because of the Camino de Santiago. The Pope had given the king of the gypsies a piece of paper to carry that gave them access to every inn and church along the way. "Please take care of these good people," it said. "They are God's children, and there will be a reward for your hospitality in heaven." The gypsies took advantage of this letter for hundreds of years before anyone wised up.

The barkeep wanted to know, Is everything all right here? Do I need to get rid of this guy for you? But what he said was, "Anything else to eat?"

I wanted to show I was comfortable with the situation. I had my backpack pinned beneath my knees and if he really wanted my walking stick, I knew I'd find another one eventually. *"Café con leche, por favor,"* I said. I would catch up to Louk fairly quickly.

"*Un bocadillo de queso,*" said Jesús. The barkeep looked at him, but he went in and made the sandwich.

I turned to Jesús. He pointed at the slip of paper again. I said, "I think you say '*Donnez-moi d'argent.*'"

"*Bueno,*" he said. "*Donnez-moi d'argent.*'"

"*Sí.*"

He looked at me with that wall eye. "*Sí. Donnez-moi d'argent.*"

I laughed, despite the situation. "Oh, I see." The barkeep came out with his sandwich and my coffee. "But you see, I don't have any. Truly, none at all. In fact," I suddenly realized in my absent-minded state, "I don't even have money to pay for this coffee." I must have looked panicky.

This is when I experienced my first true Miracle of Santiago. Jesús, my gypsy friend, who had already given me his secret list of *refugios,* pulled a small coin purse out of his pocket and motioned to the barkeep, who stood in the portal of his little shop, draped with that curtain of beads which was meant, I guess, to discourage flies from coming in. He pulled out the pesetas and motioned at my coffee and his sandwich. "*Todo junto,*" he said, "all together." And he paid for my coffee.

Essentially, a gypsy had given me money. The barkeep looked as astonished as I did.

Jesús got up, slipping on his *mulchila.* "*Gracias,*" I kept saying. "*Buen viaje.*" He said the same to me. I turned, invigorated by unlooked-for generosity and *café con leche,* and scampered off, eager to catch up with Louk, to tell him about the miraculous occurrence.

It wasn't until I caught sight of Louk on the road ahead that I realized that my pockets were full of francs, a currency now useless to me, but the very thing my gypsy friend needed.

And the gypsy's gift was one that kept giving: the piece of paper with his scribbles and ratings turned out to be dead-on accurate. We learned to avoid the places he had written *no* beside and sought out the ones he'd written *sí* next to. It became known, among my fellow pilgrims, as "The Gypsy's Guide to Santiago."

Of all the pilgrims I met on the road to Santiago—the quack Italian bone doctor, the Madrid bullfighters, the French lady who carried all of her things in two shopping bags, the Brazilian pilot—the one who haunted me most was the wall-eyed gypsy, alone, walking against the flow. His goal had come and gone, and yet he struck me as the most authentic of us, the solitary sojourner who had turned desire into longing, removed the objective from his sight, and continued on anyway.

From the very beginning of my journey, the road markers had constantly reminded pilgrims of how many kilometers there were to go. For the last one hundred, stone markers announced every single kilometer, like a countdown. It reminded me, among many other unpleasant things, of a dwindling T-cell count. It also warned us that we would all soon disperse, fly to our separate corners of the earth, and resume regular lives. One phenomenon of the past five days had been the multiplication of blisters on my fellow pilgrims' feet. I took these wounds to be a sign of reluctance, of a resistance to the coming end of our journey, a statement, by the body, of its unwillingness to reach point zero.

How free the wall-eyed gypsy must have felt, without the burden of those numbers.

Since A.D. 700, pilgrims have been coming to Santiago from all over the world, walking the same path I'm walking, complaining about their feet, sharing jokes with other pilgrims, looking forward to that day when we all arrive at the Pórtico de la Gloria in the cathedral and get our *compostela,* a certificate that gets you a third, more or less, off purgatory.

Why were we still making the pilgrimage? I'd been afraid that I'd be surrounded by religious fanatics, but so had everybody else. With a few exceptions, we were all agnostics or unsure Catholics mutually agreed that we're stuck with this religion, going to Santiago to find out if there was any way to make peace with it. Louk, forced into retirement by Shell Oil, was hoping to find something else to do with his life.

For three days we had walked along with five Belgian men, who mostly kept their distance in the evenings but were very talkative during the day's hike. I got to know Pietr well, one of the three who were taking orders from the other two. Every morning, the two order-giving ones, both short, blond, and taciturn, would say in Flemish (therefore I approximate), "O.K., you guys, time to get up, let's get moving." Pietr and I talked for three days about our mutual interests—opera, literature, travel, good wine.

We passed by Irache, a vintner famous for giving free wine to pilgrims. You simply filled your travel cup with as much as you could drink. Although we'd arrived at nine in the morning, this didn't stop most of us. But when Pietr reached for his collapsible cup, one of the two phlegmatic blonds said, "No, stay away." Pietr frowned, but obeyed.

I furrowed my brow and asked Pietr, "Why do you take orders from those guys?"

Pietr smiled. "Well, you see, I am a prisoner."

A prisoner? So were the other two men who were taking commands. No shackles, no firearms, who could tell? It seems a Belgian law that dates back to medieval days allows criminals to be punished by sending them to Santiago. My fellow Belgian pilgrims were doing penance, with the added punishment of fixing church doors along the way.

"What did you do?" I asked Pietr.

He never told me explicitly, although I heard farther down the trail that all three were embezzlers. "White-collar crime" is all he would tell me.

"So," I wondered out loud, "if you're going to Santiago as a punishment, why am I going?"

Pietr was amused. "Oh, Brian, you haven't heard?" He explained it to me: "When you reach Santiago to receive your *compostela,* you are also given a coupon from the archbishop. This coupon you may use to commit a murder." We all laughed. "One murder," he clarified, "or two armed robberies."

The Belgians stopped in Viana that day, to fix a door. I never saw them again.

My journal contains lots of reasons I was going to Santiago. For the cultural history. For the architecture, the exercise, the friendship. One murder, two armed robberies.

The main reason, the dramatic one, the true one, however, had slipped away, because I was no longer going to die, at least not tomorrow.

I'd watched my partner, Jeff, and many other friends make desperate moves to thwart death: They'd changed their blood, ingested the poisonous essence of peach pits, and submitted to the pharmaceutical shakedowns that can only be referred to as severe baroque—a term I'd use to describe the cathedral in Burgos as well—only to succumb to the virus anyway.

I hadn't been sick enough to plunge into any of these risk-taking activities, but I had had my own crazy seat-of-the-pants lifestyle: no savings, no 401(k). I'd thrown all my money into travel: I'd gone nude waterskiing in Alaska, climbed down sheer cliff faces in the Italian Alps, and stowed away on trains into Portugal. Santiago was one more—or one last—notch in my bedpost.

I'd also thought of *The Canterbury Tales.* The holy blissful matyr was said to heal the sick, if you came to see him. The cast of characters I met as I walked across Spain rivaled Chaucer's ribald gang, including Sandi, the completely deaf translator of four languages; Gabriel, the retired photographer of the great bullfighters; and Dani, the twenty-something Mallorcan who'd read more American literature than I had. Many pilgrims I met were going in hopes of miracle cures.

I had already had the miracle cure! At least, I had had the miracle stave-off-er, the antiviral cocktail of three blue tablets, one brick-red capsule, and one little white diamond that looks like the French Bar-Tabac signs I'd seen north of the Pyrenees.

Another miracle that my dead friends could never have imagined is how painless these pills are. Clean as a whistle, although a two-month supply to be hauled over the mountains and across Spain did, for a while, seem heavy. But, in any case, no stomach-rotting failed remedies, no diarrhea, no headaches, no nothing.

I am not a fan of miracles, or miracle-workers. Magicians dazzle me, all kinds—skilled writers, excellent musicians, good lovers, chefs—all those who overpower the senses and make my imagination go limp. Yes, I yield without hesitation to those with the power to allow me to slumber in the present without thought of past or future, because they don't need me to do any of their work.

Santiago's miracles are more subtle. He awakens the imagination and revives the sleeper until the past, the present, and the future are all one.

> In the Middle Ages, when a Pilgrim came to Satitiago, he made his visit to the cathedral, and then continued on to Finisterre, the end of the earth. There he would toss his old clothes into the sea and begin the long journey home.

My backpack felt light. This was supposed to have been a grueling day, but I was full of energy coming into Burgos and I couldn't figure out why. Twenty-eight kilometers must have been a miscount! I'd been so nervous about the toughness of the day's journey—and the lack of coffee—that I'd forgotten to put on sunblock.

After a shower at the hostel, my German friend Petra and

our Swiss friend Jean-Philippe went into town to shop for new walking shoes. Petra's husband, Matthias, and I suggested we meet them in the Plaza Mayor after we had visited the cathedral.

It was only when we finally met up with the other two that I really started to limp.

I ordered a fizzy lemon soda. Petra gave me an aspirin.

"You look terr-EE-blay," said Matthias.

"I feel terr-EE-blay," I said. "Did you find shoes for Jean-Philippe?"

I was in pain, but I could see that the plaza was pleasant. Everybody was out on it. Petra was wearing that damned Indian cotton-print skirt again, which she always managed to make look slightly different, hitching it up, pulling it in, accessorizing. She joked with me now and then about having her nails done or slipping out for a bubble bath or shopping for some high heels, but she loved this, the simplicity of it all. For all that, I thought, she was an amazing woman, one who could make a couple of bracelets, a little lipstick, and that same old Indian skirt look new every evening.

In the Plaza Mayor, locals talked with their friends and had a glass of wine. There's no such thing as prime-time television in Spain, and nobody seemed sorry about it. I certainly wasn't.

But I was hunched down. I must have let loose a groan, because my friends looked at each other with great concern.

I started to shiver. I said I should go back to the hostel. Petra said she would go with me, since she wanted to get some food for the next day. Jean-Philippe said he and Matthias wanted to look in one more shoe store, but then they would bring some sandwiches back and we could have an early dinner and I could go to sleep.

By then, the aspirin was upsetting my stomach. I followed Petra into the market just off the plaza. I felt achy and feverish. It must have been sun poisoning—sun stroke or sun poisoning; I always got the two confused.

In the *alimentario* it was warm and airless. All the wheels of *manchego* cheese in the room were ripe. My ears began to buzz, and I got dizzy and started to sweat from head to foot. *"Estoy muy enfermo,"* I said calmly. I had a strange out-of-body look at the situation, which, my assessment was, could not be helped.

This must be what happens, I thought, when you faint. I'd never fainted before. *"Hay servicios?"* No, there were no bathrooms, but perhaps in a bar down the street.

Time was running out. I ran into the street, if only to get away from the warmth and the smell of cheese.

Once I was out of the store the dizziness increased, and I noticed a little kid riding on a dolphin-shaped mechanical ride, the kind you put a few coins in and it bobbles up and down to carnival music. This one played a relentless, passionless version of "There's No Place Like Home" over and over and over. It was like one of those over-the-top scenes in a Tennessee Williams play, in which the main character's sanity, exposed as a house of cards, tumbles down before your very eyes, and the demented calliope toodles on and on and the funhouse mirrors shiver and all the world is laughing and jeering and there's no exit from the room and then—

And then I barfed into a planter. And felt instantly better.

Petra saw the whole thing. She patted my back and handed me a third lemonade. She'd gone through with all her purchases, even though I was vomiting in public. What else could she do? She had a loaf of bread and three small sweet buns, a can of olives, and a wedge of cheese. Ten minutes before, the sight of these things would have made me barf. Now that I had anyway, now that I'd gotten the poison out of me, I was starving. "Can I have one of those buns?" I begged her.

I think it relieved her that she could do something. I kept saying, "I feel so much better. I feel so much better."

We walked along the river. It was early evening. She wasn't saying anything. Looking back, I think she was terrified.

I said, "I forgot to put on sunblock today."

"Stupid boys," she said, blaming the foolish bravado of my sex rather than me, which didn't sound true to either of us. That's the thing about swearing off machismo: you can't depend on he-man bonehead courage, the fools-rush-in heroics of masculinity, to cover up for your idiocy. You yourself have to take the blame for your own bad judgment.

The river babbled. Petra wanted to say something, I thought, maybe to soothe me, but she was at a loss. I was trying to think of something to say to reassure her that the illness was over, that I felt one hundred percent better, which I really did. She handed me a second sweet roll. "Brian," she said, reluctantly, "We think you should stop the pilgrimage."

"Stop? Why would I do that? I just did a Stupid Boy thing, I just forgot to put on the sunblock."

"We have heard about how you are dying."

"Dying?" I sputtered, and stood stock-still under a huge stone tablet declaring that here, here on this spot, Franco took control of Spain.

O, Peregrino.

Suddenly, everything made sense. Somehow, somewhere along the way, I had told a fellow pilgrim about my HIV status. When was it? At the drunken dinner in the Basque village? Under the influence of *pacharán*, that devil's drink?

It was Louk, the Dutchman, I was sure. He had fallen behind our group about a week before because one of his feet had swollen up, and I'd probably told him when he was at his brattiest, complaining about being an old man. Probably I wanted to eclipse his little drama with my own, to shut him up once and for all. (It never did work.) But wouldn't I have told him the whole story?

For weeks now, they must have been fretting about me, always watching the poor dying boy, who was forever laughing and telling funny stories but was secretly in pain and not long for this world. Smiling on the outside, crying on the inside. Oh, brother.

I set her straight. I told her everything I knew. When I first planned my pilgrimage to Santiago, I thought it *would* be my last hurrah. My T-cell count had gone down to such a level that I had to start cutting back, doing less. I had imagined myself using the last of my strength to . . . to do what?—to thank St. James, to thank somebody, for having been allowed, once more, the chance of a full, long life. What a nice bit of closure, I had thought, an ending that I could control, no matter what fate might ultimately be delivered.

But a year before the trip I got into a study for the then experimental protease inhibitors, the drugs that turned out to work like a charm. By the time I set out for Spain my T-cell count had climbed to where it had been years before. So, although my health had never been failing, I had become a pilgrim possessed of all the strength and vitality of a man who'd escaped death, at least for a while.

Now, I told Petra, my pilgrimage was not to thank St. James for a life well lived, but for a second life, the one I didn't think I was going to have. "I can't quit now, Petra, because this is not the end for me. In fact, everybody wants me to start my life all over again."

She had torn off a little bit of bread. She wasn't weeping, but she was full in the throat with a kind of joy that I hadn't experienced myself over this revelation, because it had not, until this moment, hit me so dramatically, so collapsed in time. When I saw how she saw it—that I wasn't going to die, that I was going to live—I thought to myself, yes, you are right, what a happy ending it actually is. Let the new beginning begin.

When Jean-Philippe and Matthias got back to the hostel (still shoeless), Petra must have run out to tell them. They gathered around my bunk, where I'd already taken a sleeping pill in hope of getting a long night's sleep, since we were surrounded by a fleet of German cyclists. Matthias wanted to toast my long life—ugh, with *pacharán*. They were so relieved that they made me feel relieved for the first time in many years.

A British naval captain gives a toast: "Sweethearts and wives— may they never meet!" and we all laugh and chug our *pacharán*. We are on a postpilgrimage pilgrimage, all of us marveling at ourselves for having actually done it, all six hundred miles of it, are we crazy or what? We are on the "Paris-Dakkar run," a long alley of bars named after cities along the course of that famous road race. The point is to have a drink in every bar along the street, the last at the finish line in Dakkar.

I look down at the ground as I trundle off to the next bar, and it's surface doesn't seem important—paved, gravel, grass, mud: who cares now? I am reminded of Elizabeth Bishop's poem about Robinson Crusoe after he is rescued, how he had prayed every day that his knife would not break, but now it is useless, destined, at best, only for a museum.

There has long been an urgency to my life that, now that danger has been (at least for the moment) avoided, baffles me. Growing old used to be an impossible object of desire. Now, the promise of early death has evaporated. Now I am the wall-eyed gypsy going to Rome.

Finding something on the other side of Santiago, something on the other side of HIV, is the challenge in a life that I had decided long ago was going to be miniaturized but has suddenly telescoped out. Should I be so sad about having an empty dance card?

We are all a little sad on the Paris-Dakkar run, even though Jean-Philippe has bought us a bottle of *pacharán* and Petra has publicly incinerated her cotton-print skirt. Matthias and I take to commiserating about sex.

"Look at the Brazilian." He points to a man we had dined with a week before and who had impressed me with his ability to speak several languages perfectly. He has reappeared at a table with a handful of beautiful women hanging on his every drunken word. "How does he do it?" Matthias wanted to know, searching for the right word in English, "with his four ... four ..."

"Languages?" I offer.

"No, Brian, women!" My pilgrim friends have accepted my homosexuality in this way: Brian prefers languages to women.

Tomorrow we will have to go our separate ways. In the Middle Ages, pilgrims spent a year walking to the shrine, and then, unlike us moderns, who jump on a plane, had to walk all the way home. I wonder what that would have been like: the real point of the pilgrimage wasn't to arrive at Santiago, but to arrive back home. And going home must have seemed a lot harder, more of a penance, more of a sacrifice.

I had walked six hundred miles in two months, my own sacrifice to time. Now, time was not so much an enemy of mine, but a thing inside me like the virus.

What I want to say is that it seemed strangely easier to live when there was no life left. Manners seemed absurd. So did conserving, waiting, restraining myself.

"When it is finally seen," laments Matthew Stadler, a writer I admire, "childhood has a trajectory, a countdown aimed toward zero. This is the sickness of nostalgia."

When we reach Santiago, or mandatory retirement, or the last T-cell, that point zero has to be a beginning, not an end. Like the wall-eyed gypsy, we must go back to where we came from, armed now not with the joy of sacrifice, but only with the Dream of the Peregrino.

Philip Gambone

Invading Their Space

On the day I flew to China last fall to begin a three-month teaching job, I announced to my friends that I was "determined to find gay life in Beijing." They smiled indulgently.

I understood their skepticism. For months, I'd been trying to find information about the gay scene in China, but my efforts kept running into dead ends. A gay Chinese graduate student whom I'd contacted summed up the situation.

"There is *no* gay culture and almost no gay life in Beijing," he told me. "Gays are very invisible." He went on to say that now, at the American university where he was pursuing his doctorate, he had joined the gay student organization. "Something unthinkable" in China, he added.

Despite all this discouraging news, I remained undaunted. In a country of more than a billion people, in a city of twelve million, there had to be gay people and a gay subculture.

Once I got to Beijing, it took me two weeks to find it. But the graduate student was right. Gay life *is* invisible in Beijing. Nevertheless, it's there, pushed underground by a combination of governmental and societal antipathy. Through word of mouth, I learned of a gay bar, a gay-friendly disco, a gay hotline, and even an underground AIDS newsletter. Pirated gay videos—films like *Philadelphia, The Bird Cage,* and *Maurice*—secretly circulate.

Most Chinese gay life takes place clandestinely—in parks and public toilets. Of the thirty or so gay men I met during my stay in Beijing, most, if not all of them, frequented the parks. What most surprised me, though, was the fact that the parks functioned not just as places for quickie, anonymous sex, but as venues to make more lasting connections with other gay men. In the absence of gay clubs and coffee houses, the parks, and even the WCs, provided the arena in which gay men began friendships and romances.

It was not until my final week in Beijing that I learned of another underground meeting place, one I hadn't expected. A gay bathhouse. I'd heard rumors that such a place existed and had even met an American who claimed to have been there, though he would not tell me where it was located. (I think he wanted to keep it for himself.) Having pretty much dismissed the idea, but still curious, I casually brought it up with my Chinese friend Yuan one evening while he and I and my American friend Mike were having dinner.

"Oh, yes," Yuan said. "I've been there. It's not exactly gay. I mean, it's a typical old-style bathhouse where Chinese go to wash and socialize, but most of the guys there are gay. Do you want to check it out?"

Did I! Yuan gave us directions: take the subway to a certain stop, walk west down the main street, turn here, turn there. Finally, we were to look for a white sign on which there were four Chinese characters painted in black.

"That's the sign for the bathhouse."

A few days later, Mike and I were on our way. But Mike was nervous. He'd never been to a gay bathhouse. What would it be like, he kept asking me. Would he be accosted by a lot of dirty old men? I described my experiences at the few bathhouses I'd been to.

"You'll be amazed at how many cute guys just like you there are," I told him.

But this was *China*, Mike insisted. Maybe things would be completely different. I looked into his blue eyes.

"There's only one way to find out," I said.

Mike kept stalling. First, he said, he had some shopping to do, then we had to go back to his hotel to drop off his purchases, and then to McDonald's (there are twenty-three of them in Beijing) to grab a hamburger.

"Mike, let's go," I urged, watching him work on his second Big Mac. "It's just a bathhouse. No one's going to attack you."

I finally managed to get him on the subway, which we took to the designated stop. We got off, proceeded according to Yuan's instructions, and found the street and a white sign with four black characters.

"Are you sure this is it?" Mike asked skeptically.

I had to admit that I wasn't sure. Apart from the unreadable sign, there was nothing to pin our certainty on.

"Well," I said, beginning to feel some of Mike's trepidation, "We'll go inside. If it's not the right place, we'll go to the zoo instead."

We walked in and found ourselves in a kind of lobby. On one side was a little food shop selling sodas, beer, and snacks. On the other, a laundry and dry cleaning business. Through the plate glass window I could see someone ironing. People were milling about. No one seemed to pay much attention to us.

"I don't think this is it," Mike declared.

"Wait," I said. At the back of the lobby I saw two doors, one marked with the Chinese character for man, the other with that for woman. Just as Yuan had described.

"Let's leave," Mike coaxed.

"Take a deep breath and follow me," I told him.

Opening the door marked "Men," we were greeted by the warm, humid aroma of . . . a bathhouse! We entered a small vestibule, at the right of which was an old man seated at a simple desk. The ticket seller, I guessed. I approached him and asked for two admittances. I'd picked up enough Mandarin to know how to say this, but just to be sure I held up two fingers. The old man smiled and nodded.

We paid our money—perhaps seventy-five cents apiece—in exchange for which we were given a pair of plastic sandals, a small piece of soap, and a numbered locker key.

"Come on," I said to Mike. We made our way into the central locker area. Immediately, many of the other patrons, all Chinese, stopped what they were doing. It seemed as if every eye had suddenly and simultaneously turned to watch us come through.

"Everyone's looking at us," Mike said.

"Keep smiling and act like you know what you're doing," I told him.

Following my own advice, I tried to keep up a confident look. The last thing I wanted was to project an air of uncertainty. I didn't want anyone getting the idea that we were hesitant about being here. Our diffidence might give them a reason to ask us to leave. The words of a friend of mine echoed in my mind: "You can get away with anything," he once told me, "if you just pretend hard enough."

I turned to Mike. "Now let's see. Where do you suppose our lockers are?"

We moved down one aisle, looking for our numbers. Between the banks of lockers there were cots on which a few men—older guys draped in towels—were relaxing, napping, or getting a massage. They looked up as we passed by.

Mike and I found our lockers and started to undress. The lockers were really wooden boxes, maybe the size of a large bread box, stacked on top each other. They didn't look particularly secure, but I decided we had no choice but to trust them. This whole experience, I could tell, was going to be one where we would have to wing it and hope for the best.

As I finished undressing, wrapping the skimpy towel around

my waist, I noticed a middle-aged man sitting on a bench a few feet away. Glaring at us, he whispered hostilely in English, "How *dare* you come here and invade our culture?"

I panicked. Did all the men who had been staring at us feel this way? Had I presumed wrong in thinking that the unwritten law of universal gay solidarity would prevail here?

Managing a friendly smile, I replied that our intentions were simply to relax and enjoy ourselves. "We're here for the same reason everyone else is," I said, hoping this was a signal he'd understand.

"How did you find out about this place?" He seemed to have calmed down a bit.

"A friend, a *Chinese* friend," I emphasized, "told us about it."

I decided that introductions were in order. Holding out my hand, I told him my name and introduced Mike, who was, to my surprise, already undressed. It was a delightfully unexpected turnaround from someone who'd been so reluctant to come. The man shook our hands.

"Do you understand what this place is?" he asked.

"Oh, yes," I assured him.

As we continued talking, the man, who told us he was a university professor, began to relax more and more. In fact, he seemed almost amused that we'd come to check out the bathhouse.

"What do you think of it?" he asked.

"It seems very friendly," I said. "In fact, all the"—I decided to hazard the word—"*gay* Chinese I've met so far in Beijing have been very friendly."

"You have to be careful," the professor said.

"I have no intention of doing anything foolish," I assured him. Rewrapping the towel around my waist, I added, "But I do want to see the rest of the place."

"There's the shower and bathing area." He pointed to the

back of the locker room. "And the sauna's over there. You have to pay extra for that."

Mike and I thanked him and, flip-flopping in our plastic sandals, made our way to the showers. It was a huge place, about as long as an Olympic-size swimming pool and two stories high with a skylight above. At each end were a dozen or so shower-heads, all occupied. Most of the room was taken up by a large pool, which itself was divided into sections: a central wading area and, at each end, a few long, troughlike sitting areas where men, chest-high in water, relaxed on benches that faced each other.

Trying not to look too self-conscious, Mike and I stood around waiting for a couple of showers to become free. At last two guys moved away and we took their places. By trial and error, we discovered that a rather rickety pedal mechanism controlled the flow of water from each shower. The water was surprisingly warm. We soaped up, rinsed off, then, not knowing what else to do, soaped up again.

Our neighbors were all Chinese—guys in their twenties and thirties. Some stared at us, some ignored us. A few caught our eyes and smiled. Some of them were washing each other, lathering up backs and chests. One or two had erections.

As we lathered up for the third time, Mike and I kept up a steady stream of conversation. It was awkward babble, noise to take the place of the nervousness we both felt. Not knowing how much cruising was permitted here, I tried keeping my eyes to myself. Still, it was hard not to notice that Mike and I were the only circumcised men in the place.

"What now?" Mike asked.

"I guess it's time to test out the pool," I suggested.

We picked up our towels and walked over to the central pool, an area about as large as two or three American hot tubs and almost as deep. Although the murky water was not particularly inviting, several of the guys lounging in it were. Over-coming our squeamishness, we abandoned our towels and eased ourselves in.

There was almost no room around the perimeter, which was lined with men, but somehow Mike managed to squeeze in be-tween two guys. That left no place for me but smack in the cen-ter of the pool. I felt very conspicuous. The fact that all the men in the pool, and most of the men in the neighboring pools, were looking at us didn't help matters. I settled in to see what would happen next.

Once again, Mike and I resumed the pretense that we were having a casual, nonchalant conversation, but all the while I kept vigilant as to what customs, conventions, and etiquette applied here. On trips to Europe, I'd been to bathhouses (or to use the term Europeans prefer, "saunas") in Florence, Bologna, Brussels, and Amsterdam. These were exclusively gay places—designed for gay men and their erotic pleasure. But this place was differ-ent. Yuan had told me that up to ninety percent of the men here would be gay, but the place seemed more like what I imagined an American YMCA from the forties or fifties must have felt like: loud, hearty, fraternal, and only slightly cruisy.

I looked around at my poolmates. Of the perhaps twenty of us in this central tub, about half were young guys in their twen-ties, the other half older men, upward of fifty. A few must have been married because at least one man had brought his two sons —both under eight—who were lounging and splashing and checking us out. In such a heterogeneous environment, it was hard to feel that I could be sexual. But this was China, where it's still virtually impossible to find an exclusively "gay space." The concept of privacy, even the word, hardly exists. Gay men share most of the few venues where they meet with their straight comrades. Even Beijing's one gay bar is staffed by straight bar-tenders.

"There's a guy staring at you who is *really* adorable," Mike said. "Right behind you."

Slowly I turned around. Mike was right. The guy was a cutie: black hair that fell winsomely over his forehead; dark, bright eyes; high, sculpted cheekbones; and a smooth, hairless chest. His two buddies were equally lovely. All three of them were cozied up together, staring, then whispering, then tittering like three young queens. We made eye contact and smiled.

"They seem very amused," I said to Mike.

"And very intrigued," he said.

Until coming to China, I hadn't given much thought to the erotic potential of Asian men, but my stay in Beijing was showing me otherwise. Never a big fan of gym-buffed, big-muscled American hunks, I'd fallen for the lithe bodies and boyish looks of the Chinese.

"This is so weird," Mike continued. "We can say whatever we want and no one will understand a word."

The cutie moved toward me and reached out to examine the necklace of beads I was wearing. He fingered it tenderly.

"It's Navajo Indian," I said, knowing he wouldn't understand a word of this. "*Meiguo.* American." He was standing now, the water only up to his navel. He motioned for me to give him the necklace. When I shook my head, he pouted and returned to his friends.

I wondered if he was a "money boy." I'd seen them at the bar, boys who will keep you company if you'll take care of them—dress them nicely, take them out to dinner, maybe give them an apartment.

"They're more like mistresses," a Chinese-American friend had explained. "It's not so cheap as to say, 'For fifty bucks I'll blow you.' It's not like that. It's more like, They want to latch on to you and have you put them up. And, sure, they'll be your companion."

But a money boy was not what I was after here. Suddenly, the smile disappeared from Mike's face.

"Something's hap-pen-ing," he said, drawing out the final word.

I turned to him now.

"What do you mean?"

"One of the guys next to me is touching my dick."

I couldn't tell from the wince on his face whether this was giving him pleasure or turning him off.

"Which one?" I asked, trying not to make eye contact with either guy. The one on Mike's right was young and pretty; the one on his left was an older man, probably in his late forties, with a slightly doughy, puffy face.

"I think the older one," Mike said. And again I was struck at how bizarre it was to be able to talk about people right in our midst and know we would not be understood.

"Well, are you enjoying it?" I asked.

Mike chuckled. "I want it to be the other one."

"Oops, me too," I said, feeling a hand caress my cock.

Nearby, about two feet away, another young man was looking at me. I could tell from the way his arm was extended under the murky water that he must be the one sampling my wares.

"That one?" Mike asked.

"Yeah, I think so."

Mike expressed his approval. "Yum." He moved away from the guy who was feeling him up. "You're getting all the young, cute ones, and I'm getting all the older guys."

I suggested it was time we check out the sauna.

"Let's go," Mike said.

"Wait!" I cried. "I'm not getting out of this pool with an erection. Give me a minute."

The sauna was tucked away in another corner of the locker room. When we entered, there were maybe one or two other guys inside, wearing towels and talking idly. If the heating coils were on, they certainly weren't doing a very thorough job. As if he'd read my mind, one of the Chinese guys moved to the heating unit and started pouring water onto the coils. They sizzled, sending up clouds of hot steam. Soon the temperature began to rise. So, apparently, did interest in us, for within a few minutes we had been joined by half a dozen other guys, all crowding into a space that could comfortably accommodate only five or six. We were now ten.

"This sure is cozy," I joked to Mike.

"What do you suppose happens now?" he asked.

"I guess we'll wait and see."

As in the pool, the guys kept looking at us, smiling, commenting to each other (presumably about us), and occasionally chuckling.

"*Ni hao.* Hello," Mike said to one particularly fetching young man. The man responded with a sentence or two in Chinese. "What's he saying?" Mike asked.

"That he's madly in love with you and wants to go back to Chicago with you," I teased.

"Tell him I'm not ready to get married yet, but that I'd love to take him back to my hotel room. How many of the guys in here do you suppose are gay?"

"From the looks they're giving us, I'd say all of them."

"I can't believe this!" Mike said. "All these yummy rice cakes and me a rice queen and . . ."

He was interrupted by one of the guys pouring more water onto the hot coils. The steam became almost unbearable. We decided to take another plunge in the pool. As we got back in, a Chinese man asked us in perfect English if we were Americans.

"I'm Lu," he said. "Is this your first time here?"

It was, we said. Lu was in his late thirties, bright-faced and solidly handsome. He said he'd only been to the bathhouse once before, the previous day. He was from Hong Kong, a visiting scholar. He introduced his friend, someone he'd met at the bath yesterday. We began comparing notes, but out of the corner of my eye I couldn't help but notice that the boy who'd been eyeing my beaded necklace was still looking at me.

"You like him?" Lu asked.

"Yes, I think he's beautiful," I said. "But I think he's only after my jewels." Lu didn't get the joke. The boy smiled at me again and said something to his comrades. I decided it was now or never. I moved closer to the young man, reached out underwater, and fondled his dick. He squealed and splashed away, laughingly protesting.

"Didn't like it, huh?" Mike asked.

"Well, he could have fooled me," I said.

The rest of the guys in the pool seemed nonplussed, even amused. Whatever breech of etiquette I'd made hardly seemed to cause much of a stir. The squealing boy resumed his seductive leering at me.

It was then that I noticed that the water level in the pool was going down.

"They're draining the pool for cleaning," Lu explained. "I think it means they're closing for the evening."

Mike and I got out and managed to squeeze our way under one showerhead. Because everyone had left the pool, the showers were crowded. Even more than before, men were sharing, taking turns washing each other. The erection count seemed higher than before. I wondered what the straight men, if indeed there were any, and the prepubescent boys thought of all this. And again I was reminded that in a country where privacy is at a premium, people must develop a certain kind of tolerance—or perhaps blindness—for what we in the West would deem "transgressive" behavior.

"Let's come back tomorrow," Mike said.

"*You?* The one I practically had to force here?"

"There were so many cute men," Mike sighed.

As we were toweling off, I suggested to Lu and his friend that we all go out to dinner. He said they'd be delighted. I realized I was using the bathhouse in the same way the Chinese do, to make friends. I doubted that much sex went on there, other than a lot of touchy-feely stuff underwater. But these gay Chinese, ever resourceful, had managed to create a place for themselves where, if not sex, at least, as Walt Whitman once put it, "the dear love of comrades" could prevail.

As we were turning in our keys, the ticket man said something to Lu and Lu laughed agreeably. Out on the street, I asked him what the man had said. Lu smiled.

"He said, 'Next time you come, bring more foreigners.'"

Darieck Scott

Ride of the Centaurs

SAN FRANCISCO As the trip to Greece approaches, I decide it's only right and proper to follow the example of ancient world travelers and seek the consultation of unseen powers as to what I can expect—what mishaps along the road to avoid, what monsters I will have to slay, what deities I ought not to offend. Since my ticket to Athens via British Airways and the four-hour cab ride to Koroni on the southern tip of the western finger of the Peloponnesus has been generously paid for by my lover Stephen's father—unsolicited provenance, plucked from the air—I have reason to suspect that the universe is once again moving in its mysterious ways: setting me up for something, in other words, good or bad.

So I consult a sibyl, the late twentieth-century kind, in this case my psychic Marcus, a hilarious German expatriate whose voice shifts between melodious purrs and a Teutonic brogue that is sometimes as difficult to decode as the priestess of Apollo's incoherent mumbling and hexameter verse must have been. Marcus does not proffer his auguries in mountainous Delphi, of course, but his apartment on the slopes of Twin Peaks boasts its own dramatic and arguably divine setting. As we settle down on the floor pillows, Marcus bids me to shuffle a deck of plain red-backed playing cards and a second deck of cryptic, almost abstractly drawn Tarot cards. I take in the view through his three windows facing west, north, and east. It is a high moment of twilight, and in the sun's fading glow the city is made anew, as familiar colors that pass unremarked in the brightness of noon become both more somber and more radiant. Across the sky I see streaks the ruby red of grapefruit and curled like wisps of smoke illumined by fire; I see a strip of milky sky as yellowed as old papyrus, and a great rolling mass of purple fog slowly advancing through a cleft between the hills, like an iceberg wreathed in vapor.

Surely, I think, this is the equal of the sinuous haze of fumes and shadow in which the sibyl of old beheld the shifting and elusive countenance of the god.

"You are worried about this trip," Marcus purrs. "You shouldn't be. Everything says that you will meet very interesting people." He turns over a card: the Jack of Spades. "Here it is again: meetings."

This will not strike you as the most impressive of predictions, given that I am going on a trip, and meetings are part of the package, more or less. But meetings of the kind to which Marcus refers, "interesting" meetings, have been a source of small but persistent anxiety for me when I travel abroad. At once shy and exhibitionist, I find negotiating between my own extremes a challenge in foreign lands, where separation from the people and things I know frees me from the safety of distraction and forces me to notice what I usually keep hidden. In this context, with the inner battle raging, meeting people sometimes seems a tricky thing. (To wit: gorgeous Mediterranean man at three o'clock—watch surreptitiously? Or flaunt what you've got and proposition him on the spot? This is a *vacation*, after all, you have *gone away* to do *something else*.)

Meetings. A white gay man I know who is old enough to be my father has traveled widely but tells me that he has reached the age to embark upon a different kind of journey. "I'm tired of these sexual tours," he says, and apart from wanting to ply him for the seamy specifics I feel slightly unnerved. What he refers to is alien to me; it is a glimpse of some other existence. Perhaps the dissonance between us is simply the veil between the generations (I think of acerbic old Gore Vidal, who likens his number of tricks to the legion of conquests of Marlon Brando) or, more properly perhaps, between me and the rest of the tribe, for whom sexual exploits sometimes seem supernaturally plentiful.

"You will meet very interesting people." Marcus speaks in the quotidian terms of the everyday, as a good psychic probably should, but I think I would prefer the poetry and mystery of the charlatan's vague cliché: "You will meet a dark and handsome stranger."

Marcus concludes our session with an observation that I presume carries no predictive weight, but is reflective of another kind of insight. "You are black," he says, "so everyone will want you." My father was in the army and I lived in Germany for six years, so I know that the presence of an African American, at least in less cosmopolitan settings, can draw a measure of attention. For two years of our sojourn in Deutschland, we lived off-post and outside the city, in a small hamlet consisting of ten sparkling-clean German houses surrounded by farmland. Every day of those two years I walked my collie along the roads that passed by the fields, and every day the same German farmers would stop work and stare at me as if they had never seen my like before.

As I leave Marcus I reflect upon this, and consider that although we no longer believe that Apollo's arrows will strike us if we offend him or that there is a man in the sky who holds the lightning in his hands, we cling still to a number of myths. The racial kind are among the most powerful.

"You will meet a dark stranger."

I look upon this prospect with suspicion, with caution, with a wish.

EN ROUTE TO OLYMPIA In a comfy van driven by Stephen's uncle, Stephen, his mother, his aunt, his cousin, his cousin's husband, and I ride up and down and over the green hills of Arcadia. When not drawn into conversation or lulled to sleep by the gentle bounce of the van's wheels, I am plugged in to my Walkman listening to the gospel riffs and thrumming bass of house music and reading Alan Hollinghurst's novel *The Swimming-Pool Library*.

We have been one week in Koroni, the seaside village from which Stephen's grandparents emigrated to the United States in 1910, and now the site of his father's newly constructed summer vacation home. We have enjoyed late, lazy mornings; strolls up to the thirteenth-century Venetian castle that overlooks the villagers' and tourists' evening *volta* along the waterfront; sunny beach afternoons and forays along the coast in the family boat; we have had good food and lots and lots of it. But as yet my stranger has not appeared. There are indeed a few dark, handsome Greek men around, especially on the beach, where visitors from Athens and other sites inland congregate for weekend getaways. Yet they seem an insular group; in my presence their expressions either remain stonily indifferent or assume a scowl of disinterested hostility. I am ensconced among my in-laws, as they are cordoned off with their own friends and family, and we do not meet one another.

What is strange and new to me, however, is Hollinghurst's novel. It is stirring something in me—envy, most likely, of his success and of that euphonious facility the British have with the English language; but it also stirs me with excitement, because the voice of the novel is so lovely that I can hear it, accent and all, each time I put the book down, and frequently for a long time after. He—it—makes me want to write, makes me enthused and eager and antsy to write.

For years the novel has stood virtually untouched on my

shelf. I had often opened it, but one of the first lines reads, "I was getting a taste for black names . . . ," and I could never quite get past that. I was afraid of how I might feel to see the author objectify black men.

Yet now I have come to a stronger place; I relish the line, I imbibe it, it holds no terrors for me. Now I'm wanting to write a little sketch in answer to Hollinghurst's Lord Nantwich, an old army officer posted to East Africa who falls in love with the men he is meant to rule, falls in love, it seems, with blackness itself. Talking to the first black man he has ever known, he hallucinates that he is in the presence of "a superior kind of person." In my sketch I want to talk about black boys and white boys as the objects of my lust, and I do want to deal with them as objects, to hold them at the distance objects are held. I am drawn—guiltily, sometimes, which makes the obsession all the more compelling —to the objectification of men, not only to the act but to the contemplation of the act. There are moments when I feel that for me the whole lure and arousal of sex lies in its enactment of object relationships, the various postures and playing out of someone *using* someone else, each person dealing with the other, imagining the other, as if he were a plaything. There isn't much that's nice about this fascination, and even if there were it would soon be engulfed by shadow, for my fantasy life really gets going when I can imagine one partner taking the other, dominating him, raping him. You know the sort of rape I mean: rape with quotation marks, the kind that doesn't exist except in highly orchestrated S/M D/S B/D scenarios, where no-don't suddenly becomes sock-it-to-me-Daddy and you get exactly what you wanted and then some. Not nice, as I said. That I like to identify with the *taken* in these little fantasies means something, I suppose, but it does not mean that I don't have it in me to objectify or dominate others, for as the author of the fantasy I distribute myself in its every aspect, from the rough razor-stubble on my kindly rapist's chin and the taste of his tongue to his abusive language and the way he uses his belt on my ass. Why does this scenario move me? Isn't it bad? Would I ask the first question if I truly believed that the answer to the second was no?

I recall now the different level of sexual experience I discovered a couple of years ago with Stephen, when I woke up to the idea that one can express intimacy and love in sex, instead of just lust and passion. Naively I had believed that the phrase "making love" simply meant that the two people fucking loved each other. Somewhere in the progression of our relationship, as if stumbling across buried treasure I had never imagined existed, I found that sex was not only the symbol or the seal of a love truly experienced in other venues, but that it could be a kind of language in which things other than lust—though not necessarily more profound than lust—could be spoken. A revelation, yes. But still, when I recall the best of our sex or anticipate what is to come, what I see and what I want is to be down on my knees with my face in his crotch performing an act that feels like obeisance, like fealty and worship. I want him to pound his prick into my mouth and come loudly, I want to hear "Suck it, bitch" and embarrassing stuff like that.

In real life, of course, in this van as we slowly descend into the lush valley of the Alpheios and watch the thickets of pines and evergreen oaks rise higher and higher, I hate the idea of abdicating my power. I do not want to be sexually dominated or to sexually dominate anyone else, unless by plan and according to rules, within the drawn-curtain intimacy of a committed relationship or the enchanted chalk-drawn circle of a compact between role-players. I like to toy with the imagined scene of sexual domination; I flirt with it, I charge up to the line and dangle a prize I cannot quite see on the other side, but I do not cross over.

OLYMPIA, THE SACRED PRECINCT The site where the first Olympic festivals were held has been reclaimed from the depredations of fire, earthquake, flood, Christian zealotry, and plunder. The scars of its long decline are everywhere in evidence. Strewn about in patterns only vaguely recognizable as the foundations of fallen buildings and long-ago looted temples are stunted roofless columns and misshapen limestone bricks. The bricks, sheared in half or in quarters or thirds over the years, bristle in their interiors with protruding chips of shell like broken claws or eyeless sockets. The sight of these dead crustaceans' remains, which were already old when the stone was quarried in the fifth century B.C., makes me shudder. Here at the carcass of the temple of Zeus the bricks lie tumbled one upon the other in something resembling a stairway, the steps now too huge and disjointed to be easily climbed except by professional basketball players, or gods. There, according to the *Blue Guide*, was the gymnasium, and there the palaestra where the competitors practiced. One squints, but there are no ghosts of sweaty Greek athletes tussling in the grass. As for the gods who presided over these games and who, if the Iliad is any guide, likely took part in the contests on behalf of their favorites, their presence, too, is much diminished. I decide that the invisible deities have spread their divine essences upon the air, for, sodden as it is with heat, the air is too thick to be merely a collection of oxygen molecules clinging to one another.

In the broad shade offered by a cabal of leafy trees gather the members of a Scandinavian motorcycle gang. They are the closest thing to embodied gods, the dressed-in-flesh avatars of dead athletes. This is of course a hallucination; there are no motorcycles anywhere in sight. I call them bikers because they are all wearing black and they are sweating and long-haired and look scruffier than the old trees, and they are as foreign to this place as I and thus fair game for the invention of myth. "Motorcycle gang" suggests danger, invasion. I like that. I loiter as I pass by, hoping to catch a whiff of their bodies baking in the heat.

Only one of them interests me, a very handsome, strikingly blond, sable-eyed fellow with a nice strong chin and jawline and an arrogant way of standing and looking at me. It is his hair that really keeps my attention—it is always a man's hair that keeps my attention: how it is cut, if he has a goatee or sideburns or the shadow of a beard, whether wisps of it creep up above the neckline of his shirt or spill out from his sleeves to inch along his wrists. His is so blond it is almost white, blond like buttercream, like goat's milk. I don't generally take note of blonds in the U.S., not at least at first glance, but this man has an altogether different resonance: there is about him the perceptible but not quite namable mark of the strange, the other. He is foreign; he is—yes, that's the word—exotic. From the Greek root *exo*, meaning "outside." He demonstrates to me how truly alien a blond can be, how different and therefore desirable—as you might find it desirable to own an odd deep-sea fish with multicolored scales for your aquarium, or desirable to sample some new and fragrant food you see on someone else's plate that you have never before imagined you would like. These illusions are sexual in origin: he is a ready surface upon which I happily project. The biker biography that I have invented for him makes him seem a bit menacing, too, a bit barbaric, and that appeals to me.

We pass on from the blond and his posse, but my thoughts linger with him; I turn to watch him from time to time as he ranges about the ruins, my exotic invader from the north.

OLYMPIA, THE MUSEUM The museum houses busts of Roman conquerors, Mycenean masks, tools from the workshop of Pheidias the sculptor, Archaic bronze armor, and vases decorated with kinetic slim black figures. My attention is taken by the statues of the gods—there is the Hermes of Praxiteles, with the infant Dionysus on his arm; there is Zeus in terracotta, abducting Ganymede. It is unfair to modern Greece, which has quite enough fascinating history of its own, unfair to Byzantine Greece and Ottoman Greece and Venetian Greece, unfair perhaps to most of the history of this much-trod-upon part of the world, but I am always most drawn by anything that evokes the accounts of things that never happened but seem truer to me than history: the myths. You can tell me about Thessaloniki and Mystras and Santorini, but my ears will not prick up in quite the same way that they do when I hear those old, familiar names— Artemis, Aphrodite, Athena, Hades, Persephone, Hecate.

In the museum's central hall are assembled the surviving fragments of epic sculptures that once adorned the pediments of the temple of Zeus here at Olympia. The west pediment depicts the beginning of the war between the Lapiths and the Centaurs. According to the legend, Peirithous, boon companion of the great Athenian hero Theseus, held a feast to celebrate his wedding to Hippodameia, whose name is variously translated as "horse tamer" and "she who fights with strength." The invited celebrants came from far and wide, and among them numbered Theseus, several of the immortals of Olympus, and Peirithous's cousins, the wild, shaggy, half-horse Centaurs. Like disreputable family members at many weddings, the Centaurs were seated apart from the main party, and obliged to take their repast of sour milk (suitable for horses, one supposes) near the mouth of a cave. But, unruly under any circumstances, they raided the decanters of wine and became intoxicated and belligerent, and worked themselves up into such a horny frenzy that when Peirithous arrived at the cave to introduce them to Hippodameia, the Centaur Eurytion brazenly seized the bride by her hair and tried to carry her off for his pleasure. Peirithous and Theseus leapt immediately to Hippodameia's rescue, but the other Centaurs went mad with lust and began, as Robert Graves puts it, "lecherously straddling the nearest women and boys."

This last detail is missing from the English-language note-card affixed to the railing in front of the sculpture at the museum. We are informed that the Centaurs attempted to carry off the women, and judging from the marble figures of a woman crouched low in fear as the battle rages above her, another woman trying to escape the clutches of a fearsome Centaur who is being stabbed by a warrior, and Hippodameia herself in the grip of Eurytion, the museum's partial description would seem to be confirmed. Except that there are also male figures who are not wielding swords: one is being lifted from the ground by a Centaur, and another is trying to strangle the Centaur who has him cornered and is being bitten on the arm for his trouble. The unflinchingly precise Miss *Blue Guide*, thankfully, does not shrink from indentifying these figures as the prey that they are, "boys" who are as much objects of lust as the women, though their height and musculature is such that they resemble college students rather than elementary school tykes.

I am intrigued by this story. It takes little for me to become enamored of these loutish, rapacious Centaurs, who are said to be the mythological counterparts of a "primitive" mountain tribe that practiced "erotic orgies." I imagine them galloping through the wedding party, sweeping up trembling young men in their hairy arms as they go. The women I have to cross out of the story, unless I imagine Hippodameia arising in her strength to toss Eurytion on his flanks and start scooping up young men for herself; otherwise the scenario is unbearable rather than titillating. Freed, though not completely, from such concerns, I can ride the fantasy where it takes me. I can feel a primitive tribesman's rough hands on my exposed flesh, I can be led in ecstatic rites practiced in the shadows of fires lit in the mountain night, beneath the silver stars . . .

OLYMPIA, THE STADIUM For those of us who carry in mind the image of the monumental venues where the modern Olympic track-and-field meets are held—the graceful symmetry of their ovals surrounded by towering rows of seats arranged like a mighty choir, the green field in its center—the distinct lack of drama in the first stadium's construction is disappointing. After we pass through what remains of the vaulted entrance, an arch of bricks and two low walls that form an open-air corridor, we see grass embankments that slope gently back from a rectangular dirt track. A thin length of stone or perhaps modern concrete, ringed by weeds, marks the starting line, and further on, another marks the finish line. The distance between the two is a mystery: six hundred "Olympic feet," according to Miss *Blue Guide*, though the span scarcely looks as if it's a hundred meters.

Stephen has often told me that when he came to Greece as a child he raced his siblings in the Olympic stadium. Having a certain romantic attachment to the first idea that forms in my mind when I hear such reminiscences—I think I confused the stadium with an ancient Greek theater, and believed there were old stone seats rising up from the track and broken columns placed picturesquely in the grass—I, too, am determined to race. Presumably this is what almost everyone does when they come to Olympia, though we see no one else racing today.

I take my T-shirt off, partly because of the heat, partly because the ancient races were run in the nude, and partly because I am an exhibitionist. We run and I win. No surprise there—in high school, I was a sprinter and Stephen ran middle distance. What is surprising (or is it in fact something I was aware of all along?) is the presence of a small group of European men standing on the embankment, watching with smiles on their faces as I slow and turn, watching as I jog back, watching as I pick up my T-shirt, watching and not moving. I recognize them. They, like a number of others, have been making more or less the same circuit through the ruins as we, and they, like the others, have until this moment barely taken note of my presence. (You will recall that I have been looking for such notice: "You are black, so everyone will want you.")

I decide to keep my shirt off. It's hot, I'm sweating, I'd best wait until I dry off. We decide to rest a bit in the shade near the pedestals of the Zanes, the bronze statues of Zeus that once stood here as tribute paid for by Olympic cheaters. A young boy who has seen me exit the stadium has been staring at me, and now he turns from his course and walks back toward our party, while an adult, perhaps his father, waits. He strolls slowly by, staring, stops a few feet away, and stares. I have the feeling that he is comparing me to an image he recalls from a magazine or television, as if he thinks I'm Linford Christie or Michael Johnson. Being a world-class sprinter is of course my own fantasy, so his interest interests me; I enjoy my fantasy of his fantasy of me.

We rouse ourselves from the torpor of the heat and walk on, past the Metroon and the Heraion, too exhausted now to linger much. Miss *Blue Guide* falls silent. Men and women—they could be Italian, German, Greek or French or Russian—look at me, some staring without modesty (I suspect these are the Germans), others giving me a brief but intent regard.

The attention is delicious. It is fuel to a fire; I warm to it, I become radiant in its spell. I am also suspicious. Maybe it's the muscles of my chest that they're looking at—my physique does not seem outrageously remarkable to me, but then the various tribes of Europe are not known for flocking to the gym each evening as a certain contingent of San Franciscans are known to do. If I were to see a shirtless someone like myself, say, outside the De Young Museum in Golden Gate Park on a hot day, maybe I'd look too—but my motivations would be ho-ish and lecherous, which cannot be universally the case here. No, I believe it's my color that turns their heads, my color on display. I suppose they are seeing me as a kind of alien creature, a *black* embodying the athletic and physical prowess with which we are assumed to be naturally endowed. There is no evidence for this conclusion, except the sixth-sense tingle many African Americans have developed that alerts us to those moments when racial difference shifts from an unconscious dynamic in cross-racial encounters to a palpable presence. This learned instinct (we might compare it, in an odd way, to gaydar) is culturally and historically adaptive—that is, it might help to have a feeling you're going to be lynched before it actually happens—and it is tingling in me now.

Yet I don't feel endangered or belittled or assaulted by their stares. I feel objectified. I'm content with this feeling. One might say I enjoy it. The truth is, I'm a whore for attention, especially the kind of attention that has nothing to do with me, but with the appreciation of what people project onto and desire of my physical being. It doesn't matter to me that their cultural lens may lead them to see me as a jungle bunny, as less or other than human; I'm so unquestionably *not* those things that what they think has no real purchase on how I feel about myself—or else, or also, it is this very aspect that I like: I like being an exotic.

Sometimes, that is. At a distance. Whatever my admirers say about what they see I don't know, because they say it in a language other than English, Spanish, or German. The *silence* of their regard, the fact that we are relating to one another only through guesses, through fantasy, is the appeal here.

So I find myself wishing for my Scandinavian biker. When we saw each other before, he showed me only a momentary interest, and now I should like to parade before him shirtless and see what he'd do and how he'd look, this no doubt straight

Nordic fellow with hair the color of cream. I want him to stare. I want him to burn to have me—and as a thing, I guess, a sex thing—just as I would have him.

OLYMPIA, THE MUSEUM The beauty of slender, hairy brown legs . . . In the lobby of the museum Stephen and I spy a fresh Italian youth. We decide he is Italian instantly, based solely on his look. One of the ways in which travel works on the mind is that you become highly cognizant—or highly inventive—of how nationality can be read in someone's face and build and way of dress as much as in the sound of their language; everyone is to some degree transfigured into the representative of a national type, so that you will see a group of dazzlingly handsome Italians and think, I love Italian men, making a leap you might not make so readily if you came upon an identical group of Italian Americans in the café around the corner from your home.

Our fresh young Italian wears a white Adidas shirt piped with black racing stripes, and loose white Adidas athletic trunks. Lean and tall, he has black hair and dark eyes and an unremarkably handsome face, and all of his visible flesh is deeply and exquisitely tan. Something about his rusty copper color has the strongest effect on me. Among the many dubious legacies of modern human beings' abiding investment in reading significance in skin pigmentation is that color sometimes triggers synesthesia: the mere sight of a particular shade of brown might, by a trick of the wiring, move me to a sensation akin to being swept up in the vaulting emotion of a favorite diva at the peak of an aria. Color becomes the touchstone of a dreamlike narrative; it *speaks*. All this, of course, is filtered through the lens of idiot prejudice and racial fantasy.

Our Italian enters the museum's central hall. I stare at him, and eventually he sees me watching, because I do not turn away

when our gazes meet. I don't know what he thinks of this exchange. What I feel is a kind of hunger, and the frustration of
knowing—*believing*, not knowing, really—that my hunger will
not be satisfied. There is a sweetness in this feeling, a strange
mute joy. Our eyes and then our bodies follow the Italian
around the lobby, sometimes discreetly and sometimes boldly,
sometimes in tag team, as he drifts through the galleries and
finally, finally, we see with a surge of hope and desire, into the
men's restroom.

The restroom lies below the main floor. A tiled platform
stands like a ledge above the urinal trough, and a chest-high
board separates the length of it into two stations. There is a line
of men waiting to piss, and the Italian is directly in front of
Stephen, who is in front of me.

He steps up to the ledge. His legs are slim and hard with nice
rounds of muscle, and the hair on them is as black and as long
as the hair on his head, each strand a kind of wiry black thread.
A look like his is as intimate as a smell, as near and dear as if I
had sidled up close to him and inhaled the aroma of his sun-
heated flesh in my nostrils.

Yet I cannot linger. A trickle of panic runs through me. I
don't need to piss and it would look suspicious if I stood there
just holding my stuff, and there are only two stations and he
might leave first, maybe I'll see him better at the washbasin, and
someone is behind me in line waiting. In desperation I go to
wash my hands, and it is only as I begin to soap my hands that I
realize the silliness of my fears.

I do not see my Italian again except as he dashes from the
restroom and skips up the stairs to the lobby.

Later Stephen tells me that he could feel him taking his cock
out, he could hear the rustle of the silky polyester as it brushed
his thighs, he could sense its elastic spring as he tucked the band

below his balls. But Stephen didn't dare peer over the divider. The Italian seemed to be very resolutely focusing down and away. "It didn't feel right to keep looking at him," Stephen says.

OLYMPIA, THE WEST PEDIMENT OF THE TEMPLE OF ZEUS

The real rape that is suffered by women and men and children in the world is morally outrageous and viscerally horrifying, and not something I find erotic. But rape as figure, as a play—the "rape" that I imagine and control—excites me. So I find myself shaken when I read the history of nearby Anatolia and come upon a scene in which the Tatar conqueror Timur forces the vanquished sultan Beyazit to serve as his footstool while the sultan's favorite wife, Despina, serves dinner; and at the conclusion of his meal, the naked Tatar, his appetites not quite sated, rapes Despina before her husband's eyes. The story makes me angry, though this dark deed was done some six hundred years ago. But if I make the Tatar a fictional creature of my own, tall and cinnamon brown like my Italian, dark-eyed and dark-haired with a beautiful hooked nose and black hairy thighs, and if the sultan's beloved is a favorite serving-youth or horse groom from the Russian steppes or from the crumbling cities of Nubia—suddenly the scene becomes immeasurably fascinating. But how separate are these scenes, really? There are few true firewalls between the chambers of the human psyche.

The pediment's sculpture seems to capture something of this truth. According to the legend, blame for the battle between the Lapiths and the Centaurs cannot be laid solely on the Centaurs' drunkenness; while Peirithous asked his father Zeus and the other Olympians to attend his wedding, he declined to invite Ares and Eris, the gods of war and discord. A perusal of the old stories will tell you that it is not a good idea to leave Miss Eris off the guest list; it was she who, excluded from the wedding of the mortal Peleus and the goddess Thetis, spitefully tossed into the midst of the festivities the golden apple that led to the Trojan War. On that occasion Ares joined her in seeking vengeance, and together they incited the Centaurs to rampage. Thus the chief responsibility for the resulting deaths must be attributed to Peirithous's ill-considered lapse in courtesy.

Ares and Eris's intervention remains unseen in the fragments that have come down to us from ancient times, but there is one god who is visible, mighty Apollo, the sun god from whom the light of reason and moderation flows. Apollo, enemy of all barbarism, stands tall at the sculpture's center, hovering above the fray. According to the story he comes to the aid of the Lapiths, but his stance here is not active or wrathful; it is regal and removed, and in his cool marble face there is a lofty equanimity. Neither outraged nor surprised by the carnage he beholds, he presides over the scene, as if there were nothing untoward in the coexistence of a celebration of love and the outbreak of violence, as if he were a knowing witness to the fact that even in the highest and best of our moments it is wise to acknowledge and give due to that which is rampant in us—the wild, the hot-tempered, the heedlessly gluttonous and cruel, the rage of discordant desires.

That the appeal of this rapturously violent image might bear some relation to the primal scene of the Atlantic slave trade, the horribly destructive and unintentionally creative act that produced my ancestors, does not escape me. There is a trauma three centuries old that I am trying to catch by its horns and ride as I guiltily take part in the scene in cracked stone before me, though I do not recognize this now. I cannot yet see that as I identify with the Centaurs and surrender to the dark passions of rapine, that as I identify with the youths and revel in their terror tinged with forbidden desire when they are snatched away from the bosom of the tribe by lusty, horse-cocked men, I have chosen a safe site in which to restage, rework, and redistribute the emotions and effects of deeds otherwise too horrible to contemplate.

EN ROUTE TO SAN FRANCISCO Aloft. Below—is it Iceland? Greenland?—an awesome landscape viewed all out of proportion: brown and evergreen mountains and hills and lakes—it's like looking at the top of a huge cake that has fallen and been singed, or like walking amid sand-drifts on a beach after a tumultuous tide and finding gorgeous, intricate, intimate tidepools of cobalt blue.

This view of the familiar made strange returns me to that old and truest cliché: The true stranger one meets is, of course, intimately known. He is indeed dark, and his attractions, though perhaps not those of a gorgeous face, are to me endlessly beguiling. He is me.

Joe Orton

Tangier Diaries

MAY 25, 1967 Kenneth decided not to go to the beach. His boils slightly better, but still painful. "Imagine how Job felt," I said, "and you'll forget your troubles." "Piss off," he said, "and get down to The Windmill." Arrived at beach at about eleven. Weather perfect though a cold wind by the shoreline. On the way to The Windmill I met the boy I'd had at Bill Fox's and at the baths. I had already warned Kenneth that I intended bringing him back if I met him. "Hallo," he said. "Hallo," I said. "*L'amour* today?" I said. "Today," he nodded slowly. "What time?" "Come to The Windmill at two o'clock." He nodded and went away.

I lay in the sun till twelve. Went for a swim. Talked to Frank. "My mask of that young Moroccan," he said, "came out rather well. I'm engaged on doing the eyes. I color them the best I can." "What color do you use for the face?" I said. "Oh I try and get it as exact as I can," he said, "though I'm afraid my efforts could hardly compare with the works of the divine Madame Tussaud.* At one o'clock Ken rang. "Your waiter's just turned up," he said. "But I told him Friday at one." "He must have lost his appointment diary then," Ken said. "I said you were at the *plage*." A few minutes later Nasser hovered on to the scene. He hadn't understood the day. "Come tomorrow at one for *l'amour*," I said, "to the apartment at one." He smiled, tossed a few remarks about how "wapu" I was, and how he liked *l'amour* with me, didn't "go with tourists." All of which may or may not be true.

*Madame Tussaud (Marie Cresholtz) (1760–1850). Swiss-born modeler in wax.

After he'd gone, the boy Larbi brought round last night appeared. I returned his greetings and approached him. He was an English schoolboy too, but the tall blond type who looks fetching in tennis flannels. I was pretty vague with him. I then saw Mohammed (the one that was coming at two—he wore a yellow jersey and, to distinguish him from the rest of his kind, I'll call him Mohammed Yellow-jersey). So I had a couple of poached eggs and a coffee, and nodded for Mohammed Yellow-jersey to follow.

I went onto the Avenue d'Espagne and Mohammed Yellow-jersey was still following. I let him in and he sat on my bed smiling. Kenneth came out of the bathroom. I went in for a shit. When I came back Kenneth was sitting in a dressing-gown. "Do you want tea?" I said to Yellow-jersey. "Yes, please," he said. I made a pot. He had condensed milk in it and three spoonfuls of sugar. Kenneth and I talked. He had a piece of hash cake. I wasn't going to risk it fucking up the sex. I took a couple of Valium though. I usually find a mild muscle relaxant helpful. I took the boy (who is about fifteen) into the room. We took off our clothes and lay together. I stroked him, kissed his nipples. When I'd got a spanking good hard on, I turned the lad over and, using a little grease mixed with my spit, I put my prick up his arse. I found he wouldn't take the cock up the arse. He cried out as it went in. But he allowed me to have the prick between the buttocks which, as I fucked, he agitated in a most alarming way. At this point I, my hand well-greased, put my hand under him and took his medium-to-large tool in my hand. While I fucked him, I pressed his prick between my clenched fist and had a truly satisfactory orgasm.

We dozed for fifteen minutes or so and then he had a *douche.* We smiled a lot and I gave him six dirham and he asked for another, so I gave him seven. We displayed more affection and then he went and drenched himself with a cheap kind of eau-de-cologne which Kenneth had bought for midge bites. I made a pot of tea, had a largish slice of hashish cake, and came into the living-room. "Very good," I said to Kenneth. "Just my type." "You must let Nasser fuck you occasionally," Kenneth said, "or otherwise we shall not be able to get the hashish."

When Larbi arrived at five, I went to the boulevard to get some tablets for Kenneth. I bought them and sat on the Place de France drinking mint tea. Nearby was a quartet of English tourists and one woman was saying "Well, the best holiday we ever had was in Plymouth, but we didn't have the weather unfortunately."* As I walked back a Moroccan approached me. "You English?" "Yes," I said. He looked at me. "You want girls?" he said. "No," I said. He paused and coughed a bit and said in a tentative tone, "You like boys?" "No," I said. "OK. Good-bye," he said.

I had a very pleasant stroll back, the hash and Valium working well. Met Ian Horrible. "How are you?" I said. "Alive, I regret to say," he said. "Has anything exciting been happening?" he said, and I told him of my Yellow-jersey episode. "Yes," he said, "he's quite a nice kid." "A very valuable addition to my collection," I said. He chortled to himself and gave a spin into a café, leaving me relieved by his departure. I found Ken and Larbi still in the bedroom when I returned. After a while Larbi came out quite naked parading up and down in front of the long mirror in the hall admiring himself. I gave Kenneth the tablets. He took two and said they gave him the most odd feeling on top of the hashish.

*Orton to Peggy Ramsay, 30 May 1967: ". . . Hardly any tourists. Occasionally a cruise ship docks for a night and then we have clumps of the most terrible English middle-classery in flowered frocks sitting at the cafés looking as though rape was imminent. On one of these occasions I overheard a woman, with the sunlight dappling her C and A Modes hat, the exotic palms and the Arabs in their fezzes around her, saying in a loud voice, 'The best holiday we ever had was in Plymouth.' I felt like pouring my mint tea down her neck."

We sat talking of how happy we both felt and of how it couldn't, surely, last. We'd have to pay for it. Or we'd be struck down from afar by disaster because we were, perhaps, too happy. To be young, good-looking, healthy, famous, comparatively rich, *and* happy is surely going against nature, and when to the above list one adds that daily I have the company of beautiful fifteen-year-old boys who find (for a small fee) fucking with me a delightful sensation, no man can want for more. "*Crimes of Passion* will be a disaster," Kenneth said. "That will be the scapegoat. We must sacrifice *Crimes of Passion* in order that we may be spared disaster more intolerable."

We went to the Alhambra for dinner. I had a glass of wine because it works well with hash. Kenneth already with hash and Valium inside him decided *not* to risk vino as well. We went for a stroll. Sat on the boulevard at the Café de Paris and, at ten, rose to go, only to meet Nigel, Frank, and Kevin who persuaded us to stay a little longer. In the reallotment of places, I sat next to a rather stuffy American tourist and his disapproving wife. They listened to our conversation and I, realizing this, began to exaggerate the content. "He took me right up the arse," I said, "and afterwards he thanked me for giving him such a good fucking. They're most polite people." The American and his wife hardly moved a muscle. "We've got a leopard-skin rug in the flat and he wanted me to fuck him on that," I said in an undertone that was perfectly audible to the next table. "Only I'm afraid of the spunk you see, it might adversely affect the spots of the leopard." Nigel said quietly, "Those tourists can hear what you're saying." He looked alarmed. "I mean them to hear," I said. "They have no right to be occupying chairs reserved for decent sex perverts." And then with excitement I said, "He might bite a hole in the rug. It's the writhing he does, you see, when my prick is up him that might grievously damage the rug, and I can't ask him to control his excitement. It wouldn't be natural when you're six inches up the bum, would it?"

The American couple frigidly paid for their coffee and moved away. "You shouldn't drive people like that away," Nigel said. "The town needs tourists." "Not that kind, it doesn't," I said. "This is our country, our town, our civilization. I want nothing to do with the civilization they made. Fuck them! They'll sit and listen to buggers' talk from me and drink their coffee and piss off." "It seems rather a strange joke," Frank said with an old school-teacher's smile. "It isn't a joke," I said, "there's no such thing as a joke."

Nigel, who was drinking some strange brandy, got very excited by a girl who passed. She looked like a boy. She was German. We discussed women for a bit and I wrote them off as a mistake. "Who wants a girl to look like a boy?" I said. "Or a boy to look like a girl? It's not natural." "I really think, Joe," Nigel said, "that you shouldn't bring nature into your conversation quite so often, you who have done more than anyone I know to outrage her." "I've never outraged nature," I said. "I've always listened to her advice and followed it to wherever it went." We left at eleven. I feel so content.

I slept all night soundly and woke up at seven feeling as though the whole of creation was conspiring to make me happy. I hope no doom strikes.

Rondo Mieczkowski

Bodies in Motion

Lane divider stripes stretched toward the horizon. My roommate Danny, tired, lounged in the passenger seat while I drove.
After a long holiday weekend in San Francisco we were on our
way home to L.A. On the 580 now, I was gearing up for the te-
dious trek south on Interstate 5. Reflector dots winked as we
zipped past. Modern windmills on the hills spun their high-tech
arms.

It was Monday, Presidents' Day. Dead Presidents' Day. Unseasonably hot for February: earthquake weather. I should have
guessed something would happen.

Back in Ohio, my grandmother was always leery of holidays
that celebrated the dead. She refused to travel on Memorial
Day, always missing the annual family picnic by Lake Erie.

Grandma grew most agitated as Halloween approached. She
would start a novena days before to protect my younger brother
and me on Halloween night when, defying her vigorous disap-
proval, we'd go out trick-or-treating. "Boys, the earth splits open
and the devils reach out and grab you," she warned us, as we
squirmed. She insisted, until we grew old enough to refuse, that
each Halloween night before we went out we recite with her the
Prayer to My Guardian Angel.

My brother and I would drop to our knees in whatever cos-
tumes Mom had made—spaceman, hobo, clown—and pray with
her, heads lowered, hands reverently folded, Grandma keeping
one eye open on us—

> *Angel of God, My Guardian Dear,*
> *To Whom God's love entrusts you here*

Ever this day be at my side
To light and guard and rule and guide.
Amen.

The two of us would rise and run out into the night, willing to risk Grandma's demons for sacks of sweetness that seemed to last nearly forever.

After four days in San Francisco my thoughts were still sticky with sex as I drove down the freeway. San Francisco was where I came out after college as a gay man—not bisexual, not androgynous, not asexual, all appellations I tried to wear without much success at Michigan State University.

San Francisco is webbed with desire. Walking just a block can tangle you up with a dozen potential boyfriends. The cruising is immediate, up close and personal, unlike in L.A., where offers of assignations are perpetrated from within the protective shells of autos. As an Angeleno I've become expert at making U-turns; deciphering the code of brake lights, rates of acceleration, eye contact at twenty-five miles per hour; and reading the depth of desire as it retreats in a rearview mirror.

After this visit I've realized there's no longer any point in night cruising Collingwood Park in San Francisco. The park is small, part of a square city block in the Castro that also contains a school, cute shops, and a twenty-four-hour supermarket. Guys head there after the bars close at 2 A.M. and pursue each other around the block, maybe making a new friend for the night or just a few hours, while the louder queens hold court on the street corners. Unfortunately, most of the men cruising there do not have a place to go—they're from out of town and the friend they're traveling with is asleep in the motel room, or they have too many roommates and too little privacy, or they live way the hell in the East Bay, or they're cheating on their lovers.

I stand halfway between the street and the school wall. Flush against the school seems very posed, and right on the curb could be interpreted as too tweaked out or too desperate. The chilly spring air is heavy with the sweet tang of mock orange trees. A warm front is supposed to arrive tomorrow.

I'm wearing a cockring. But it's so cold tonight there's no chance of my dick getting hard. Almost no chance.

A pickup truck pulls up to the curb, stops just beyond my sight line so I can't see the driver. I walk over to look into the pickup's cab, and the electric window on the passenger side rolls down.

"What are you up to?" the driver asks.

"No good," I answer. He is lean, wears a long-sleeved thermal T-shirt that shows off his pecs and tight belly.

"So, what are you into?" he asks me.

"Mostly top stuff," I answer.

Back in Michigan, no one wanted to be fucked. Everyone wanted to do the screwing. I was shocked when I moved to San Francisco and all these butch, bearded men were throwing their legs up in the air. I didn't realize that a man would *want* to get fucked. Not just as a favor to a buddy, but because he liked that more than anything. There was a lot to learn about being gay.

He nervously pushes the brown hair back from the clear skin of his forehead.

I start to grow hard.

"Definitely top stuff with you," I add. "What do you like to do?"

"I'm mostly a bottom," he smiles. "You want to get in?"

I open the truck's door, making sure the streetlight catches the outline of my cock in my jeans.

I follow my dick. That's another thing I've learned. Generally I have a type of man I'm attracted to, but sometimes just the way a man laughs, the resonance of his voice, or the way light spills a shadow on his face can start me raging.

Something in me is responding to this person. So I follow my dick like a divining rod, to see what treasure I can discover.

Of course, it works the opposite way too. While chatting with some available stud all he has to do to make me wilt is proclaim how much better things would be if Bush had been re-elected.

I reach over and pinch his right nipple through his shirt. He closes his eyes and moans, "Do you have a place in the City?" My dick ceases its throbbing, because I know he doesn't have a place and I don't have a place. That's why we're out here at three o'clock in the morning.

He suggests sex in his truck, which causes my hard-on to retreat completely. The idea of a law enforcement officer breaking up a passionate interlude may be a scene that tickles some libidos, but it scares me limp.

We say good-bye. I step back into the sweet night air.

I hear a bang from under the car, then another. The car shudders violently. I try to hold the steering wheel straight, aim in a straight line. Danny tells me, "Hold on . . . Hold on . . . Hold on . . ."

I'm getting fucked for the first time. It's Michigan, 1977. I don't even remember where I met this man, but he was a rarity back then, an out gay person in Lansing. He was sweet, pleasant, and already a college graduate. He managed to talk me into anal sex.

We drove back to his place. I was surprised how tiny and stark it was. Being a student, I was used to economical living arrangements, but I thought a gay man out of the closet would have a more "mature" type of apartment.

Very calmly and gently he placed my legs over his shoulders. He lubed himself up and entered me. "Hold on," he coaxed. "Just hold on."

God, it hurt. I tried to focus on something else and settled on a bowl of fruit on his table—a wooden bowl with two red apples, a banana, and two oranges—the one touch in his apartment that seemed grown-up, like something out of a 1950s *Life* magazine photograph. The fruit bowl represented an image I had of the perfect adult life. It promised that yes, I would have many friends, any one of whom might unexpectedly pop by my perfect home. Amid laughter and good cheer, the cool, perfect fruit, unblemished, carefully selected by me, would be ready to assuage my friends' hunger.

I think we were airborne for a while. We discovered later that both passenger-side tires had blown out. The highway patrol officer found a chunk of metal back on the highway, which is probably what I ran over. I never saw it.

The car floated and bounced at the same time, like one of those amusement park log rides that climaxes in a scary descent into a drenching explosion of water.

David was the last person I dated seriously. He had a season's pass to Disneyland, and in our short courtship we went there twice. He was also a print model—your standard tall, dark, and handsome hunk. David had really chewable lips, and the thick type of hair that allowed him to change hairstyles as often as his moods—which shifted at least twice daily. He was also in a couple of twelve-step programs. After we broke up, I vowed never again to date a model in recovery.

David loved just about everything at Disneyland, but especially Splash Mountain. We double-dated with his older brother, who I thought was cuter than David and definitely less manic. I insisted on riding in the front seat for the best view of our fall from the heights. David was behind me, his brother and his brother's boyfriend behind him. With David's arms snaked around my chest and his legs on top of mine, we floated and bumped our way into the mountain.

As soon as our eyes adjusted to the darkness of the cavern, we rounded a bend and were assaulted with a Dayglo-bright landscape dominated by Uncle Remus characters. We slid on, while "Song of the South" blared over the speakers. I could feel David's hard-on under his Banana Republic walking shorts press against the butt of my black 501s. Zip-a-dee-doo-dah, indeed. He squeezed me, "I love you," he said. "Oh, thanks," I said. He gave a nudge, "I love you," he repeated. "Oh, look," I pointed out, "there's that silly Br'er Rabbit." "I love you," David insisted.

I knew David wanted me to say, "I love you." That wasn't so hard. I just hated being trapped in a boat with him, his arms tightening around me, waiting for me to say those three little words. But what harm could it do?

"I love you, too," I mumbled.

David was so excited he bounced up and down in our floating log, almost tipping us over. We exited the mountain and started to hurtle toward the earth.

Steering proved impossible. I held the wheel as firmly as I could while the car jumped and shook. Suddenly it swerved toward the concrete median and hit it head on.

I couldn't breathe. A cloud of glass from the remains of the headlights rose up, catching the California sunshine. The engine screamed as it scraped sideways against stone.

Some Hindus say that what you think of at your moment of death determines what you will come back as in your next life. A powerful king in ancient India was thinking of his pet deer when he died, so he was reincarnated as a deer. The recommended plan is to always chant "Ram," the name of God. If you die with God's name on your lips, you will come back to a better life.

I wasn't thinking of anything alive or anything as big as God when we hit. I just saw the sparkles of the shattered glass shimmering up through the air. Would I come back as something glittery? Maybe a spangle on a female impersonator's right hip? A drip of pre-cum rolling off a cockhead under the streetlights at Collingwood Park?

Perhaps your next life's fate is not determined by what you think, but by the outfit you're wearing when you die. I was dressed all in black, poised to fall back into the void. Or perhaps ready to be reborn immediately through the dark tunnel of a birth canal.

Could it be your after-death experience is determined by what you last ate? Oh God, it was a bacon cheeseburger at lunch for me. I'm sure to fry in hell, or come back as one of those clueless cows outside the giant slaughterhouse up there on Interstate 5, wandering through the stink of manure and death.

Well, it could have been worse. At least I didn't say, "Oh shit," when the concrete wall appeared in front of me.

Or maybe your future in the next life is determined by who you last had sex with.

It was Jerry. Redhead Jerry with the ivory-smooth body. I met him a couple of Thanksgivings ago. I've never had sex with someone who laughed and giggled so much. He had just moved to San Francisco from Texas after serving a few years in the army, where he achieved the rank of master sergeant. He got the nickname "Smiley" in the service. His grin was big, and he had perfect teeth. A sweet man with a honeyed Texas accent, full of energy.

On his chest, over his heart, bloomed a tattoo of a stemmed rose, half opened. I asked him about it. One night, he said, all the men in his unit went to the tattoo parlor off base and had the same rose inscribed on each of their chests. All of them, I asked? All of them, Jerry giggled. Well was everyone in your unit gay? I wondered. Oh no, said Jerry. Then he paused and laughed again.

I ran into him this Presidents' Day weekend. Jerry's smile had noticeably faded, though it still shone brighter than most on Castro Street. Things were hard. He was only working part-time jobs, had been ripped off by a couple of gay restaurant owners. The friend he'd initially stayed with in San Francisco had died of AIDS. As had others.

Our sex was simple—kissing, and hugging. We shoved our tongues down each other's throats while we jacked ourselves off. Then we held each other.

Earlier that night I went to see Holly Hughes in performance, one of the infamous NEA Four. Still a target for the fire of God-fearing conservatives.

In her new piece she spoke of her father's recent cancer diagnosis. How when someone manifests a disease, that disease rises up in the middle of the night and enters the bodies of all those who care about the ill person. Everyone is affected.

Jerry felt heavy in my arms. The Market Street traffic was noisy outside his bedroom. It's a wonder how anyone can even stand up in San Francisco, carrying the weight of all those AIDS verdicts, the hundreds of people cared about over the years now gone, from lovers to clerks at the corner grocery. And more leaving every day. How can anyone function at all?

This visit I noticed that San Franciscans had a sad twist to their faces. Fifteen years of a plague can do that.

I pulled Jerry closer to me.

We smashed off the wall. I could see debris hovering in the air where we had been. Where was I? The car seemed to collapse. I couldn't breathe. We kept spinning.

The Teacups at Disneyland used to be my favorite ride. Keep Space Mountain, the Matterhorn. And David, keep your Splash Mountain. The whirling Teacups gave me more of a buzz than those other rides combined. And they were interactive! You controlled the speed of your rotation by how quickly you turned the wheel in the center of the teacup. There was something delicious and subversive about watching the perfect Disney landscape dissolve, like in an acid trip, into colorful blurs.

The last time there, I became ill from the Teacups. I broke out in a sweat and grew clammy, cold. After the ride, it took a few minutes before I could walk without dizziness. Was it an indicator of a declining immune system, or just the advance of middle age? I haven't been back since.

Finally stopped, pointing the wrong way on the freeway, I saw a host of horrified faces behind windshields. I don't want to die looking at someone looking at me like that.

Nobody hit us—no tanker filled with gasoline, no tractor-trailer—and apparently we didn't hit anyone—no school bus, no Volkswagen bug. Without incident the river of vehicles on the Interstate gingerly slowed, then halted.

I still couldn't breathe, was gulping for air, the center of my chest a hole on fire. "Relax, just relax," Danny told me. I tried to breathe, in and out. Slowly; little breaths at first.

People ran up. "Are you all right? Are you all right?" I didn't think I was.

Two women appeared, one in a dark tailored suit, on Danny's side of the car. She punched numbers on her portable phone, dialing for help. Later, Danny told me she said, "Don't worry, you boys will be all right."

Her friend came over on my side. All I could see was her blue and white checked dress and long blond hair. She held my arm and started massaging it.

I heard somewhere that the most important thing to do for someone in an accident or other trauma situation is to touch them. Words aren't enough. The physical contact lets them know that they are not alone. I'd promised myself that if I ever found myself in a situation to give help like that, I would be sure to make contact with the injured person. Now this stranger was doing it for me.

My breathing came easier, grew deeper. "It's a horrible thing to happen to anyone," she said, "but especially you guys."

I wondered, "especially you guys"? Who was this person? I wanted to see her face. Was she a dyke? Did she know we were gay? I tried to turn, but she said no, just relax, as she kept up a gentle pressure. I forced myself and looked to where her face would be, but all I remember is a halo of bright blond hair.

"Man, your car is gone," someone said, then the CHP officers came up, then the ambulance. The stream of traffic resumed around us, a temporary annoyance in the flow. We could walk. Our seatbelts had limited our injuries to pulled and battered muscles, though our car was totaled. I could breathe again. But those two women had disappeared. I wanted to thank them. No one saw them leave.

Everything would be all right. We were alive.

Perhaps those tense faces on the sidewalks of San Francisco were simply reflecting stress over the many days of rain this winter. Maybe everyone was anxious for sunshine and spring, for life again.

It was unseasonably warm the evening of the Holly Hughes performance. The rainbow colors of the sunset glowed garish as popsicles. The first stars blinked on.

Hurrying to the performance I passed pairs of men strolling, holding hands. In all my years of living in and visiting San Francisco, I never noticed so many men walking hand in hand, smiling, enjoying each other's simple touch. Walking brightly into the approaching night, as if guided by angels. Protected, for the moment.

Adam Klein

A Desert Shade

Bijay, the proprietor of Shiva Lodge, stood at the door in his underwear, shaking his head sadly and telling me not to pay the boy. "I don't hire commission boys to bring people to my lodge, but you still end up paying." He led me inside, shouting something in Hindi as he closed the door.

I took the room at the top of a stone stairwell, and when the large wooden shutters were opened I had an unobstructed view of the Ganges and the pilgrims descending to its edge. Sometimes the monsoon rains would cool the room and leave the floor around my bed wet, and the moonlight glinting from the floor and the Ganges would connect them so that it seemed I was floating on its slow, gray surface. I remember a dream I had after falling asleep during one of the rains. In it, my bed was a raft on the Ganges and I saw religious people bathing in the waters. The water was silver, like a daguerreotype, or a mirror. And the people were bringing the water up to their faces, which would change by that contact, suddenly bearing the immutable expressions of old photographs. I remember putting my legs over the side of the raft and the water not being liquid, but ash. And when I cupped my hands and brought it toward my face, the ash began to separate like mercury, revealing a scalp and teeth. And then my legs were brushed by something and I was certain it was the rest of this body I had in my hands. I woke up sweating and would not let myself fall back to sleep. It was five in the morning when I left the lodge and began walking.

The ghats were silent except for the boatmen calling me

down to the water. The sadhus sat meditating under large umbrellas, and from the temples I could hear a singer and the tanpura. I walked to the burning ghats, where the cremations were well under way, and stood above the bodies being prepared with clarified butter and broken sticks. The men who prepared the bodies and the people who mourned were all eclipsed by the smoke and the fires, which burned all day. And I remember feeling haunted by a loneliness that made me want to get too close to the body on the pyre, as though I'd found a reason and a place for grief.

I sat down. The sun was bleary on the horizon. A boy walked toward me carrying a rolled-up mat under his arm. He squatted down behind me and I felt his knees in my back. He put his hands around my forehead. Then, still gripping, he drew his hands back across my temples, pulling my hair back tightly. "Indian head massage," he whispered in my ear, "twenty rupees." I closed my eyes and let him continue. He pressed around my eyes with his fingers. The fever made it feel like he was shaping fire in my head. I felt myself sweating and breathing hard. I imagined his mouth on my neck and on my ears while his hands covered my eyes and his fingers pinched my eyelids. And then I let my strength go. His fingers pressed at every indentation of my skull. I felt so weak that it seemed he was holding my head up, that his hands had gotten inside my skull and were opening my eyes from behind.

I felt his hands on my shoulders and under my arms. "Take off your shirt," he said, but he was already lifting it off. Then he rolled out his mat and laid me down on it. He touched my stomach and I winced with pain. "This is all swollen," he said uncomfortably.

"I'm not well," I said, trying to lift my head.

I felt his fingers on my legs and at my thighs. I felt embarrassed by how sexual I felt, and looked down the steps of the ghat; only the boatmen were out, the sun bleeding over the Ganges. I looked at his eyes, dark and troubled. He was smiling as his hands came to my groin. But I wasn't sure of his smile, if it wasn't the smile of someone who will have his revenge.

He put his hands under my neck and lifted me slowly into a sitting position. "I am finished now," he said. "You must feel better?"

"I feel dizzy," and I gripped his arm.

"Eighty rupees," he commanded. "For the full body massage."

"Twenty," I said, but I suddenly felt choked, like crying.

"Eighty," he persisted.

"O.K., eighty. But please, I need your help," I pleaded. "I don't think I can get back on my own."

But with the rupees clenched in his hand, he was gone.

I walked up the steps of the ghat and came to the marketplace, but I was already slumped in exhaustion. I was still haunted by his hands. Wherever they had been, I ached. The vendors, just setting up, called me over. Someone's hand was on my sleeve, I heard, "My brother's shop." I felt myself being pulled along. I was seeing only the ground, the feet passing, a woman's toe ring, the slime on the stone. I was pulled through the market, but they were forcing me, so I pulled away. I imagined my face looked bloodless and terrible like a mask. I no longer saw the man who had entreated me to follow, just the blank expressions of the rushing crowd. They watched me walk up the street, then I fell forward, everything went black, and I hit the stone.

Bijay asked me how it happened, how I came to be so sick. I told him I had an Indian head massage on the steps of the ghat. I wanted to ascribe my sickness to the boy's hands.

"How much did you pay?" he asked.

"Eighty rupees for the full body," I told him.

"You paid too much. You could have paid forty rupees for an hour in your own room."

"I don't care about it," I said. "I'm not an Indian, and I've never paid an Indian price for anything."

He frowned at me. "You should care," he said. Then he closed the door behind him.

I slept restlessly while the shutters banged. I remember waking up at intervals and the light being different in the room. And then it was extinguished. I felt nauseous and walked to the bathroom. I stood over the squat toilet, and liquid, like rusty tap water, began to drain from me. And then the vomiting started. I felt everything convulsing and crumpled weakly to the floor. I lay curled on the floor a long time, shivering and dehydrated. I told myself to keep quiet. I was afraid of Bijay, of his concern.

The next morning I heard a rattling at my door, and I lay there watching it, amused, thinking it was Bijay carrying curd and not wanting to wake me. Then it burst open, and a monkey baring its teeth stood aggressively in the doorway, watching me. I sat up, though not quickly, frightened but not wanting to scare it. It shot forward into the room and leapt up on the bedframe. Its face was horrifying and compelling. It reached down near my foot and began gathering the blanket in its hand. It drew the covers slowly off me until I was naked there with it. I watched my heart pounding under the skin; I imagined the animal tearing it out. Maybe I would have screamed for Bijay, but the animal became spooked and darted from the room, leaving the covers strewn over the floor.

"I think it would be better for me in America," Bijay said. "Indians are very nosy, they watch you all the time." For three days I had been in bed and no more active than he. I would watch him from above, lighting his chillum and filling his clay pots with bath water. There was nothing here in his tower of silence, nothing but talks with foreigners he couldn't fully understand and who couldn't understand him. No, it was more than language; it was life that kept him apart. He was completely alone, as far from India as I was, and no closer to America.

"I can do whatever I want," he said, "I am still a bachelor. I have no wife and no dowries to pay. But what good is freedom in India when everyone is watching you, waiting to see what you will do, what mistakes you will make?"

~

I rode first class on the way to Jaipur; the berth was empty for most of the ride. It was too hot at night to use the blankets they supplied. Instead, I took a cotton lungi from my bag and wet it down with water I'd brought from the bathroom, then stretched it over myself, and it was cool for a while. I kept the windows open even as we made our way across the desert and the sand began to cover the floor. Eventually the monotonous sound of the train became secondary to the silence of the desert. It seemed as though the tracks were buried behind us like the bones of an animal. During the day I'd see the women coming off the horizon in their brightly dyed veils carrying stones in wide baskets on their heads. From far off they appeared like sails, their saris beating in the wind. It seemed impossible that they could find their way to the tracks, to the specific spot where they would lie and break their stones. They made their way through the emptiness, over the hot, white sand, as though it were in them, as though emptiness was what they were most certain of. I imagined myself walking out into the desert. Could I read the lines the wind left in the sand, or the snake tracks one sees in the mornings? I knew for certain I'd be lost in the desert silence. But as I lay there staring out the window, the landscape seemed more and more familiar, and I felt for the first time a connection to India and all its unknowable miles.

I let the sand pepper my face. I felt it stinging at the corners of my mouth. The moon had risen, a perfect disc, and the desert stretched out blue-black in the darkness like a mirror of space. We traveled three hours before we came to the next village.

There were lights strung in the station, and a rush of faces and hands pressed against the grilled windows of the train. Some were offering food or chai, others just hung on the window, staring, smiling. They seemed hypnotized by these faces moving across the desert. I smiled back at them, their faces glowing under the yellow, swinging illuminations of the lanterns. This stream of faces was a mystery they toiled to keep alive with their endless breaking of stones and shifting of iron.

A young man, an Indian in a Western-style suit, entered my berth. There was a crowd of Indian children outside the window by now, pushing their hands through the bars, talking and laughing excitedly among themselves. The man went to the window and shut the glass. "They're laughing at you," he said.

"Why?" I asked, stung, looking briefly at their cruel faces.

"They're just children," he said, smiling and sitting across from me. "To them you are something new. And then, of course, you're wearing only that lungi over yourself, and you are covered with sand."

"Here," he said, reaching out with a handkerchief. "To wipe the sand from your eyelashes and your lips."

I began to wipe the sand away, but as if I were a child without any understanding of my face; he came and sat next to me and took the cloth from me and rubbed my face. He smiled down at me, his eyes observing and comforting at the same time.

"You have a fever," he said.

"I thought so."

"Do you want chai?" he asked, smiling more comfortably when the train began to move out of the yellow generated light of the station. In the dimness he sat facing me, and his eyes were charming.

"No," I answered. "Where are you going?"

"To Jaipur. My family has a business there, gems."

"I'm also going to Jaipur," I told him.

"Did you know it is famous for its gems? Look at my ring. Do you like it?"

"Yes," I said, "but I really don't know anything about gems." I looked out the window. *I don't want to go to your jewelry store.*

"This is a Star of Burma."

"It's pretty," I said. My eyes were on the desert, empty.

"Maybe it's not as beautiful as the stars you're looking at." He joined me at the window.

"You can't set them in gold and wear them on your finger," I said somberly.

He laughed. I was surprised to hear it and turned to look at his face. His eyes were brown and warm in the shadow, and he stared at me as though my sadness had contour or meaning. Before I turned away from him I felt his hand move up my back, and with a gentle but determined force, I felt him draw me toward him.

"Have you taken pleasure with an Indian man before?" he whispered.

"No," I answered. *Taken pleasure*—I smiled.

"I will write you my address in Jaipur."

"What's your name?"

"John," he said. I did not ask him for his Indian name.

After a silence I asked, "Can you tell I'm sick?"

"All tourists get sick. Even I get sick when I return from Europe."

"Please open the window."

He hesitated. "The sand is blowing all over the cabin."

"I'm so hot," I said, almost panicking. "I can't breathe."

He opened it. The desert invaded immediately. The sand slid across the table and gathered around the water bottles.

I asked him to take a water bottle and wet down the lungi I was stretched naked beneath.

"You don't want to waste your drinking water," he said.

"They're refilled with the water from the bathroom." I pointed to where he should start, the top of the lungi, just below my neck.

He was nervous turning the bottle up, as though it were blood. He poured lightly at first, thin streams that I felt stretch over the fabric, cooling my body down. He poured the water heavily over my crotch and thighs. He looked closely, but didn't touch me.

Finally, rubbing two of his fingers over my lips, he said, "I will get us chai."

He left the berth and came back with a large thermos. He poured out a cup and held it to my lips. It was too hot for tea, but I drank it for his effort.

He let himself stroke my hair and I closed my eyes, trusting him enough to fall asleep, leaving everything unlocked and unguarded.

I woke up some hours later. The sand had covered over everything. I could feel it on my cheeks like a stubble. I could feel it under my nails. It had gathered on the lungi between my legs, and between my fingers. John was gone. It was easy to imagine he had never been with me. My possessions, becoming fewer and fewer, were untouched.

I looked out the window then, and in the darkness I was able to see the outline of homes just a few yards from the tracks and people out on their doorsteps, the wind blowing their hair across their faces. It must have been after midnight, so it was strange to see them there, as though they'd roused themselves so as not to miss our passing.

In the distance behind them I saw a sudden series of colorful lights flashing and rotating, a carnival a few miles from the tracks. Jaipur. I gathered my things in case the signs confirmed it when we pulled in. When I took the water bottle from the table, I found his address on a small torn square of paper. I rescued it. The ink had begun to run.

The train moved slowly into the station as though it were nudging its way through the throngs of people. The crowds were taking refuge from the rains, the first in three years. I watched them with their umbrellas and sheets of newspaper over their heads, running from the rain but with expressions of excitement and joy. The rain affected them like a prophecy or a promise. I watched others staring out at it as though it were a theater curtain.

People began to jump from the train, and I watched them moving through the crowd until they were taken up and embraced by family, or took seats on the floor, waiting for the bicycle rickshaws to commence service. I looked out over the crowd to see John, but I didn't trust my memory of his face. I remembered the Star of Burma and how he'd shown it. He was lost somewhere, and when I gave up searching for him I was shocked by the part of me that had ventured out like a tentative root.

In the hotel I discovered a rash covering my side, like a continent mapped on a globe. I was feeling better, but now my body had this marking, and I could not reconcile the two. There were moments when I could imagine wellness, but the long red patch remained. It was impossible not to think of the sickness and how far it would extend. It became a vigil, to watch the borders.

I took a rickshaw into the old city, the pink city, the walls around it cut from pink sandstone. Brightly painted suns crowned the lampposts. The streets were wider here, and for the first time in an Indian city I did not feel cramped. The rickshaw driver let me off at the Palace of the Winds, and I stood back from it so I could see its ornate edges and honeycombed windows. The women of a historical court were once kept here, and I could imagine their eyes flashing behind the filigreed bars on the windows.

I thought of John and called to a rickshaw driver. We passed through the city's gates, and already I remembered these places, the fruit stands and bookshops. The rickshaw driver was practically stoic as he drove; he was trying to convince me that he knew this address. But he'd consulted with five other drivers, and I felt I had to keep asking just to keep him from pedaling to exhaustion. He swerved suddenly and took us down an unpaved side street that kept the rickshaw jumping and put an unbearable strain into his face. At the first square we reached, he stopped pedaling and turned hesitantly toward me.

"We are here," he said.

"Where is here?" I asked with some amusement in my voice.

"The address you want to go."

"I see." I looked around, and there were so many children and they were moving toward me with their hands already outstretched. I stepped out of the rickshaw and paid him the price we'd discussed.

"No, sir," I heard him say as the children took hold. "It is forty rupees, not twenty."

They were shouting and pushing each other to shake my hand. Some of the young boys shook my hand elaborately or with such force I began to worry that they would overpower me.

I pulled out the address for one of them who was eagerly asking, "Are you lost?"

He stared at the square of paper for some time, rubbing his thumb across it as the others looked on.

"English?" he asked finally.

I read the street name off the paper. The children just looked enthusiastic and confused. I put it away and started walking, losing some of them to their street games and to the ice cream stands. The streets were dominated by the gem trade. Workers sat crouched over rotating wheels, refining gems at the ends of sticks. Men stood in doorways calling me in.

I would see him in a doorway, too, and my recognition would be immediate, and he would know by the way I hesitated to step any further that I had come for something impossible.

I did not see him, though, and when I asked the other shopkeepers they did not know the street I tried to pronounce. I began to think he must have written this name to confuse them —when they said it to themselves, their minds went blank.

I wanted to look into every doorway, see behind every curtain. The address he'd written was a hoax, a screen. But there was a part of me already resigned not to find him. I thought of us on that train—had we spoken at all? When I imagine us speaking now, there is a subtext of futility that drowns out our words.

I entered a shop. The man in the doorway offered chai. His expression was gentle and assuring as he put his arm around my shoulder. I realized that I wanted John to tell me I wasn't sick, no more than any other tourist, and that I wasn't alone. The man displayed a tray of rings.

I was looking at the stones. I was crying. The shopkeeper noticed my tears.

"It's just dust in my eye," I told him, and took the tissue he offered. I pointed to the center of the tray. "Is this a Star of Burma?" I asked.

"Very good," he said excitedly. "Do you know how you can tell their value?" He didn't need to be a good salesman, but he was.

"Can't someone wire you the money from the States?" he asked, when I told him the price would break me.

"I can take your traveler's checks at a very good rate," he persisted.

I shuffled the last of my checks. This is another three months in India, I thought as I endorsed them. Somehow, I felt free of the burden of watching them diminish.

The white star is like a blossom trapped in the pink stone, like something alive in a glass ball. You judge the value of the stone by the fullness of its star, by the spears of light it emits.

"You can sell this for hundreds of dollars back home," he said. It fit my finger perfectly.

In my room, I rolled my clothes into my suitcase. I went through my money belt. It scared me then—when I realized how little money I had left. It was as though I had put pressure on myself to expire before it did. I almost hoped that I would, so I would not have to depend on mercy.

⌒

The driver was distributing the baggage alongside the bus, and the vendors wove their way through the new arrivals, strung flowers hanging from their arms. The boy offered to take the bag for me.

"I will take you to my uncle's lodge," he said. He was wearing the customary earrings of the Rajasthani villagers, six-petaled flowers with rubies, sapphires, or diamonds on each petal. The men wear them in both ears, and it seems to make them soft around the eyes. His long black eyelashes made him look both feminine and sad. We walked silently together. There are no rickshaws in Pushkar, and the road was quiet and untraveled.

Pushkar is a small village, a ring of civilization around a lake. The lake is holy; it is claimed to be the footprint of Brahma, and businesses have sprung up around it like mushrooms. But the businesses are seasonal operations and haven't destroyed the lake as a place of prayer and worship. An almost hypnotic gentle rippling marked the surface of the lake, manifesting itself in the pace of life around it.

We arrived at the Lotus Lodge, a small establishment of maybe eight rooms and a courtyard that sloped down to the lakefront. The boy dropped my bag and called out to the owner, who approached me with his hand extended. He shook mine enthusiastically and asked the boy to make chai.

We sat at a table on the lawn and he pulled his accounting book from under his arm. His name was Acharya. He was balding on top of his head and wore wire-framed glasses, which acted as his business attire. The only clothing he wore was a pair of underwear and the Brahmin string, a janai, which hung loosely from his shoulder.

He began writing in his book and simultaneously telling me of the difficulties he'd had getting someone to fix the fans in the room. As he talked I looked over at the storage room, where the boy was squatting before the fire, making our chai. There was no light on inside and it seemed like a cave in there, the boy's eyes like an animal's.

Acharya explained that the room would be only ten rupees a night, since the fan was out and I'd most likely prefer to bring my cot out on the lawn and sleep there.

"Then you have only to worry about the monkeys in the

morning," he said. "When they come down from the trees they like to run along this back wall." Even then a family of monkeys was playing on it. "The boy did the painting there," he continued. "It is the symbol of the Om."

Just then the boy emerged with a tray and two cups of chai. He bowed with a strange formality as he served us, and his uncle asked him then to fill the shower tanks with lake water. Acharya and I sipped our tea in the heat, watching the boy trudge with the water buckets from the lake to the top of the hill, where a cement shower room was built for guests.

By the time we had taken our chai I was ready to lie down, and the boy walked me to a room and placed my bag inside. I stretched out on my cot and closed my eyes, and the boy started singing one of the popular Indian songs I'd heard reproduced in every wedding procession and played in the streets from every radio. He sang it very quietly as he began to sweep the corners of the room.

The fever escalated rapidly; it felt like fingers on my throat, and soon I was gasping. The boy was sitting by me; next to his bare feet he had a pail of lake water, and using an old rag, he wet me down with it. He did it with patience, as though tending to me was all he had to do that day, and he continued singing, a melody that wove its way in and out of my delirium.

He did this for days that I could not keep track of—keeping me in the shade during the day and at night carrying first my cot and then me out to the lawn, where it was cooler. He fed me curd and bananas in the afternoon, dahl at night. Finally the fever broke, and he quickly took the bedding from my room to wash.

At sundown I left the room and sat weakly in a chair facing the lake. The sky was divided—a band of fiery orange and, just above it, a night sky, black and heavy with stars. There was no one on the lawn, just the long shadows of the trees from behind me. A cool breeze was coming off the desert, and the patches of grass felt cool on my bare feet. This is how I will die, I thought, just after the pain breaks and I can feel again.

I sat there silently until Acharya drew up a chair beside me. "You feel better?" he asked.

"Yes," I said, "and thank the boy. He was a great comfort."

"He is a hard worker; I was lucky to have found him. He was very sick when I first saw him. It cost me a great deal to have him taken care of."

"You are his uncle?" I asked.

"I suppose so," he laughed. "He is convinced of it."

"He must be grateful to you."

"Yes," he said. "I let him live here. He cooks and cleans. He is quiet."

Just then I heard some music, faint but beautiful, which made our shadows on the lawn and the surface of the lake seem as luxurious as life depicted in a miniature painting.

"That's him," he said. "He is a good musician. All of his family played."

I remembered the melody. He had been humming it at my bedside. I looked over my shoulder and saw a fire burning in the storage room, and in that light the boy was playing.

"Both of his parents died. They were villagers, musicians. His father died when he was young. His mother died slowly; she was very sick. She could not see; she could not walk. He would come miles by foot to Pushkar to play the instrument his father left him. He would make money and bring back food and medicine to her. He was always playing, and he was always serious. Then one day he came out of the desert. I noticed him, from far off. He looked so broken and so old, like a sadhu. But he was just a boy, crying over the loss of his mother. I could see he was very sick himself. I told him he could work for me when he got well. He has worked for me for five years."

He turned toward the storage room, where I was watching the boy's shadow flicker along the wall, and shouted out for chai. The boy put his instrument down and went for glasses.

Acharya leaned toward me from his chair. "I have alcohol," he whispered. "The boy picks it up for me in Ajmer because Pushkar is dry. It is not acceptable for a Brahmin to drink." I could smell the liquor on him then, and his eyes were deep with his confession. "That makes me an unacceptable Brahmin."

The boy came with chai in tall glasses. He handed us each a glass and smiled at me as though he were pleased with his nursing and my recovery. He said goodnight and walked back to the room where the fire was burning. I saw him take his lungi off and spread it on the floor, and that is where he slept.

In the morning I awoke to the shrill cries of peacocks, hysterical in the trees, as though they were stranded there. Acharya was still sleeping, in a cot near mine.

I walked down to the lake. There were groups of monkeys huddled by its shore, and a swimmer at its center. I took off my shirt and pants and left them in a pile at the edge of the lawn. I walked down to the water and put my foot into it, and watched it, blurry under the surface. I worried that someone would take notice of my illness, which seemed to afflict my whole body in one way or another. The patch on my chest had grown, and there were small irregular marks on my legs and thighs.

The swimmer had made his way back to the shore and was only a few yards away before I recognized him as the boy who'd taken me here and nursed me. He began to call for me, waving his hands above his head.

"The water is good for you," he said, laughing. "Don't be afraid."

I stepped carefully into the water, then pushed myself away from the edge using my feet on the algae-covered rocks. He swam toward me and grasped my hand when he could reach it.

We kept ourselves afloat with just our legs paddling in the current beneath us. He put his hands on my shoulders.

"Try to stay still," he said. He was smiling and drawing me close to him.

"What's that?" I asked, almost jumping out of the water.

"That's the fish," he laughed. "They're kissing us."

It felt suddenly as if there were hundreds of them, brushing between our legs, lightly connecting their mouths to us.

"I should go back," I said.

"I'll go with you." He offered his hand again and we swam back together. He pulled me up on shore and carried my clothing down to me.

"Do you want chai?" he asked.

"No," I said. "Today I am going to walk and see the rest of Pushkar."

"Let me take you?"

"Yes," I said.

He was wearing Rajasthani shoes that point at the toe, his lungi, and a turban with multiple knots and gatherings. He carried his instrument with him. The shops were quiet. The tailors sat on their folded fabrics smoking bidis and reading newspapers. Cows wandered through the streets with flowers in their mouths. When we passed a tourist, the boy lifted his instrument to his chest the way country musicians in America hold their violins. And he started to play, something that repeated itself, as the bells dangling on the bow kept time. It was a sad, serial melody that developed slowly and slightly, music that was sweet and painful, that returned mournfully to its themes like a memory of childhood.

He kept his eyes averted as he played. He wanted to slip behind his sorrowful invocation, invisible. He wanted the music and not his eyes to make the listener sympathetic. He wanted the music to ask for coins.

The woman he played for stopped and watched him, then handed him a five-rupee note. When she had walked off he continued playing for me.

We sat down in a restaurant boasting pizza. "The prices are too high here," he said.

"I'll buy," I said. I was already out of breath.

When the food arrived, I couldn't eat. I was sweating heavily. Suddenly, my circumstances terrified me. I would barely be able to afford another week here before the money ran out, and there was perhaps less time than that before my health would fail me entirely.

I sat there squeezing my head in my hands, trying to stop the anxious thoughts. But I couldn't stop them. I could not accept the arrangements I had made for myself. I had cornered myself. I had to die or beg for charity. But I couldn't beg.

The boy asked me, "Are you going to be sick?"

"Yes," I told him, and I put my hands over my eyes so he wouldn't see me crying.

"What's wrong with you?" he asked.

"I'm tired."

"We will go back now," he said, standing.

He took up his instrument and walked a few paces behind me, playing. It seemed as though I was walking through my own funeral procession, with people turning their heads as we walked. The desert whistling behind the awninged shops made the whole town seem like a painted curtain. He followed me halfway around the lake before I turned to him and asked his name.

"Sanjay," he said.

Someone called out from a chai shop, and I turned around. It was a German I'd met in Jaipur. I walked back to see him. He was sitting in a large wicker chair, smiling.

"It's good to see you here. The last time I saw you, you were telling me how much you needed a rest. It's restful here, though I can't say you look any better for it."

"It's worse," I said, joining him at the table.

Sanjay sat down too, but looked uncomfortable and kept his attention on the street. Eventually another musician boy, a little older than him, approached. They spoke to each other, often glancing back at the German and me, until I asked Sanjay to go on without me.

He looked sadly at me but didn't question my suggestion. He gathered his instrument and bow and asked if I would see him later. I assured him I would, and he and his friend walked off.

"Have you seen a doctor, yet?" the German asked.

"No, I don't have the money for it."

"There's a public hospital in Jodhpur, just across the street from the train station."

"I don't need a hospital. The boy is taking care of me."

"He's lovely," the German said, winking. "How long have you had him?"

"A few days. He helped me through a fever."

"What kind of medicine is he treating you with? Are you in pain?"

"No medicine, just cold rags and simple food."

"If you're in pain I can help you, " he said. "I have an opium connection here."

He offered to bring it by the Lotus Lodge later that evening.

"I'll have to leave India," he confided. "My permit ran out years ago. I read tarot cards to make a living. Tourists sometimes pay me in American money. I tell them my story, and most of them are horrified by the idea of being trapped in India and they sympathize with me. But I've loved India. It changes you. In Hamburg, my goal was to work in a bank, or to sell good German cars. In India, I'd be content to have a group of young boys who would follow me out into the desert like a holy man."

He laughed and looked over his shoulder as though he expected the desert to present him with a mirage, a preview of his enlightenment. "They'll catch up with me soon," he said, growing more serious. "Otherwise, I'm afraid if I do stay in India, I'll be tempted to walk out into the desert, even if I can't find anybody foolish enough to follow me. It sounds crazy, but it's a fantasy of mine."

It was late afternoon when I left the chai house. Sanjay was waiting on the street. He hesitated, though, until I called him over. Then he quickly took my arm and asked me if I would write my name on the face of his instrument.

"Write it under that tree," he said, pointing.

It was a beautiful spot he had chosen. We sat in the shade and he handed the instrument over to me. I took out my pen and scratched my name over the bleached leather. My markings were tentative. He watched over my shoulder, and I could hear the anticipation in his breathing. I felt at first I was defacing the beautiful instrument, which had four taut strings running along the wooden neck and over the gourdlike body, but he squeezed my arm to encourage me further. I thought it strange that he might remember me, sitting there and writing under that tree, by some markings he could not read.

We stretched out under the tree. He lay on his back with the instrument on his chest, plucking the strings with his long fingernails. He inclined his head so that it almost touched my chest. His eyes were closed and he was smiling.

"What are you thinking about?" I asked him.

"My mother let me play for her like this. When my father died, she wanted to die too. There was no rain and we lost everything. Then she got very sick and she stopped eating. Every meal I would force her to eat. She stopped being able to see, and then she said that she was already dead and she told me to go to

Pushkar and not come back. But I went back anyway," he laughed, nodding his head, "and I would play for her because it reminded her of my father. Then before she died she asked me to play the song I was just playing for you, and she started to sing, only quietly, but like she did when there was food to cook and friends still in the village."

I was trembling at his closeness. I wanted to lie beside him for the rest of the day, but there was only a short time to enjoy him. His friend approached and stood over us, laughing, then took his bow and began jabbing at Sanjay with it. He stood up and they began arguing.

Finally, Sanjay said the other boy wanted to play for me. He stood silently by the tree. I couldn't understand his expression, whether he felt ashamed of his friend, of me, or of himself. But his friend started to play and tapped his foot as he did. And it was the same melody I'd heard Sanjay play, but with none of the sadness, with a strange mockery instead. When he finished playing, he reached his hand out to me.

"You don't play as well as him," I said, looking over at Sanjay's quiet face. Then I stood up to go.

Sanjay walked beside me, apologizing. I told him it didn't matter, that I was tired and wanted to nap.

"I'm going to help you get better," he said.

I grasped his arm with a strength that surprised me. "You're not going to make me well," I said. "I'm dying, and you're not going to make me well."

He pulled his arm from my hand and ran off.

By the time I arrived back, I had cramps so severe I couldn't stand straight. I went into the shower room, took off my clothes, and let the water run. I stretched out on the floor beneath it and didn't move until the water tank had emptied. I sat on the shower floor, my teeth chattering. I prayed for the German to come with the opium—indirectly, it was the first time I'd prayed for medicine.

It was Sanjay who found me. He looked astonished by my condition. "You should go to the hospital," he said. His eyes were sadder than usual. I imagined him thinking, *Because you won't let me make you well.*

At that moment I wanted to tell him to try, that I would try also, but it was too unfair to do that to him again. His mother had waited too long before she sang with him. Even if I wanted to, I couldn't remember that tune.

"My medicine is coming," I said. "My friend will be here soon."

He woke me when the German finally came.

"Thomas," I said, already delirious with fever, "I can't believe you're here."

"This is Heinz," he said, taking my hand. "I don't know if I should give you this."

"Give it to me," I said. "It's like morphine, right? That's what they give soldiers when they can't help them."

He nervously paced the room and asked Sanjay to bring us chai. "I'll mix it in your tea. Drink it fast. It's bitter."

Sanjay brought the tea, then hesitantly left the room when the German asked him to.

The opium affected me powerfully, but not in the way we'd hoped. It stunned me. I threw up. I was nauseous at the slightest movement and sat still at the edge of the cot.

"Hospital," was all I said, gasping for breath.

The German paced nervously. I was throwing up in a bucket by the side of the cot, and the smell was pungent, like a hospital. I think he smelled death on me, and that propelled him to action. It wouldn't be easy getting me to Jodhpur, and I know he was worried that I wouldn't make it. How would he ever explain himself to the authorities, traveling with a long-expired visa and a dead American?

Under the influence of the opium, I didn't make much sense. I remember Sanjay coming into the room and taking out the bucket, and touching my face with his hands. I twisted the ring from my finger then, and put it in his hand. He was crying when the German finished packing my bag and led me away.

I saw an omen in the streets of Jodhpur. In front of a store I saw a white horse staggering on a mound of trash. It was tethered to a post by a rope tied around its neck. Its front leg looked broken, but it was made to stand by the short length of rope, and it seemed to have been in this condition for some time. Something like gangrene had set in, and the horse's flesh was putrid.

I was wheeled into the emergency ward of Mahatma Gandhi Public Hospital. They pressed me to lie down on a rusty stretcher with rubber wheels. The wheels squealed and turned off in odd directions so that the short, nervous intern who was guiding me through the hospital corridors had to run along the sides of it to save us from hitting a wall or one of the many spectators.

I was wheeled into a room where a woman and her daughter were standing. The little girl was weeping, her face pressed into the hot pink fabric of her mother's sari. Behind a green curtain, a man was screaming and crying.

They cleaned me up, brought me into the ward, and put me on IV for dehydration and malnutrition. The German saw me after I'd settled in, a crowd of interns gathered by my bedside, prodding me.

"I apologize," he said. "I can't stay with you. The hospital will drive me crazy."

"So will the desert," I told him.

"Get well," he said, "and come back to Pushkar."

In the bed near mine, an old man from a village not far from Jodhpur was connected to tubes. The men of the village had been sleeping on mats around his bed since he'd arrived. Old-world loyalty. They'd marveled at the beeping and pumping machines that kept the old man breathing. But an American was even more interesting. They spoke no English but gathered around my bed, smiling and bowing and excitedly talking among themselves.

The villagers are trying their turbans on my head, one by one. The fever sweeps over me. I no longer make any sense to them.

One of the sisters is crying at the bedside. Sanjay squeezes out a cloth and puts it on my forehead. I know his song now, and I hear my voice intoning it. The villagers stand at the foot of the bed. They look like a hundred grandfathers. They're patient with me. I keep looking back; I keep stumbling at the start of the desert.

Hanns Ebensten

First Night in the Promised Land

My arrival in the Promised Land was not very promising.

Plowing through high seas and winter fogs for four days and nights in November 1965 on the Zim Line's MV *Moledet* had been uncomfortable and dull. The Israeli government had used part of its German reparations to have a fleet of passenger ships built with which it planned to compete in the lucrative transatlantic and Mediterranean vacation markets, but had failed to realize that neither American nor European tourists wanted to be transported like immigrants—six to a cabin, a bathroom along the corridor, dismal meals, and no entertainments. The only pleasantly appointed room was a nursery reserved for children under the age of twelve, of whom many dozens ran screaming and shouting all over the ship and made life hell.

The smaller the country and the more recent its creation, the more complex and tiresome are its entry formalities. Endless forms had to be filled out, and long lines of fretful passengers formed in the lounge as the ship approached Haifa.

My passport and tourist visa were in order, but the immigration officer was not happy with my form. It had been foolish of me to have facetiously entered "Human" against "Race." My interrogator did not consider this amusing. Worse, "Religion: Christian" and "Place of Birth: Hamburg, Germany" gave him cause for concern.

"Where are parents?" he asked me.

"Dead."

"Any relatives living in Germany?"

"Yes, an uncle."

"His profession?"

"Colonel in the army."

This incongruous truth was clearly most unpalatable. A considerable delay ensued as others in line behind me were processed, until, after a whispered discussion among three officials, one of them led me away to a distant cabin. A security officer, wearing a short-sleeved shirt and with an impressive diver's watch on his hairy wrist, made me stand awkwardly before him as he lounged in an armchair, legs wide apart and crotch thrust aggressively forward, enjoying an obnoxious cigar while he flipped slowly through the pages of my passport and surveyed me.

"You have an uncle in the German army?"

"Yes. My mother's brother," I admitted.

"Other relatives in Germany?"

"No."

"They live elsewhere?"

"No. My father's relatives all died in concentration camps."

This was reassuring at last. Scrawling something on my form, he slipped it between the pages of the passport and handed it to me. "Enjoy your visit."

I thanked him and walked down the gangway to face the customs officials ashore.

The Israel Government Tourist Department had invited me to visit Israel's part of the Sinai Peninsula and make recommendations for tourism there. (It was not until 1984, when the whole of the Sinai Peninsula was Egyptian territory, that I led my first group across the peninsula in the way I had planned to do it more than twenty years before.) I had learned on previous visits that although the country was striving to attract not only pilgrims but tourists, Israelis were too busy with more important problems and projects to spare the time and make the effort to cosset visitors. Israel is very high on history, but sadly short of charm.

A representative of the Tourist Department met me outside the customs area and took me to an impressive car; it was to drive me to Tel Aviv, where I was to spend the night and meet my official hosts next day—but first, he said, we would make a little deviation to pick up some friends of his in order to give them a lift.

We drove north instead of south for more than an hour toward Safad and collected two women and three noisy, unruly children, who crowded into the back of the car and removed my suitcases from the trunk and filled it with their parcels and packages. I was not introduced to them, and no one spoke to me during the long drive back to Haifa and then to Tel Aviv. I sat between the driver and the government representative, who both smoked cigarettes and talked to each other in Hebrew as though I did not exist. It was almost midnight when they dropped me off outside the Dan Hotel, the pride of Israeli tourism.

The listless doorman made no attempt to carry my luggage into the lobby. The receptionist did not disguise his contempt. "Only one night?" he asked. After a great deal of searching in drawers and turning of ledgers, he found my reservation and handed me a key.

With a suitcase in each hand and my overnight bag tucked under one arm, I took the elevator up to my room—and was amazed to find that it was not merely a bedroom but an exceptionally grand suite on the top floor of the hotel, taking up the entire width of the building.

There was a huge sitting room filled with sumptuous furniture and a long terrace overlooking the Mediterranean; a corridor led to a magnificently appointed dressing room and bedroom, beyond which I found another balcony overlooking the city. Elaborate floral arrangements graced every table throughout the suite; there were lavish pyramids of fruit under cellophane and a box of chocolate mints and a bottle of water on a bedside table; books and magazines were neatly set out as in a library; on the writing desk stood a model of what looked like a town development.

I was bewildered. This display of luxury seemed most unsuitable for a single, unimportant guest. Why, I wondered, am I being treated like a visiting cinema actor or an expensive whore?

I walked from room to room, from the ocean view to the city view, and felt sad and lonely. Then I unpacked, tried out different light effects, and counted a total of twenty-three lamps, including four ceiling chandeliers that were fiendishly ornate, nibbled at the fruit and gorged on the chocolate mints, and went to sleep.

"Breakfast 7:00 to 10:00 A.M.," stated the hotel information sheet in my suite; but when I entered the dining room at five minutes past seven, I was not welcome. Waiters made ineffectual gestures to lay tables in a parody of slow-motion-movie style, and the members of a tour group filed into the room and settled down with resignation to await events.

After twenty minutes, a waiter approached me. He was an elderly Central European and doubtless possessed the highest qualifications to perform brain surgery or judge a court case, but he resented having to wait at table. He was unshaven and sickly pale.

I asked for tea, toast, and honey.

"*Toast?* Toast must be made; rolls are ready," he admonished me.

"But I prefer toast, please—"

"Why make me troubles? I give you rolls."

He also brought two kinds of jam, artificially colored red and green like traffic lights. I reminded him that I had asked for honey.

"I give you jams; why make me troubles and want honey?"

"But isn't Israel the land of milk and honey?" I asked him. "And I prefer honey."

"You *prefer!*" His whine rose to an anguished scream. "*Toast* you want! *Honey* you want! Who do you tourists think you are?"

After breakfast I went back to my suite, laid out my clothes for the luncheon meeting with the officials of the Tourist Department, put on my swimming trunks, and took a towel, a book, and my room key to the hotel beach.

It is always fascinating to arrive at a beach very early in the morning and watch as it becomes animated. I was the only hotel guest at that hour; the few other people were hardy year-round swimmers and gymnasts going with intense concentration through their morning gyrations.

Israeli women do not exercise—they become trees, tenderly putting out springtime buds, swaying in the summer breeze, shedding leaves with calm acceptance in the fall; they are lotus flowers, opening their dewy petals to welcome the sun; they are birds, free as the air, fluttering to and fro. Old ladies without an ounce of excess fat on their trim bodies, with sun-scorched skin like leather, and with their hair pulled back from their faces like a ballerina's, twisted slowly this way and that, raised arms to heaven, moved fingers like Indian palace mimes, stood for amazing lengths of time like storks on one trembling, varicose-veined leg. Old gentlemen ran up and down the beach, singly and in packs, encouraging one another and puffing with pleasure and exertion. Tough young men pranced and postured and turned somersaults, raced one another into the ocean, swam vigorously, then changed to go to work.

Later, as the December day became warmer and when the

good people of Tel Aviv were at their toil, less energetic women arrived. They greeted one another with screams of delight and rubbed one another's beautiful bodies with pungent oils. Their swimsuits were extremely abbreviated, and necklaces of bleached seashells or of gold set off their impeccable suntans. They flicked their fingers to the rhythms of portable radios, posed on bright towels, and hid their roving eyes behind dark glasses.

Later, a stunning tall man appeared on the beach and spread his towel near mine, pulled off his trousers and shirt, and surveyed the scene around us. He was very blond, muscular, and deeply tanned. Occasionally our eyes met. "English?" he inquired. I told him that it was my first day in Israel and asked him whether he was Scandinavian.

He was deeply offended.

"Me—Scandinavian? You think I am tourist? I am Israeli, born here, a Sabra."

I apologized for my blunder but said that I had been misled by his blond hair.

"So you think all Israelis must be thin little men with white skin in black suits and hats like in the old Polish ghettos?" he said. "We are a nation now; we have everything other nations have." He looked toward the young women in their bikinis, soaking up the wintry sun. "Even prostitutes: in the day they come here outside the Dan Hotel; at night, they are in the coffeehouses and bars on Dizengoff Street." He seemed proud that Israel was so advanced as to have ladies of easy virtue, yet disapproving.

Presently he leaned back onto his elbows and gave me a very meaningful look. "I wish—" he said.

"Yes?"

"I wish to go with you."

"Go with me?"

"Oh, you know what I mean. But I cannot take you to my house. My wife did not go to work today; my daughter is home sick with ear infection."

I told him that I had a place to go and showed him the key of my suite, with its massive metal Dan Hotel tag.

He was delighted and immediately began to pull on his clothes and roll up his towel. *"Maher, maher,"* he cried, "I only have forty minutes; I must be at work at one o'clock." It suited me fine—I, too, had only forty minutes before my luncheon meeting.

We walked through the underground passage from the beach into the hotel basement and took the elevator to the top floor. How impressed he will be with my opulent suite, I thought, with its flowers and fruit baskets.

We came out of the elevator and I began to lead him toward the suite at the end of the corridor; but there was a soldier sitting on either side of its door, and as we approached they rose, grim-faced, and pointed their automatic rifles at us.

"Hara!" shouted my golden Sabra, and ran back to the elevators.

I was totally bewildered and, barefooted and wearing only swimming trunks, felt extremely vulnerable and intimidated.

"That's my room," I said, and showed the key, but I did not take a step nearer.

A chambermaid came running up behind me. "Please, mister—other room for you!" she called out.

"But *that* is my room—"

The Sabra was frantically pressing the elevator buttons; one of the doors opened and he disappeared.

The maid led me back along the corridor to a small room, where I saw my clothes neatly laid out on the bed, my teddy bear propped up against the pillow; my books and maps lay on the dressing table. I found my shaver, my toothbrush, my 4711 eau de cologne, and my bottle of Dr. J. Collis Browne's Chlorodyne on the bathroom shelf. The maid handed me the key of the room in exchange for that of the suite from which I had been evicted.

At the luncheon meeting, my government hosts explained to me what had happened. They thought it was a great joke. I was not, happily, no longer a welcome guest in Israel, as I had feared. The night clerk had a made a monumental error and had given me the key of the suite that had been prepared for Mr. Levi Eshkol, Israel's prime minister, who had arrived from Jerusalem early in the morning.

The mistake had been noticed when the day staff came on duty, and the hotel management had tried all morning to contact me. Unable to find me, they had removed my belongings—and, presumably, quickly repaired the damage I had inflicted on the splendid fruit basket and the box of mint chocolates.

"We hear you travel with a teddy bear," my hosts said. I blushed.

They drove me up to Jerusalem in the afternoon, and before taking me to the King David Hotel made a detour through pretty, tree-lined suburban streets and slowed down the car outside a modest villa behind a high wall.

"We thought you might like to see where our prime minister sleeps when he is in Jerusalem," they said.

Edmund White

Shopping

We read a book by Mario Praz, an Italian critic, in which he describes all the objects in his palatial apartment in Rome, giving their pedigree and provenance and all his personal associations, including sometimes quite shocking revelations about his unhappy marriage and estranged daughter. Hubert and I keep thinking it would be funny to do a sort of comic version about our own apartment and all our junk, but I'm sometimes worried he won't have enough time left to do the pictures.

I say "junk," but Hubert would bridle at such a word. To him our place is a treasure house where we store up all the marvels we've unearthed on our trips. Or rather, *his* marvels, since his finds are all discoveries of museum-level artifacts, whereas poor old gullible Ed gets taken to the cleaner's every time.

Take the misshapen little jug with its elephant-gray hide and mold-blue inner glaze, the pure product of an arts-and-crafts class taught in an asylum by an incompetent to an indifferent on Thorazine, a three-dimensional daub Hubert seized on in what used to be East Berlin at a street fair across the canal from the Pergamon Museum. "It's obviously a . . . yes, a *honey pourer* from the late eighteenth century. I've *studied* such objects in paintings of the period. Laugh all you like, you'll see, an expert will come here one day and offer us a fabulous sum for it." He grows quiet and, irked, adds, "Funny that you can't see it. Usually your taste is rather good."

On the same trip Hubert bought me a Russian icon being hawked by a gentle young Slav. Hubert rejected other lacquered, highly colored icons in favor of this one, which has a warped wood back and a tin cover snipped into small openings to reveal paintings of Christ, his mother and various angels, all hopelessly rotted away or blackened with candle smoke except for one ineffaceable angel on the left with a consoling little salutation unscrolling from its mouth like ticker tape.

Hubert was racked with remorse for nights after this purchase; he thought he'd virtually stolen this masterpiece out of an impoverished Russian home of fallen aristocrats.

In a Toronto shop (which the French would say was run by a *brocanteur,* to mark a midway point between the noble antique dealer and the ignominious junkman), Hubert bought a 1930s lamp, now in his bedroom, with a chrome tango dancer dipping beside a clouded glass column—an obvious Original, which the pitifully unsuspecting dealer had let slip out of his careless hands for mere pennies. Curiously, the same shopkeeper became a cynical exploiter of a shockingly naive American when he sold me, at an exorbitant price, a green bowl of 1950s Finnish art glass (now filled with walnuts in the sitting room)—a worthless and ugly folly that Hubert keeps hiding away in the kitchen to spare me further embarrassment.

Hubert has a shelf of horrors he loves to show squeamish guests—a scorpion under glass, a tarantula in a paperweight, a Chinese portable cage in which to carry crickets (presently empty), and best of all, an immense ostrich foot outfitted with a very nasty-looking claw—which resembles a lethal homemade weapon cobbled together by a Road Warrior.

Showing the foot always provides Hubert with an opportunity to discuss his two years in Ethiopia. On our sitting room walls we have two large paintings, as impressive as they are grim, which Hubert bought in Addis Ababa, where he taught architecture for the French government. One painting depicts a squadron of men in blue-and-green uniforms marching and waving huge red banners. The other shows three military dictators in army uniform on a podium. They are staring directly at us while their followers, all identical men, avert their eyes either to the right or to the left. As Hubert explains, these canvases were done by a man who'd been one of Haile Selassie's official painters, but after the emperor was replaced by communists the artist gave up royal jousts and lions as his subjects and turned to dispiriting Marxist parades. Hubert met the painter, bought his work, and took his picture. In the photo he's shown in front of one of his paintings, but the African sunlight is so bright that the canvas is bleached white; only where his shadow falls across it are the colors and shapes visible.

Ethiopia remains such a reference for Hubert that he compares almost everything with it. When he went to New York for the first time he surprised me by comparing Manhattan to Addis Ababa. I was even more confused when he thought the New Mexico landscape looked like that of Ethiopia. Whenever Hubert's in a cross mood, our friend Christine (who lived with us in the States for a year) can get him out of it by diplomatically asking him a question about Ethiopia.

Nothing about that exotic, hermetic country seems excessive to Hubert or his ex-wife, Fabienne. She's an expert in Ethiopian culture and speaks three of the country's languages. She once showed me a photo of a strangely *hairy* arch of triumph. As she explained, since Mussolini's invading troops kept building Roman arches to celebrate their Abyssinian victories, the Ethiopian army decided after a victory of their own to put up an arch to which they tacked the severed testicles of their Italian prisoners. A photo (*this* photo) was duly sent to Mussolini. Hubert keeps wangling for a Xerox of it to add to his shelf of horrors, to be placed next to the ostrich foot.

If Hubert is guilty of exaggerating the importance of his purchases, I'm not above my own fudging. An orange-and-black lacquered coffee table in the sitting room comes from Chicago, so I've somehow decided to attribute it to Marx, a famous Midwestern designer of the 1940s, though I have nothing but wishing to substantiate my claim; in a similar spirit of optimism I've assigned the green-and-gold wrought-iron French end table to Poillerat, though my only basis for such an attribution is a near likeness I once came across in a photo book about 1940s furniture designers.

Hubert's brother has dubbed the bedroom the "White Museum" since Hubert has put up dozens of photos of me, everything from the two Mapplethorpe portraits (one screaming), taken in 1981 when I was still thin, to a more recent double portrait by Arthur Patten of Fred and me, each of us sporting three chins. I'm so embarrassed by the Musée White that I call it "Hubert's Room" and pray he won't say it's ours.

Although Hubert gets skinnier and skinnier, he likes it that Fred and I remain so robust. Sometimes, however, when I'm too hardheaded, he'll say, "You're just like Fred"—a reference to the basset's notoriously singleminded character. But since he loves Fred so much, I can't take the reproach as a genuine insult.

When I look around our "House of Life" (the title of Mario Praz's book), I feel a bit apprehensive. Hubert has said from the beginning that he's decorating it for me so I'll have a place to live after he's gone, though I can scarcely imagine rattling around it alone.

Cary Alan Johnson

Obi's Story

At seven A.M. he looked upon her, a fantastic bas-relief against a sea of smarting blue. Brown, open, a thrush of mountains plying down her spine, into a crack, a gully of darker. He had risen from a wet July night in New York, solid black and white with the genies of rising steam on JFK's tarmac, and broken through to a clear African morning. Through the porthole he watched the coast of Mauritania transform itself into the groundnut sand of Mali, only to be replaced by the lush Nigerian bush. The plane fell east and south.

The only black passenger in the first-class section, Stu had expected at least an African diplomat or two, or a businessman flying Air Afrique back home to Doula or Libreville after parlaying gold, diamonds, or oil into VCRs and expensive cars. He was alone with the Burkinabé flight attendant and felt a strange guilt each time one of the coach passengers, overwhelmingly Black Africans, would wander into the first-class cabin by mistake or out of curiosity.

As the Belgian woman in the aisle seat slept, a haughty nasal buzz came from her mouth. Back in New York, he had thought her French as they attempted the ad hoc friendship eight hours of flight necessitated. During the night she had spoken in her sleep, an ugly Flemish Afrikaans sound, he had thought, and remembered how frightened she was when the plane took off, crossing herself repeatedly, gripping her crucifix, the divider between their seats, and finally his arm as they lifted high above Long Island.

"*Pardon, Monsieur.* Flying makes me so nervous."

"*De rien, Madame,*" he responded with the magnanimity he always felt at the beginning of a long trip.

"Oh, you speak French? I thought you were *noir américain.*"

"Yes, I'm an American."

She shrugged. "But you speak so well. You've lived in Europe?" she stated her question.

"No, in Africa . . . and Haiti," he added the last for emphasis, though he'd never been to the Caribbean. It was just the next deepest, darkest, blackest place he could think of.

She clucked to herself and smiled. "But you speak so well," she repeated. "You are a diplomat, perhaps . . . no, no, no. A journalist." She had decided.

He debated momentarily about which answer would most likely shut her up. Both opened a can of worms particularly savory to expatriates in Africa when they have a captive audience. He had already determined that this woman had lived in Africa for many years and was probably more at home on the verandas of private clubs in Kinshasa than in a Paris boutique. He knew her type, hated them, therefore hated her.

"Yes, journalist."

She smiled comfortably. He signaled the handsome Burkinabé to bring him more champagne. Journalist was as good as anything. What was he after all? A tourist, an invader? What had he ever been here?

Now, several hours and bottles of Moët later, he turned back to the unfolding map below. It had been too long since his eyes had feasted on this sight, and he'd grown weary and red-eyed from a night of expectation and twisting in anticipation of this particular arrival. Five years since he last set foot on the continent, since that wonderful and vicious summer with Kate and Obi on the coast and all that had happened since.

He wondered if anyone would be at the airport to meet him. He imagined Kate, drinking tea, her tanned face and red hair amid the crowd of fiercely turbaned heads and crisp robes on the observation deck. He imagined Obi, a black mountain of a man, calm and imposing in the sea of activity that always reigned at Ntala Airport, its red and black flags flapping in the harmattan. The images disquieted him, and two Valiums and the alcohol could not dispel them. Now as the earth approached the plane, miles at a time, his anxiety turned to fear.

God, she must hate him. The years of no words had methodically grown into a wall of dispassion built to shield him from the pain of that summer, of losing Obi, then Kate's friendship, and finally himself. But in New York, and then later in Washington, the losses, the liquor, and finally the drugs had come crashing down on him, leaving him with no choice but to return to the scene of this crime, to Ntala, to the coast, and to what was left of that summer's memory.

Five years ago it had been so different. It was he on the observation deck sipping not tea but *Mbusa*, the national beer, the "water of champions," as its advertising proclaimed. The sun was a cruel slash in the sky that day, its rays releasing the copper in his skin. Ruddy, it had turned him, tanned just like a white boy he remarked when passing reflective shop windows in the capital. He wore a safari suit: Khaki and large, it hung comfortably on his thick shoulders, a gold chain lying casually among the hairs of his chest. His short, well-oiled afro picked up flecks of intense light and shot them back. He was twenty-nine at the time and unremarkably handsome. It was his eyes that set him apart. They had an intensely sad quality to them, as if they'd witnessed too many bitter scenes already at that young age, as if they belonged to a small child who'd been left out of too many games. It was this pain in his eyes that lit his face when he smiled, making his joy all the more important for its viewer.

At the table with him, Obi sat drinking a bottle of the same. Among the handsomely dressed and well-bred Africans in the terrace café, Obi was a commanding figure, tall for a Ntalan, with skin so dark it approached true black in its reflection of light. He did not appreciate the sun in the same way Stu did and sported a blue cap with a visor to shield his eyes. He wore a pair of plaid walking shorts, very fashionable at the time among the *"jeunes premiers,"* the West-looking youth of the capital. Hairless, muscled legs ended in clean white Nikes. A small brown tanned leather pouch hanging from around his neck seemed to be the only vestige of the traditional in his image. He quietly hummed along with the crackling radio tuned to Gabon and Africa Numero 1 until a fast track came on.

"Papa Wilo," his eyes brightened. "He's in town tonight."

"I know, I know. Best high life on the continent. We'll be there if Kate wants to go. She may be tired after the flight. Damn, must this thing always be late?"

Obi looked at his watch, a black face with tiny silver chips where the numbers might have been, a gift from Stu only last week. Stu wagered it was the nicest watch Obi had ever owned. Obi downed half the bottle of beer and leaned back in the white wire mesh chair. The sight of his body unfurling flipped a switch in Stu; he summoned the waiter. The man came, dressed in a clean white coat and beach sandals. Stu ordered more beers in Kindoma, the words falling easy and light off his tongue.

Obi smiled. "You still speak Kindoma with an American accent."

"How many Americans do you know can speak Kindoma?"

"Just you and the Great White Fathers." Obi laughed loud and killed what was left of his beer. "They're Americans, aren't they?"

"Of a sort."

"But you know more curses."

"You're damn right. That's 'cause I hang around you and Zamakil too much. Too many high-life concerts."

Obi straightened in his seat. "Does Kate speak Kindoma?"

"No, she's never been here, but her French is fantastic. She's great. I can't wait to see her."

Obi reached across the table and pulled the pack of Okapi from the pocket of Stu's shirt. "I think you like her."

"Of course I do. We've been friends for a long time."

"That's not what I mean," He lit two cigarettes, handed one across the table and returned the pack to Stu's pocket.

Stu smiled at the boldness of his lover's actions, amazed at how comfortable Obi had grown over the past six months. "Now Obi," he lowered his voice, "if I didn't know you better, I'd think you were jealous. You know I'm not thinking about anyone else, okay homeboy? Kate is an excellent engineer. We work well together. I need her on this project if I'm gonna get that water pumped in before the river goes down. We want to be in the States by Christmas, right?"

"Right."

"So we'll work together. We're a team, okay? Okay, chief?"

"Yeah, okay, Stu." He answered this last in English. Stu slapped him lightly on the face, letting his hand linger imperceptibly while the noisy chatter on the terrace was broken by the sound of the DC-10 approaching the city.

Dear Kate,

Hey sweetheart! Trust this letter finds you well. I sure hope, however, that you've had a lousy winter and want to totally change your lifestyle, 'cause I've got a proposition. The engineer on the water project just quit and we need a replacement fast. I've been doing such a damn good job on these quickies, that I've got the Minister of Works eating out my back pocket, so to speak.

So the other day, we're sitting around talking about how to get a top-notch, crackerjack engineer with small irrigation experience to spend the summer on the beautiful coast of Ntala. Well hon, we thought and thought and couldn't come up with anyone. So I decided to ask you (ha ha).

No, but seriously, you've got to come out. We'll be in the middle of the short rainy season, and Katie, you've never seen anything like this coastline. It'll blow you away. I've really fallen in love with this country. So different than the years we spent in the Peace Corps. Do you remember how frustrated I was? Loving my work, but hating the rest. My God, I couldn't wait to get out of our village, but do you remember how I cried like a baby on the truck? But I seem to have worked things out. Or they've worked out for me.

Most of the reason is probably this gorgeous mothafucka lying in bed next to me. I swear, Katie, I'd given up all prospects of falling in love over here and had resigned myself to taking some desk job with AID in Washington. But meeting Obi has changed everything. He's just so honest and genuine. He really cares about me as a person. You'll see. If you come out we'll be working together. He's the liaison man. Most of the projects I've worked on that means glorified interpreter and chauffeur, but I swear Katie, the guy is so bright. I'd never get these folks working so fast if it weren't for him. And now everything else seems to be falling into place, too. I'm going to bring him back to the States for a few months, spend Christmas in Detroit. My parents will love him. And then we'll see. See how he adjusts to life in the States. Or maybe back out here. Or, there's a job with Catholic Relief in Harare.

Anyway, I'm going on as usual, letting my imagination run away with me. Let me stop. I really hope you'll consider the job. You need to be out by first July. Cable me as soon as you get this. My love to your dad.

Best love,
Stu

"Katie, you look great. How's Washington?"

"Same old bullshit. Summer was hot as hell. Thanks for the rescue." Kate was a modest and attractive woman in her early thirties, with angular features and a full frame. She had a playful quality that at times made her seem much younger than she was, and at other times her up-front brashness made her seem

years older. Her no-nonsense, down-to-business attitude sometimes alienated people, particularly the staff under her, but she
was easy to respect, a hard worker, and committed. The last ten
years of her life had been divided between graduate school in
engineering and work in India and Bangladesh. "Something
about the faces of the children," she had confided in her letters,
"I just can't stay away."

On the drive from the airport, Obi removed the top off the
jeep. Kate's hair caught the wind and rose. "It's dry as a bone out
here." She pulled from her bag a pair of punk black sunglasses
hanging on an old-fashioned silver link chain, and surveyed the
dusty maize fields sprawled along the road. Single huts and
larger compounds, all washed a sandy brown, dotted the landscape.

"Two years. No rain." They were the first words Obi had spoken since the initial introductions on the terrace. He seemed to
be brooding.

"The U.S. and France are doing some famine relief in the
North. Soviets mostly in the South," Stu filled in. "Most of the
grain's been going to the cities, but what else is new?"

"That's stop-gap shit. What's the solution?"

"That's what we're here for. The government decided a few
years ago to dam this great big monster of a river, change the
whole ecosystem, and then tell folks to dig irrigation canals.
You've seen the plan."

"Yeah, I read through the stuff you sent. It's not hopeless.
Water table's high enough. How many teams have we got?"

"Ten. Locally trained engineers on every one."

"Who's your anthropologist?"

Stu shook his head. "Ain't got none."

"Sociologist?"

"Couldn't get anyone on such short notice."

"So you're gonna go in and tell people to stop eating millet, start growing rice, and sell half of it to the government, all by your lonesome." She looked at him over the top of the glasses. "You're cute, dear, but not that persuasive."

Stu smiled, put his hand on Obi's shoulder and squeezed it. "No, I've got a little help." Obi stirred uncomfortably under Stu's grip, raising his eyes slightly to catch Kate's reaction to the small gesture in the rearview mirror.

"So, Obi, you're the man with the plan," Kate quipped. "Care to share it?"

He returned his eyes to the road. "No plan. The land is dry. People have no food. You will come with pipes and canals and pumps and help grow food. People will welcome you. You want them to grow rice. They'll grow rice."

"That simple?" Kate looked doubtful.

Obi sighed almost imperceptibly and continued, "Years ago, the French told us to grow peanuts. We grew peanuts. Everywhere peanuts. You took them. The land died. Peanuts killed the land. Now you want us to grow rice. We'll grow rice. What do you want us to do?"

The crush of the gravel underneath the wheels of the Land Rover and the turn of the motor Obi had tuned to mechanical perfection underscored the silence. An ancient Mercedes truck, loaded to twice its height with bags of imported grain, lumbered by. Perhaps this was food on its way to government soldiers squelching the warring bush guerrillas in the interior. The truck, leaning dangerously to its side, kicked up a great cloud of smoky stinging dust as it headed to the airport.

"Here Obi, you need these more than I do." She removed the Greenwich Village specials from around her neck. Obi hesitated, then looked hard at her reflection in the rearview mirror. Finally he turned to Stu for a reaction. Stu provided his most encouraging smile, lighting his face with eyes that had found their way into Obi's heart at other times, trying now to break the wall that Obi was carefully constructing. With a slight release of breath, Obi put on the shades, his dark face opening into a wide gulf of white teeth as he laughed appreciatively at what he saw.

"You look great," Kate smiled with him through the mirror.

Cameroon John Little was a large, affable, blue-eyed man. He lived in an opulent villa on the peninsula where the river turned its mighty attention to entering the city. Stu had grown to tolerate Cami, probably because he had come to understand him. It was not easy to be a man who liked men on this continent, he reasoned, though being white made it easier. Cami had learned early in his life as a businessman in Africa that he could have almost anything he wanted for the right price. He participated gleefully in the free-market economy of the capital, filling his home, its manicured gardens, poolside, and numerous bedrooms with the most attractive young men Ntala had to offer.

There Stu had met several law students from the university, Mohammed, a friendly military parachutist visiting from the north, and Zamakil, the goalkeeper for the national football team. The men Cami kept in rotating residence were always obliging, most quite openly. A few begrudgingly relented, but these were never invited to return. All were in need. The university and high school students were mostly poor fellows struggling through an academic and social system hard-pressed and unwilling to meet their most basic needs. The soldiers were living mean lives with large families on meager government salaries that were always late and occasionally never came. Some, like Zamakil, came out of no particular financial need, savoring only the pleasures that Cami's house offered.

Many found that they could live their sexual lives openly within the walls of Cami's compound. For some, the sex, with each other or with the various expatriates who also passed through, was an amusing addition to the life of decadence and excess lived there. For others, it was what they were forced to give in payment for the relief from difficult lives, or for the few dollars Cami would slip into their pockets when they left.

Cami's had originally been a refuge for Stu, who had lived in enough countries to know that such people were necessary, that to be befriended by the Camis of Africa meant entrée into a world it might take a man months or even years to discover on his own.

Stu's life as a gay man in Africa swung violently between the poles of the erotic and the neurotic. It swung between the attraction he felt for most of the intensely sure men he saw on the streets and in villages and his mistrust and hatred of the power they had over him. He was quite clear that the men of Ntala had the ability to validate him, to make him feel totally at home and accepted in this foreign land. But he knew all too well their willingness to reject him, to cripple him as a man, and even worse to betray him to a society that tolerated only silent difference. He knew that any unwise act—the wrong man approached, a pass unsuccessfully completed—could be his downfall, could mean in fact the end of his career abroad. When he first arrived in a new post, he would live a life of abstinence, carefully surveying the sexual landscape until he felt safe enough to venture out. Nevertheless, his future often hinged on the whims of his dick, not a healthy prospect for a man of his sexual appetite.

But he knew that Cami could, if he so desired, change the entire nature of his time in Ntala. So just as he'd done in Botswana, Togo, and then Zaire, he subjected himself to the scantily cloaked racisms, the thin jokes, the greedy stingy generous use of men as objects in this city that Cami and his expatriate friends called temporary home, one they hated with a passion and could not wait to leave when their fat contracts came to an end. In the meantime, they ate, drank, and fucked heartily at the villa on the peninsula.

Cami's place was known for its orgies. Stu would sometimes arrive after several weeks in the bush, stopping only to drop his bags off at the InterCon. He would find parties in full swing: Ntalans ranging in age from sixteen to thirty, in various states of undress, would be lounging by the pool, entertaining Cami's friends in tangled liaisons of two, three, or more.

Mostly people seemed to be having fun. These were the times when Stu could enjoy himself the most. Other times the commerce was too visceral. Cami would call a new invitee over.

"Isn't he a beautiful boy? Look at him." Cami would run his hand over the boy's head, under his shirt, and finally, always end by stroking his crotch. The boy would invariably smile, knowing what was expected. Stu's skin would crawl, he would struggle to maintain composure as he vicariously felt Cami's hand on his own body, as he felt a chain tug at his neck. But Cami knew better than to try it. Stu was, after all, his equal in every way. An honorary white by these twisted standards.

Yes, the boy was beautiful. Cami entertained nothing but the best. "What's his name?" Stu would ask and then regret. He did not wait for a reply from the white man. "What's your name?"

The boy had a name. He was from a place. Had a history which Stu tried to discover in between bouts of lovemaking, at dinner, or while frolicking in the pool at his hotel where he sometimes took them after leaving Cami's house. The boy was most often not a boy at all, but a man with children, or a wife, or both. With dreams. And at the end of the day or the week in the capital the boy/man always wanted money from Stu, cab fare to go back to his place, to pay his kids' school fees, once even to buy a taxi. Stu gave what he could, took a furtive kiss (he had after all paid for it), and crawled back to the project site, back to whatever distant village he was working in, feeling alone and betrayed, but never knowing exactly by whom.

It was Zamakil who brought Obi to the house. Zamakil was the only African who seemed to approach Cami as an equal. And Zamakil and Obi were friends. They had gone to primary and secondary school together and separated only when the athlete's fate turned him into a national hero. Obi, too poor to continue on to the university, had taken up carpentry and then finally had become a mechanic for a large transport company in the capital. He'd always been good with his hands. Now, both nearing thirty, their memories of childhood games on beaches, of shadowy touches as boys, brought them together as men with hardened bodies and adult needs. They were fast friends once again, two men who shared an intimate past.

On the day Stu met Obi, he was in a difficult mood. The trip into the city had been particularly annoying. He'd been stopped seven times by knuckleheaded soldiers demanding bribes to tide them over through the first of the month. It had been hot, a day that had desperately needed a strong rain which never came to break the sun's anger. He was exhausted when he rang Cami's doorbell.

"You look a mess, man." Cami ushered him in. "Rough trip?"

"Exceedingly."

"Well, put on some trunks and come for a swim, old man. I've got something outback I think will perk you up a bit." He smiled lasciviously and slid out the back into the yard.

Stu found Cami and Zamakil downing Scotch and soda by the pool. They were enjoying a good laugh about Zamakil's recent trip to Kenya for the Africa Cup finals. Zamakil stood up when he saw Stu. They had always liked each other very much, had even had an affair which ended when Stu realized that the athlete liked fresh trade as much as Cami did and could never be tied down to one man.

"Stuart, where have you been so long? Out working in the field from the looks of it." They embraced and kissed one, two, three times on the cheek. "We've missed you."

"Zamakil was just telling me about the coach of the Kenyan football team," Cami said.

"Not the coach, the manager."

"Coach, manager, whatever. You probably had them both, knowing you, whore."

"I tried." They both laughed. "But the coach was sleeping with the goalkeeper and that bitch wouldn't let me near him. Stuart, what are you drinking?"

Stu headed to the poolhouse. "Whatever's wet, and mix it with something cold."

"Don't hurt yourself," Cami called from his lounge chair and chuckled.

"Huh?" The door to the poolhouse opened, and a black man walked out wearing only a bright white bikini and a smile that matched in color and brilliance and left Stu speechless. The seconds before either of them spoke seemed both few and long.

"Excuse me," Stu said finally, "I just wanted to change."

The fine young man, tall, muscular, twenty-five or twenty-six at the most, moved away from the door to let Stu pass. "Yes, sure. How are you?" The voice was earnest and warm.

"Fine," Stu responded, feigning nonchalance, but his voice clearly matched the warmth. He entered the poolhouse and shut the door slowly behind him. Carefully sliding on his trunks, he counted backward from one hundred in threes, thought about tombstones, asparagus, and car wrecks, waiting for the bulging nylon to recede.

He found Zamakil and Cami smiling conspiratorially. The tall perfect one with the hair a bit too long for his round face was doing laps in the pool. Stu decided to say nothing in response to the obvious plot.

"What's new?" he asked Cami.

"Your reticence, for one," Cami, always master of the sharp tongue, answered.

"Okay, okay. I'm impressed. Who is he?"

Zamakil laughed and pulled off his shirt. "Who is who? Oh, you mean him there swimming. Just someone. Just a boy." He slipped out of his shorts and dove naked into the deep end of the pool. Cami followed suit, playfully wrestling with Zamakil in the warm chlorinated water. Zamakil fought off his opponent and swam to the shallow end, where he hiked himself up and sat on the edge.

The tall one got out of the pool and sat on the grass under a shaded palm near Stu, who watched him watch Zamakil as Cami's head bobbed methodically between the goalkeeper's legs. The stranger's face, a nearly impassive mask, broke only at the corners, which twitched uncomfortably. Was he excited? Should Stu move on him? He was here, he knew the game, the unwritten rules of the house. Stu made what seemed like an interminable trip over to where Obi sat in the shade. He reached his hand out to touch the water beading on the taut chest. A black hand darted out and encircled his wrist. The man looked at him confused, betrayed. The warm look of invitation was gone. A shield had gone up. He let go Stu's hand and pulled on his pants over the wet suit. He stood and shook the water from his thick hair, then walked around the side of the house onto the path which led to the street.

Stu rubbed his wrist. It did not hurt nearly as much as his ego, newly bruised. He felt small and ashamed. He cut through the house to the front yard, racing to catch the man at the wrought-iron gate.

"Wait a minute. I'm sorry, okay?" The other was silent. "I didn't know."

"Didn't know what, nzuma?" He used the Kindoma word

which had come to signify foreigner, stranger, but translated literally as white man.

Stu felt as if he'd been slapped. "Is that what you think of me?"

"Is that how you behave?" He threw open the gate.

"Wait, I'll give you a ride."

"I'll walk."

"It's a long way to town. Lots of hungry soldiers. Let me give you a ride. I'm sorry, okay. Okay? What's your name?"

Perhaps it was the earnestness of Stu's voice. Or the memory of the first few moments of their meeting. Or perhaps merely the fear of soldiers on the long road to town, but Obi relented. Stu drove.

That night at the hotel, when Obi took him, he felt warm and full, safe in a forest of circling lions. As the momentum mounted, Obi built a fire of black logs for protection. In the morning, so much later, when he took Obi, the fire was replaced by clear white light as he gasped at the shock of entrance, an entrance so tight and fitting, so perfectly unforetold that he came before he could pump or slide or ride. These would come later, of that he was sure, from Obi's sighs, from the relax in his body, from the wet he felt running down now over Obi's hard black belly.

"Are you married?" The room was lit only by dawn creeping through Venetian blinds, under doors, and across pillows.

"No, are you?" Obi propped himself up on his elbow, slid his other hand slowly down the long of Stu's body.

"I'm gay."

Obi laughed. "I, too, am sometimes very happy."

Stu scanned his face in the scattered light for a trace of sarcasm and found none. "I'm trying to understand your country. How to be happy here. I would like to find a friend. A special friend."

"I will be your friend. Zamakil says you will go to work on the coast. It is very beautiful. My oldest nephew will be baptized there during the short rainy season. I will take you to meet my family. They have never met a *noir américain*. Would you like to go?"

"Of course, I would love to meet your family. You aren't afraid they will suspect?"

"They could never suspect such a thing. And your family . . . will I meet them?"

"They're in America. Do you want to go to the States?"

"What do you tell us? It's the biggest, the best. What fool would not want to go?"

"I mean what's in this for you, Obi, before I let myself go? What *do* you want from me?"

Obi seemed to consider, lay down on the bed, raised himself up again, took Stu in his arms, and held him. His hand was hot and moist on Stu's thigh. "Your ass, right now, would make me very happy."

Outside the hotel grounds, at the port, market women waited impatiently for the arrival of the barge from up-country. They tied and retied silk wraps over rotund bellies and generous hips, dreaming of dried fish, French perfume, and moonlit nights unalone. They stared intently north, shielding their eyes from the sun's riverdancing glare.

All day the sun had burned white-hot in an unbroken sky. The evening had fallen slow without cloud cover. Stu had spent the afternoon working budget figures in the small hut they used as an office. The last canals had been dug, the pipes were laid, and two business-class tickets to Detroit via Frankfurt lay in the safe. The visa had been simple. Marc, a friend at the embassy, had made all the arrangements, and now Obi's new passport lay on top of Stu's old one. All that was left was to close out the accounts, and Kate could do that in a pinch.

Obi's absence that afternoon weighed on him. Late in the day, Cissé, the night guard just coming on duty, had informed him that Obi and Kate had taken the Jeep and gone to the baptism on the hillside.

"Great, just when I need him, she's got him traipsing all over the goddamn bush." Cissé smiled uncomfortably. Stu slammed the door and immediately regretted revealing so much of himself to the man, an elder from Obi's tribe. He returned to his desk and looked at the papers in disarray: figures, elevations, men and their salaries, debits ran together in black lines, red dots. His head swam.

Shutting and locking the bamboo door behind him, he took the back roads that led to the beach, down behind the small *pailotte* Obi had had the crew build for him. Pretenses had, after all, to be maintained. The path, like the hut, was mainly unused. Milky thornbushes cut shallow grooves in his bare legs. He didn't care. The beach was empty except for a group of a dozen or so fishermen returning with the day's catch.

In this part of Ntala, the coastline was a study in natural drama. Within a half-hour's walk, the fine yellow sand lifted to tenuous cliffs and then hilly bluffs at the mouth of the river where the interior of the country drank its thirsty fill and opened itself up to weary passage.

He sat on the sand, wet with the approach of evening, and watched the fishermen. Night fell in patches around him; bits of sky turned themselves in, gave themselves over to higher powers. He could hear the drums from the baptism, urging but not urgent. What was ever pressing in this land of uncountable yesterdays and impossible tomorrows? The wind itself seemed to scoop percussion from the hillside where Kate and Obi surely danced and deposited it on the beach where Stu watched the sea alone now, the fishermen gone.

Tonight, he was waiting for a sign, a word telling him to go on. He got this way sometimes, lethargic, no motives. Earlier in the season,

Obi's presence had kept him moving, prodded him to work the teams at twice their normal speed. Kate had set up evening training sessions for the Ntalan engineers, sharing techniques she'd learned from local crews in Asia. Obi was a native of this region; he was related somehow to everyone. He used his contacts to speed up the delivery of supplies for the canals and spare parts for the jeep and pumps. The three of them worked like a well-oiled machine, turning to each other at the end of each day, falling steadily into the arms of a growing friendship. Most evenings they sat out by a fire, dodging mosquitoes and sharing stories, smoking and feeling the vastness of the night consuming them.

On a mid-season trip to the capital, they had danced all night to a band at an outdoor club. Kate was arhythmic and knew it, swallowed it with a laugh and a beer. Obi had guided her across the floor through a sea of black faces with one sure hand on her waist and the other supporting the lifted curve of her spine. In his arms she appeared capable and weightless. To Stu, at a table in the corner, methodically getting sloshed on dark rum, the song seemed interminable.

Slowly, through the course of the season, something had been changing. Stu felt this instinctively before he ever admitted it. There was a resistance developing between him and Obi. Despite Stu's admonitions, curses, cajoling, Obi would not allow him to caress, hold, or even touch him when Kate was around. Kate's presence brought out a shame in Obi which Stu could not penetrate, as hard as he tried. When Stu demanded more time alone with him, Obi resisted. "What will the workers think? Some suspect now. We are too much together alone. They want to know why you have no children at your age. No wife."

Stu became angry. "But you're only five years younger than me."

"They begin to ask me the same questions."

"You never cared before!"

But Obi seemed to care now. "Perhaps in the city I am more free. But here, in my place . . . and around Kate . . ."

"Kate is my friend. She wants us to be happy."

Obi smiled slightly and looked him square in the eyes. "Be patient with me, Stu."

Leaving the beach, he headed back up the path. Things would be better once they were in Detroit. Once they left the country of dying soil for the city of dying steel. Obi would be overwhelmed by the strangeness, Stu would be there to comfort him, to be relied upon, to translate their new lives into English, into American. Stu would be there.

Coming up behind Obi's unused hut, his eye caught on a flicker of light from inside, and then a sound of something hard hitting something soft. Robbers, he thought, as he stopped in his tracks. Where were the guards? The sound again, only this time it was more human, a groan, perhaps a moan of pleasure or pain. He crept up to the windowless cabin and with a push of its door exposed its two occupants to the night air.

What he saw seemed cloaked in a smoky gauze. His life was in fact smoldering around him. Obi and Kate lay tangled in each other's arms, legs, and twisted white sheets. Heat gushed from the room, it whelmed him. Obi stood up, the words coming quickly from his mouth were incomprehensible, his sex was still hard and wet.

"Shut up," Stu cried. Kate tried to cover herself with the sheet, which was caught up in her legs. Obi continued talking, explaining what could not be explained. "Shut up," Stu roared and felt his fist make contact with the soft squish of the man's eye. He was suffocating and the room became a blur. He had to get out, but to go where and to do what, he did not know. He left the door agape, swinging on broken hinges.

"Stuart." Kate came into his room after several minutes, wrapped in a flowered green pagne covered with jungle beasts. "Stu." He started packing, savagely throwing his belongings into a suitcase. Carvings from the region, carefully chosen, a woman's head in bronze, fell at his feet.

"Stu, look at me. I know you're upset."

He stopped and looked at her, slowly focused on her blue eyes, her tanned, healthy complexion, skin still gleaming with sweat.

"You bitch." He hated her completely, there was no question, no holds barred. He wanted to hit her, the way he had hit Obi, to push her to the ground, permanently to mar the beauty—female, Caucasian—that he knew had drawn Obi to her.

"I don't know how it happened. It just did."

"Save it, okay. I don't understand you, Kate. You've got your choice of whomever you want. These men would do somersaults for white pussy." He glared at her.

"Stop it."

"Even back in Botswana, you got whatever you wanted. Why do you have to take the only piece of this damned country that ever loved me, the only thing that's ever mattered to *me?*"

"Obi is not a thing, damn you. He's a man with feelings just like you or me. He has a right to make choices. You don't own him."

"Oh, don't make yourself sound so innocent." Her seminudity seemed to weigh on her now. The pagne looked light, as if it were nothing. "Look at you."

"Oh, so you can sleep with half of Africa and you call it getting in touch with your roots."

"Just what the hell do you know about it?" He slammed the suitcase shut and hoisted it toward the door.

She glared at him, looked into his eyes, and then softened as the years of their friendship came back to his. "Enough to know that you're better than this. Stu, you're not going to find yourself this way, running from one country to another paying for affection."

"Obi loves me," he stopped. "He loved me. It's not about money." He sat down on the bed, confused, his hand still smarting from the blow he'd struck to his lover's face. Kate sat down next to him and tried to take his hand. He recoiled from her touch. "I'm going. I can't stay here. This hurts too much."

She took his hand and held it. He didn't draw back. "Do you want me to leave, Stu? I'll leave. Our friendship means more to me than—"

"Than Obi's love? I don't think so. It doesn't to me. I love you, Kate. But I needed him."

The numbers of the combination lock fell silently into place and the safe clicked open. He immediately erased the numbers from his head. He would need them no longer. He retrieved the two airline tickets and shoved them into the side pocket of his overnight bag. He picked up both passports. He fingered the brilliant red and black of the Ntalan flag embossed on the cover of Obi's. He wondered how the thick raised paper would look burning in a fire, how neatly the seal of the country would tear into two, ten, twenty pieces and then scatter onto the floor of the hut. He wondered of the possibilities. He placed it on the table.

Outside, the fresh of night evaporated the sweat on the back of his neck, dried the wet streaks on his face. Obi stood in front of the Jeep, his eye swollen. He'd been crying, but Stu knew that it was not from the physical blow he'd struck. As Stu approached the Jeep, Obi reached out and gripped the handle of the suitcase. Stu resisted, holding on, their hands touched; Obi won, taking the suitcase and tossing it deftly into the back seat.

"Where are you going so late? You know the road is dangerous this time." Obi got into the driver's seat.

"The city. What are you doing?"

"I'm driving you. I'm the chauffeur, remember?"

"The project is finished. Your services are no longer required."

"I'm driving. I'm your friend."

"You're fired." He replaced Obi in the driver's seat and shut the car door. "Give me the key." He turned it in the ignition and the motor began coughing, spitting, and then finally hummed its familiar tune.

"Be careful, Stu." Obi touched the back of his neck and rubbed it lightly.

"Be careful, homeboy." Stu shifted the car into first and rolled out the compound toward the main road. At the gate the ever-dozing guard woke up. He opened the gate and waved, bewildered, as Stu passed. He did not wave back.

On the road, the Ntalan sky opened before him. It struck him as serenely beautiful, untouched. Perhaps he'd never thought of Africa as anything more than a life-sized postcard, a moving breathing tourist brochure. And even the years he'd spent living and working in the villages, towns, and major cities, crossroads of black life, were nothing more than stepping into (and then out of) still life. There was never a sense of belonging, only of tolerance, mutual, guarded, and temporary.

He was glad it was night. He knew that in each of the tightly knit villages scattered along this main artery lived young black men with big chests and open shirts. In the light of day, they tantalized him with smiles and the aroma of dust and work and hidden, dark places on the body, their physical closeness deceptive in its inaccessibility.

If he made good time he'd be in the capital by morning. It was Tuesday. He could catch a flight to New York on Thursday. And then? And then. The wind whistled past his ears. His hair caught it. It did not rise. It did not move.

The plane touched down heavily and after a series of runs and turns came to a definitive stop in Ntalan soil. The Belgian dowager sighed, relieved, and crossed herself again. Stu reached into his travel bag for a mirror. He brushed his hair forward, the slight thinning in the front hardly noticeable. He looked out the window to the terrace.

He spotted them amid the crowd. They had come. Kate and the beautiful little redheaded boy he recognized from the photos she'd sent year after year (despite his lack of response), a walking replica of his father in everything except color. The scene on the terrace was familiar. Waiters in white coats darted between tables to catch the fleeing customers running to meet their cousins, brothers, lovers coming from America, from the land of plenty. Only one person was missing.

It was the Fever that had taken Obi, the four-letter thing that had come to mean death and destruction in the States, that had ravaged Stu's circle of friends and left his address book bleeding with gaping white sores, victims of white-out, numbers remembered but disconnected, no longer needed. It was the thinning disease that had taken Obi. That had left Kate an uncertain widow and had left this beautiful caramel-colored boy fatherless. And now Stu had come back to turn a new page in his life, to help his best friend, a white woman, raise a black boy to manhood, to perhaps rediscover his own manhood, lost somewhere between the coast of Africa and his youth.

The Burinkabé stood at the door of the first-class cabin, saying good-bye to the passengers. "Welcome home," he said to Stu and smiled, engaging, promising with teeth and a decidedly warm handshake.

"Thank you," Stu returned the warm press of flesh. But this was not the time. On the tarmac, Ntala buzzed with languages he'd not heard for years. He listened to the world as he walked to meet those who awaited him.

Andrew Holleran

Sleepless in Mexico

Traveling with my sister and niece in Mexico last February, I seemed to belong to a nuclear family. In Ixtapa my sister tipped the maid who cleaned the hotel room; when I went back to shower, the maid handed me a small bag of candy and said, "Para su esposa." For your wife. She thought, as everyone else no doubt did, that my sister was my spouse, my niece my daughter. Momentarily part of the vast normalcy that heterosexuals presume but gays feel only when they are in a gay place, I temporarily belonged to the order of things in all Latin cultures: the Family. In other words, I was passing for straight; and the taxi driver taking us to our hotel in Mexico City was surprised when I told him who these women were.

My last time in Mexico City, I'd been part of a family too—the Mexican one I lived with for an entire summer. They lived in a neighborhood that was neither rich nor fashionable; the father was a middle-class attorney with seven children. I was there not as a gay man—at nineteen I was not even out—but as a Catholic college student. Each day I took a bus to the National University and then walked to Copilco el Alto, a community of tin-roofed houses built of rocks where the Catholic Club of my university was engaged in a summer project whose goal was to get the quarry workers, who drank their wages away in *pulque* every payday, to start a credit cooperative instead. It was an idealistic scheme; the priest whose retreat we attended in Cuernavaca, the famous Ivan Illich, told us we would have done more good had we sent the money we'd raised for our trip and stayed home. As the summer wore on, our shock on hearing this pronouncement gave way to a grudging realization that he was right. The dispensary the project had built the year before was hardly used; the people we visited received us only out of politeness. Soon I was sleeping later and later in the mornings, delaying my arrival in Copilco el Alto as long as possible, until finally the maid gave me a rude nickname implying I was too lazy to move. By the end of the summer we had given up, and so we hijacked the station wagon for a long drive to Fortín de las Flores, Mérida, and Isla de Mujeres.

On Isla de Mujeres, one day after walking for hours down a long empty beach on that then-remote, untouristed island, I was astonished to come upon two sleek, suntanned men in identical Speedos lying in identical hammocks reading identical biographies of Betty Grable. I thought: these men must be homosexuals. More than thirty years later, returning with my sister and niece to Mexico, so was I —though I was also a bit older than the men in the hammocks. Age was one of the reasons I was going to Mexico with my sister and niece in the first place. In my thirties I would never have done this—exchanged traveling as a gay man, free to cruise, for a sexless vacation with relatives. But now that I wasn't comfortable going into bars in New York City, I didn't much want to go into them in Mexico either. That, at least, was the grudging rationale I'd arrived at when wondering why on earth I was traveling with family at all.

They were very good travel companions, as a matter of fact, and we worked well together. Horrified by Mexico City from almost the moment our plane landed ("I can taste the air on my tongue" my sister said), we rented a car after two days touring museums and headed for the coast. My sister drove. That alone was reason enough to admire her. But she was a seasoned traveler, and that included a confidence in demanding value for money that I, the guilty gringo, supersensitive to other cultures' pride—still the exchange student worried about being an Ugly American—did not have. If the hotel room was bad, as it was in Guanajuato, she demanded another; I would have suffered in silence. My sister was also willing to spend money, where my frugal, spartan self was not. She wanted her fish grilled just so, her room to be spacious and quiet, her tourmaline ring to fit. The first time her forefinger appeared on the glass countertop of a jewelry store in San Miguel, I cringed. That imperial American digit with its nail curving downward like a bird of prey's beak, beginning to tap a staccato accompaniment to her debate with the saleswoman, summed up a whole approach to travel that horrified me. Then I saw that the saleswomen she dealt with appreciated her curiosity, rigor, demands; recognized a smart shopper and respected her intelligence.

My niece, a tall, blond, good-looking, unmarried attorney of thirty-five years, had inherited many of her mother's outgoing traits, though with an edge of impatience that verged on arrogance—until her laughter dissipated it. She seemed happiest joking with the kids selling Chiclets, was obsessive about reading, smoking, and shopping (for watercolors, jewelry, blankets, furniture), and was insistent that at some point she be able to lie in the sun and toast herself to a dark brown. In San Miguel she spent an entire day negotiating for an armoire, while I stood by wondering if a very handsome young man with two older gentlemen was a kept boy or simply a relative. In Taxco I spent an afternoon sitting in church while the women shopped for silver. Shopping was an advantage they had over me, something they could do anywhere—which left me with a lot of time to brood. There was lots to brood about in Mexico: the changes in the country since I'd lived there, the changes in me, even the fact that my niece was still single—until I reminded myself that it was her family's annual question, "When are you going to get married?" every Thanksgiving and Christmas that made me hate to go home in my twenties and early thirties. Now I was the gay uncle in his fifties, sitting in a church in Mexico, wondering why my niece was not seeing anyone and if she could possibly be happy living by herself.

Such are the thoughts one has traveling with blood family. In Guanajuato I watched as two handsome young men approached my niece (with her blond good looks, it was their patriotic duty) as we sat having drinks on that beautiful jewel of a plaza; I wondered if my sister, still attractive herself, was in any way envious of the attention her daughter was getting, and what these young men thought their attention might possibly lead to. Nothing more than restaurant recommendations, it turned out; a harmless flirtation. In the Oaxaca airport we met two gay men, each traveling solo. I felt sorry for them, so snug did I feel in my family pod, so much do I dislike traveling alone. One, a retired schoolteacher from upstate New York, had come to study Spanish for six weeks. The other, a tough U.N. attorney looking for a place to retire, latched on to the three of us for company until, at the door of a disco in Puerto Escondido, we lost him to his impulse to cruise. The next day he did not call our hotel, though we'd agreed to go to the beach together; I assumed he'd met someone and did not want to waste his time with a group that would only hold him back. I, meanwhile, spent the day making friends with an eleven-year-old on the beach who told us his father had ripped up his birth certificate so he couldn't go to school; then I developed a crush on a man in the surf I thought was Mexican until later that night, at a restaurant on the beach, I watched and overheard him and a male friend seduce, in English, a Danish woman who ended up walking off with them to their tent down the beach.

In Ixtapa I was plunged further into heterosexual life at a hotel we would never have booked except that all others were full: a big high-rise on the beach, filled with busloads of tourists from Winnipeg and Minneapolis competing for beach chairs under the thatched *palapas* or harnessed to parachutes floating overhead. At one point, out of the shimmering distance, two men appeared down the beach, wearing beads, long hair, backpacks, and Speedos—the reincarnation of the pair I'd encountered on Isla de Mujeres thirty years ago, and the only homosexuals I spotted all day.

They were followed by a stylishly dressed middle-aged black couple who held hands as they walked along the beach. There are, for historical reasons, virtually no black people in Mexico, and the sight of them made me think how difficult it is to be different. Gays, unlike blacks, can pass whenever they want to—as the latter often point out. Here I was among straight people on holiday, trying to read my niece's paperback *Prince of Tides,* watching the heterosexuals at play. The longing to be what you are, to see your own kind, to make contact, however, is so powerful that I struck up a conversation with a beautiful Canadian youth wearing an earring, but then he moved away to talk to two Mexicans his age, and I felt rebuffed. (How absurd.) Sitting in the lounge at happy hour watching the folks for the most part ignore the strolling mariachis, I felt like a superior imposter. The feeling returned even more strongly at breakfast the next morning, when my sister and niece erupted in a brief contretemps about what seemed to me a minor matter (who took the hotel key and forgot to return it); I was reminded of the ups and downs of this mother-daughter relationship, the conflicts and hurts that make so much of family life something I always wanted to stay away from. But their argument subsided as quickly as it began, and I went back, under the shade of a *palapa,* to watching my niece sacrifice her complexion to the sun.

It was awful, this vast consumer tourism (though the swimming was superb), this incredible turnover of mouths to feed in the breakfast room, of vans disgorging new visitors, of guests who come and go by the planeload, of sunburns and paperback books and souvenir T-shirts. How horrible for the Mexicans who have to work in this industry, I think; but then, they need the money. The guidebook says the remote village of San Blas, north of Puerto Vallarta, is favored by gay tourists—wild, jungly, with waterfalls—but it's the Family that brings in the big tourist bucks: it's also the reason the national capital is a twentieth-century nightmare of urban sprawl and overpopulation. The country in the interior, when we drive back toward Mexico City, is beginning to look like Ohio: high-tension wires, expressways, factories. I tell my sister not even to stop in Cuernavaca, a fantasy resort thirty years ago, now subsumed by the suburbs spreading out from the capital.

A few hours later, though, when we leave our hotel in Mexico City late on a Saturday afternoon to go for a walk, we realize that a lot of people have left town for the weekend: the air is cleaner, there is much less traffic, and the spacious, elegant atmosphere of the city I once loved is still there—as is my sense that there must be sex here, somewhere.

For instance, I feel sure that the handsome young man standing under the portico of the Palacio de Bellas Artes is waiting for another man. The fellow who was on our flight from Houston, whom we come upon entering a stucco mansion with five other bearish men his age, is, I'm certain, part of a Bear convention, about to participate in an orgy in a room upstairs. The young men with buzz cuts and baggy clothes talking to one another on street corners in the Zona Rosa may not be gay—earrings mean nothing, the look of international youth is uniform —but the queen coming down the sidewalk in hot pants, leather jacket, and studded bracelet, with three Dobermans on a leash, is clearly a throwback to "Boys in the Band." Somewhere, gay Mexico City surely exists.

Ironically, I will learn on my return that a friend from New

Orleans was in San Luis Potosí at that moment with his lover, visiting Mexican friends who own the gay bar in that city; they drove down to the capital the very Saturday I was there and went to a club near the Plaza Garibaldi to watch three drag queens emcee a show where the strippers sang mariachi songs and audience members had sex with the transvestites on stage. (On the other hand, he also told me about a leather bar he went to, which looked like a set for "The Addams Family"—candles and fog, not one man in leather. The only humiliation, he said, was asking the bartender to call him a cab.)

Meanwhile, I'm taking my sister and niece to see the Zócalo. I've never wanted to go on an all-gay cruise, or even to an all-gay resort—that would be as bad as an all-straight one, I suspect—but this time I seem to have gone to the other extreme. I can only keep my eyes peeled for signs of my tribe.

Riding in a taxi to the center of the city, I look out the window at an improbable wedding party waiting to cross the street, and then at a doorway where people are lined up to get into a club, and I recognize, in the dark streets, the breezy, deserted downtown, what I used to feel on such streets in lower Manhattan in the seventies. But now I'm on my way with my sister and niece to the Templo Mayor, where, under spotlights, we see the stone on which the hearts of the sacrificial victims (only the best-looking, the noblest, were chosen) were burnt to propitiate the gods. And walking back across the vast square I am grateful for the darkness. On a side street near the museum we enter a church where a play by Lorca had just been performed; outside, a balcony and a lighted window make me think of a friend, now dead, who was obsessed for years with a Mexican painter not in love with him, and remember what another friend said years ago about hustlers here: "In Mexico, they pay by the inch!" This huge, sophisticated city must hold a vast ocean of eros; but I am returning to the hotel with my sister and niece.

Back in the hotel we say goodnight and retire to our separate rooms within the suite we've rented (triples are the best deal, I've learned), but I can't sleep, so I slip out of the hotel and walk for a long time through the eerily empty embassy district to find the baths from an out-of-date Spartacus list. I'm the only person out, my footsteps the only sound. The walled embassies, the strange, dingy light of the streets, conjure up the whole romance of Latin America: the idea that behind the drab cement façade is something wonderful—a young intellectual reading Trotsky or Neruda, a pale youth with a big black moustache in a dark gray sweater, someone I can only experience by having sex (the ultimate form of travel). But the street where the baths are supposed to be comes to an end in the abrupt cauterization of a massive expressway ascending to an overpass. I turn back and retrace my steps—past the forlorn garages, the apartments and embassies, in the deep silence. Then, on a quiet street across the Paseo de la Reforma, a car full of young men goes by, and one of them sticks his head out the window and calls me a cabrón! or maricón, I'm not sure which. In any case it's an insult, one that reminds me of the other side of Mexico: the arrogance of rich adolescents (Mexico has its billionaires), the contempt for gringos or homosexuals or whatever it was they saw in this thin gray-haired man walking by himself down a street at eleven-thirty at night. I feel, of course, in my present demoralized state, that only the camouflage provided by my sister and niece have protected me from such treatment.

Back in the hotel, safe, angry, I still can't sleep—so, having failed to confront the city directly, I turn on its pale surrogate, the television. To my amazement, I find a talk show devoted to homosexuality. Ten young men are dancing in pairs before a high-spirited young straight audience while a solitary lesbian looks on. Then the hostess asks the men, "Which do you prefer —a man's or a woman's chest?"

The most evasive answers to this clear-cut question are given by the two handsomest young men, both wearing fake moustaches and mirrored sunglasses (the cuter of the two—who says he made a porn film when he was sixteen—keeps pressing the moustache to his face, afraid it will fall off.) Finally, three men and the woman are strapped into a machine that allegedly measures pulse rate and heartbeat, while a man in a white coat stands by to interpret the results; a voluptuous lady in a bikini and high heels comes out and sits on each contestant's lap, followed by a tall, buffed man who strips off his shirt and flexes in their faces. It is a scene from a gay nightmare—or a Pedro Almodóvar film: Which one turns you on, dear, the guy or the girl? There is something cruel, crude, and creepy about the show, but at the same time something frank and unembarrassed —all elements you can find in Mexican culture. What I can scarcely believe is that I am seeing it in Mexico at all. The devout son of the Catholic family I lived with in 1964 was horrified to find condom machines in the restrooms of truck stops in Texas when he and his siblings drove north the next winter to visit me in the United States. Thirty-three years later, condoms are distributed in bars, and I am watching a talk show in Mexico City devoted to homosexuality.

The man who made the porn film typifies the whole situation of gays in Mexico, I suspect: modern and hip, but traditional and closeted—trapped in the Mexican ideal of machismo, like the culture of the capital city itself—this incredible tattered sprawl of pre-Aztec, Aztec, colonial, modern; of parks, fountains, slums, garbage; of live sex shows and Catholic churches people still visit at all hours of the day to kiss the feet of a statue; all of it, animate and inanimate alike, reproducing beneath a sickening patina of dust and leaded gasoline. Mexico—so populous it is invading my own country, so young it could export human hair—is now, alas, acquiring the hectic identity of American consumer culture. Fast-food restaurants and shopping centers straddle the previous strata of pyramid, convent, and plaza in an atmosphere of relentless hustle. It still remains, despite its surface sophistication, deeply Other. But less and less does it offer another way of seeing things, which is why I went there, years ago, as a student to live with a Mexican family.

Where that family is as I lie in bed watching television thirty-three years later I do not know. I still remember them all, in that chilly green dining room under the little cut-glass chandelier, the parents at either end of the table, the seven children and myself in between—Fernando, the intellectual who read Bach scores the way I read books, and who was appalled that I liked Chopin, telling me that he was only for little old ladies; Elena, who startled me halfway through the summer by entering a convent; Emilio, only fifteen and already terminally handsome; Cecilia, as frail and delicate as a porcelain figurine; Maruja, who looked like Nastassia Kinski but was as smart as Fernando; and José and Bernardo—all variations, physically and psychologically, of their parents. I'd love to know where they all are now, what they've become, who's happy, who isn't, but I can't imagine a reunion. In today's paper I saw a Fernando Betancourt quoted as the spokesman for some government ministry. It is quite possibly my Fernando: he was that bright, that ambitious, that congenial. He studied and taught at a law school in Germany after I left, I recall from the letters we exchanged. I could call the ministry and ask if he once lived at Avenida Cuautemoc 156, or still does. I could take a cab there now and peer through the gate. But I won't. I'm not going to in part because I imagine we've led very different lives, in part because I would not want to explain mine. I'm not going to contact the Mexico of my memories at all on this trip, apparently, and I'm not sure I'll ever be back.

I've waited too long to come to Mexico as a gay man; I'm doing some sort of penance, I think, with this trip. We travel, after all, in various emotional states at different points in our lives; it's a wonder more tourists don't have nervous breakdowns abroad. Our suitcases are the only visible baggage we take with us on a trip; the rest becomes clear only once we're on our way.

So I shouldn't be surprised at finding this return to Mexico City so melancholy; Mexico has always been a place gringos go to lick their wounds. The vanity crisis I'm having is the least of it. I think of Maximilian, who died, and Carlotta, who went mad here; I think of Graham Greene, Malcolm Lowry, Leon Trotsky, Tennessee Williams; I think of Richard Burton in *Night of the Iguana*, fleeing the busload of American church ladies, the sort I breakfasted in the midst of in Ixtapa. It's a classic place to collapse and crash. The end of the road, for so many characters. Octavio Paz, in his famous book *The Labyrinth of Solitude,* says the Mexican, burdened with a self-fulfilling cynicism about politics and life, always wears a mask. But Mexico is where foreigners come when their own masks are coming apart. I feel doubly chastened lying here this last night in Mexico City—a gay man traveling with straight relatives, a tourist who has returned to a place that has changed as much as he, and neither, apparently, altogether for the better. But then that's what travel is for: to confront the self. I turn off the TV and look out the window at the roofs of this gray, sleeping city, half wondering if I should come back and live here by myself, deeply grateful I'm leaving tomorrow.

Michael Nava

Journey to 1971

An English novelist named Hartley wrote a book that begins
something like, "The past is a foreign country; they speak a
different language there." I don't know that memory speaks a
different language, but the past *is* like a foreign county, though
a strangely familiar one; the kind of place you've read about
your entire life, filled with much-photographed landmarks that,
when you finally stumble upon them, seem simultaneously
more and less than what you'd expected. The traveler to such
places may journey in eager and innocent anticipation or affect
a world-weary sangfroid, but it is as impossible not to be moved
by childhood photographs you have not looked at in twenty-five
years as by your first prospect of the Golden Gate or the Statue
of Liberty or the Pyramid of the Sun. You think, "I know this
place" and in your next thought realize that you don't. You've
only seen the pictures, you've only remembered.

A couple of years ago I began to write a memoir about my
childhood and adolescence, which were spent in Sacramento,
the state capital of California, a medium-sized city at the edge of
one of the world's great agricultural valleys, the Central Valley. I
was born in 1954, and the book ends when I leave home for college, in the summer of 1972. I was raised in poverty in the kind
of family nowadays called dysfunctional, though I prefer to describe it as Dickensian. The latter term better expresses the particular combination of squalor and sentimentality, brutality and
bathos, that characterized my upbringing. Moreover, many elements of my childhood came straight out of a Victorian melo-
drama: our poverty, a weak but loving mother, a villainous step-

father, my illegitimacy, encouraging schoolteachers, and, at the end, the Unexpected Opportunity, which arrived, in my case, in the form of a college scholarship. All I wanted from Sacramento was to get as far away as possible from it and my family and never return.

And yet, of course, those years in Sacramento have haunted me my entire life. They haunted me during the decades when I tried to maintain some kind of relationship with my family, and in the years after I finally abandoned the effort. They haunted me as I vaulted through college and law school into the ranks of the upper middle class, where I thought I would be safe and happy but was neither, for long. Because, as it turned out, my destiny was to become a writer, not a rich, gay lawyer. I was destined to become, moreover, the kind of writer who is incapable of imagining anything that he has not experienced, whose themes emerge from the things in his life that have "hurt" him, as Auden said of Yeats: "Mad Ireland hurt you into poetry."

I spent many years denying that this was my fate. Believe me, I would have preferred to be a rich, gay lawyer, but I could never shake off the dust of my childhood home. I could never stop trying to make sense of those years, and so finally I started to write about them—tentatively, at first, but then with firmer purpose. I would explain me to myself, then I would be all right. My notes show me that I began this writing in 1980, or seventeen years ago, but only in the past year have these scraps of memory, impressions, feelings begun to form a picture, a book. In all that time, from 1980 until a few months ago, I had been back to Sacramento maybe half a dozen times, and never for longer than a single night, and never at my mother's house. Nor had I visited the friends I had when I was growing up there or the sites where my childhood unfolded. No, I went for meetings, a wedding once, and to demonstrate for gay rights a couple of times. But as I began to write the section of the book that deals with my last year in high school, I felt the need to return, to try to step into my seventeen-year-old skin and remember what the world felt like to me then.

The significance of 1971 is twofold. It was the last year I lived in Sacramento, and it was also the year I began telling people I was homosexual. This happened because I fell in love with my best friend, a boy whom I call Joey Spencer in the book. He, like me, was a smart, poor boy pursuing the classic rags-to-re-spectability story that is the backbone of what was then called, without irony, the American Dream. I was going to be a lawyer, he wanted to be a doctor. We needed each other's reinforcement that such aspirations were not absurd for the stepson of a con-struction laborer and the son of a machinist. We were partners on the debate team, the kind of nerdy activity that looks good on college applications. Joey was a year younger than me, and during my last year in high school, over long nights at the li-brary studying together, on bike rides along the banks of the American River, and driving around in his mother's car smok-ing pot, I fell as deeply in love with him as I have ever loved any-one in my life. I had known I was queer from the time I was twelve and spent a great deal of my adolescence hiding behind the gestures and postures that I copied from observing other boys. But with Joey I forgot my lines, or what kind of touching was permissible, or how long I was allowed to look, and it didn't seem to bother him. He didn't appear to have that internal gauge by which teenage boys monitor their behavior against the soul-constricting model of the masculine that makes men's lives silently miserable. His nonchalance encouraged me to hope he loved me back, and, as it happened, he did, but not the same way: "I'm not a homosexual, Michael." Anyway, that was the country of my seventeenth year, and last summer I went back for a visit.

I take a map with me the morning I drive to Sacramento, but I don't use it. I easily find my way to places I hadn't visited in a quarter-century. I come in from San Francisco over an elevated section of Interstate 80 and I am reminded that the city's proudest civic boast used to be that it had "more trees than Paris." That was the kind of dorky, embarrassing claim that used to make me cringe, but now, on each side of the road, gigantic trees give me the sensation of soaring through the top of a forest. Beneath this cloud of trees lies the old part of the city, dating from the late Victorian era. How had I failed to notice, when I lived here, how pretty it is? Unlike wealthy San Francisco, Sacramento, since its beginning, has always been a middle-class town, and the houses that line these dappled streets (which, laid on a grid, are numbered and lettered—nothing fancy there) are not grand rococo Victorians but modest Queen Anne cottages and Edwardian bungalows.

I exit the freeway and make my way through the quiet, canopied streets to D Street, to the small wood-framed white house where Jack and Lauren Hart lived. Jack was my debate coach, and Lauren was an art teacher at another high school. The two of them were small-town bohemians who identified more closely with their students than with their colleagues and opened their house to a crowd of youthful misfits. It was at a party at this house, twenty-six years ago this month, that I met Joey, who had just transferred to my high school and whom Jack thought would make a good debate partner for me.

I remember the Harts had beanbag chairs and Boston ferns and liked jazz. Jack once bought a John Coltrane album that the three of us listened to as if we would be tested on it later. I formed my ideas of sophistication by watching them, though they were both from working-class families and only had state college degrees. Perhaps because they had come from those roots, they understood the intensity of my desire to get ahead.

They abetted me in my ambitions. Public speaking was more than résumé fodder for me; it was also a way to earn college money. On weekends, Jack and I traveled all over northern

California, to Lions Clubs and Elks Lodges and American Legion Posts, where I could compete in speech contests for scholarships. On those long weekend trips to Turlock or Fresno or Palo Alto I came to trust Jack as I had never trusted another grown-up in my life, so it is not surprising that it was here in this little house that I came out the closet. It was to Jack and Lauren that I first said the words, aloud, "I'm a homosexual." It made no difference to them. They still loved me, and when Jack teased me later with, "I thought you were going to tell me something really bad, that you got some girl in trouble," I could joke back, "You won't have to worry about that."

The concrete steps that lead to the porch are painted green. The yard is covered with brown leaves that rain down from the trees overhead. The windows are dark. The Harts have been divorced for twenty years. I talk to Lauren occasionally, but Jack I haven't seen since. I take a couple of pictures of the house, get back into my car and drive on, noticing again the cemetery calm of these old streets.

Trees. Mostly oaks. I'm crossing the American River and I look down at the thickly wooded banks where Joey and I used to ride our bikes to Discovery Park. Joey, who was something of a naturalist, would reach up to the trees and grab handfuls of leaves that he jammed into his pockets. Later, over a joint, he would spread them out on a picnic table and try to teach me to distinguish the different types of oaks by the shapes of their leaves. At least a half-dozen species grow by the river, and though I never remembered which was which, I've never forgotten their names —valley oak, scarlet oak, turkey oak, willow oak, Burr oak, blue oak—and I've noticed trees ever since, wherever I am. In exchange for the botany lessons, I tried to give Joey a taste for poetry, presenting him that first Christmas with a book of poems by e. e. cummings inscribed with lines from "pity this monster manunkind" that went:

— listen: there's a hell
of a good universe next door; let's go.

My destination is my high school, Los Rios. It sits in a neighborhood where the anxiously maintained dwellings of working-class families share the same streets with ratty apartment houses filled with single moms and crack dealers. The neighborhood wasn't like this in the prosperous sixties. Back then, Los Rios was a middle-class school virtually untouched by the tumultuous times. The biggest social event in 1971 was a week-long affair called "Hillbilly Hassle" that culminated in a Sadie Hawkins dance where, daringly, girls asked boys out to the dance floor.

I want to remember high school as having been excruciating, but in fact I was president of the student body, and I had a gang of vaguely hippie friends with whom I hung out at lunch beneath a grove of maple trees in front of the school. There was a handful of teachers, like Jack, who gave unstintingly of themselves and who, when it came time to apply to college, wrote endless letters of recommendation for me. And that last year, when I let my mask slip a little and allowed the people closest to me see me as I really was, no one turned away. Even so, my pain was real enough. I carried around more secrets than my homosexuality: there was the grind at home of alcohol, poverty, and violence that didn't seem to improve no matter how well I did at school. At the time, I saw myself as being alone, when in fact many hands reached out and guided me.

My high school is no longer a high school. A few years ago it was closed, refurbished, and reopened as Martin Luther King Diversity Junior High. "Diversity" is a euphemism for a racially mixed part of the city with enormous problems of poverty, drugs, and violence. The school's hallways are fenced and gated, the pool is drained and plastered with warning signs, and all the lockers have been removed. As I walk around with my camera taking pictures of water fountains and doorways, a janitor comes up, looks me over, and asks somewhat tensely, "Can I help you, sir?"

I explain that I am reliving my high school days. Clearly, with my expensive camera and Gap khakis I am a respectable citizen, so, however odd my explanation may sound to him, he decides to humor me.

"Yeah, I bet it's changed a lot."

"Not really," I reply. "But what happened to all the lockers?"

"Kids bringing guns to school," he says. "They just decided to do away with them."

Later, as I drive away, I notice for the first time the signs posted around the school: You Are Entering a Drug-Free and Weapon-Free Zone.

I'm not sure I'll be able to find Joey's house because there's been so much construction around his old neighborhood, including the expansion of what was once a modest shopping center into a behemoth that now consumes a half-dozen blocks. I stop to buy another roll of film and can't find my car afterward in the five-story parking lot. But Joey's street is unchanged. His neighborhood was cut up by Interstate 80 in the 1960s. Most of it was bulldozed and paved over; the handful of blocks that survived terminate in a concrete wall beyond which is one of the busiest freeways in the city.

A huge oak raises its dense and intricate scaffolding in Joey's front yard. Valley oak, I think. His father built this house in the stucco, ranch style of the late fifties. I remember orange shag carpeting and the smell of dirty diapers; Joey had six siblings, one of them still a toddler. His room was a rectangular cell at the end of the house with a window that looked out on a backyard of dirt and rubble. He loved his family but itched to get away from them; on one wall of his room was a map of Europe, with which he daydreamed fantasy trips that he, after we became friends he and I, would someday take. Meanwhile, we stuffed a towel under the door, opened the window, turned on the fan, and smoked pot while, in the living room, his family gathered around the TV to watch "Gunsmoke." Escape of one sort or another was a theme of our friendship.

Sometimes, that year, I slept over and we shared his bed. No, nothing ever happened. I was too repressed to make a move on him, but even the remote possibility, not to mention the incidental touching of our bodies, made those nights more erotic for me than most of my sexual encounters have been since. Before I met Joey I wasn't aware that every person's body has its own, individual odor; that some part of our personality actually oozes from our pores. He had a bright, clean smell, like sun-dried cotton. I snap pictures of his house and wonder who lives here now. Not his parents. When I was at the shopping mall, I looked for their listing in the phone book. They weren't listed.

As for Joey, he did become a doctor, and a rather prominent one. He married a girl he met a few months after I left Sacramento for college. They're still married, with a couple of sons who must now be in their late teens or early twenties. I doubt that Joey remembers me with the intensity with which I remember him. I wonder, in fact, if he remembers me at all.

Time travel is even more exhausting than geographic travel. When I get home to San Francisco that night, I'm completely wrung out. The next day I develop the pictures I took and spread them out on the kitchen table. Is the past a place? I wonder as I examine these images. Can you really go back to visit? Or is it a row of fading pictures in a dim gallery that has no power over us and no relevance to our present lives? Does the past exist at all, or do we just make it up to explain ourselves to ourselves, out of bits of what we remember but mostly out of what we wish had been?

Achim Nowak

Jungle Fever

"Hi, white boy."

Tony stares me straight in the eyes as he says it. His face twinkles with mischief, and tonight I find it impossible to hold his look. Light streaks through the open windows of my bedroom, it falls on us in blistering blue shafts. Tony's body shimmers, smooth and supple and charcoal like the glimmer of the distant sky. With a reckless toss he swings the shock of black hair from his face, then his tongue swoops down and continues to caress my chest. His touch is gentle and tender, his breath sends a chill down to my gut, it's so generous, so unafraid. Tony gives and gives without performing, he has not yet become one of the acrobats of sex, hasn't learned how to put on a floor show. His tongue circles my navel with the fury of a puppy-dog who's just been unchained. I get the giggles, and Tony grins at me again: "Hi, white boy." This time I hold his stare: "Hi, Indian boy."

So this is the game we play tonight. I feel my spine twist into a sudden clamp. No, I say to myself. No. This is not just another case of jungle fever. My friends in New York have all teased me. You're just going down to Tobago to get some black dick. Well, the twisting feeling lingers in my bones. Though, that of course is exactly what I am: a white boy. And this summer I'm doing the look—Blond Nordic Hippie Surferboy God. Here in Lambeau, in this slumbering village of five hundred on the windward side of the island, I'm the only white boy.

Tony and I flip-flop, he lies down and I start to caress his body, every inch of his delicate bronze chest with the baby black hairs that look so innocent and sweet. But suddenly he seems distant and tight. Tony does so much better when he's the one who gives. I turn him over, knead his back and the cheeks of his butt, and then we just sort of give up. I curl away from him, he curls into me, laps his arm across my shoulder, and I feel his stomach heave into my spine, so beautiful and helpless, as if he were a runner who had just crossed the finish line. This, of course, is the finish line tonight, this pressed-in fold, it's the moment we have raced toward ever since he rushed off the plane from Trinidad this afternoon. My eye catches the light as it falls onto the tiles of my terrace, it looks like a neon light that's cracked, murky and numb, and then I just hear the ocean, roaring, brandishing, pounding into the rocks below the house, so unstoppably powerful, and for a second I feel so very light, as if Tony and I were floating high above the water, to a place that drowns out all such noise.

"You don't know how to drive!"

Tony starts to protest the moment we leave Lambeau. He looks amused as he speaks, he trills with an air of superiority, but I also catch a glimpse of genuine fear in his eyes. I must admit, Tony has a point. It's early the next morning, and Tony and I are sputtering down the Old Road toward Carnbee. I'm sitting behind the steering wheel of our jeep, and I still don't quite know how to drive on the right. There isn't a lot of traffic but sometimes I get confused and end up entirely on the wrong side of the road. I think Tony simply can't stand to be so helpless, here in Tobago, can't stand to turn himself over to my care, just as I was helpless that afternoon ten days ago when we first met. I had just stepped out of the main post office in Port-of-Spain, back in Trinidad. His island. Dropped a letter to David, my ex in New York, a boy with AIDS who I couldn't have here in Trinidad, just as I couldn't really have him back in New York, because David didn't want to love anymore. I skipped and dashed across Wrightson Road, found the gaps amid the flow of the cars, and there he suddenly was, marching toward me in his immaculately pressed shirt, the shoulder-length hair that whipped from his face, the chestnut sparkle of his skin, the three-day stubble that spelled danger. Our eyes grazed as we passed, and my heart felt like it was about to erupt. Because I recognized this look; it is the universal look, and I knew that I had found him. My first island queer boy. My GQ Indian fantasy man. Tony's been to Tobago before, but Trinis are as provincial about Tobago as New Yorkers are about the rest of the States. Tony knows the hotels by the airport, the beach at Store Bay, the food shacks and the picnic tables. I left New York less than a month ago, but Tobago already is my world a lot more than his. No native ever roams his island as resolutely as a foreign traveler.

Just past the Gulf station where the chicken run wild, I stop the car and relent. We switch seats, and Tony's face brightens at once. He's happy, I can see it so clearly, to claim the role of the driver, he can relish the illusion that he knows where he's going, just as I relish the illusion that I, indeed, know this island.

There's a part of the North Road on the very far end of the map that is marked by a dotted line. Dotted lines I know from my years of studying my atlas at home. I was born in a small town in Germany and attended German schools, and my atlas was a German atlas. It began with maps of Germany, just as an American atlas begins with maps of the United States. Dotted lines have a double meaning. The Germany of my childhood, the Germany of the sixties, was marked by dotted lines that separated the east of Germany from the west, the eastern border of the east from Pommern and Schlesien, the parts that belong to Poland today. Dotted lines, I had learned, were separations we didn't accept, divisions that were temporary. These maps are relics now, these dotted lines have since disappeared. But the other dotted line, of course, is that which marks a road that's impassable, or a road that is yet to be built. Such is the line we face now, on the final stretch of the leeward drive to Charlotteville, the very last village of the island. This is a road the locals claim doesn't exist. It's the road, my British friend Edward told me just yesterday, into the *real* Tobago. It's the only drive I have yet to make on this island, and it's clear to me this is a ride we must make together, Tony and I.

WARNING. DO NOT GO ANY FURTHER. THIS ROAD IS CLOSED!

That's what a large black sign with fading letters declares, right as we pass the last shack in the hamlet of L'Anse Fourmi. It reminds me of the sign that used to precede the wall at Checkpoint Charlie in Berlin: WARNING. YOU ARE NOW LEAVING THE AMERICAN SECTOR. This sign, of course, cuts to the core of how I maneuver through life; it banishes any lingering doubt. I must make this journey.

Gliding over potholes more than a foot deep, swerving where there is little room to swerve, Tony and I enter the jungle. We see no more houses, no more cars, no more grazing cattle, no more light poles. The dense green of the trees and the grass has swallowed the path. I watch Tony behind the steering wheel, his brows clenched into a tunnel of concentration. To our left the terrain drops sharply to the sea. Branches strike the jeep, sweep across our bodies. We reach places where the earth seems simply to fall away, where the path disappears entirely, where the act of going forward becomes a guessing game . . . where Tony stops the jeep and refuses to go on.

"Go on," I yell at him and get annoyed. "You wanted to drive, so drive. If you slow down we get stuck in the holes, if you speed up we'll fly over them. You can't stop now."

Tony flinches, but he does it. The jungle, I've heard it said, is a loud place. I'm struck by the utter silence that surrounds me here. Not that it's really silent, no. The thicket mutters and screams. Maybe what I really feel is the stillness, the absence of all others. The absence of any of the symbols of my life. The shattering emptiness. There's a turn where we stop and rest, an hour or so into this drive. We climb out of the jeep. I look at Tony as he stands next to me. He looks startlingly beautiful here in the jungle, a Trini preppie, squeaky clean, painfully out of place. Yet he's the one who's steering both of us through this ride, he's showing a grit and determination I didn't believe he had. I think to myself, I don't know if we'll ever get to Charlotteville, I don't know if this road actually goes through, don't know if we'll make it back to L'Anse Fourmi if we have to turn around. I don't know that there's room here to turn, I don't know what we'll do if we encounter another car; we haven't seen one for hours now. I don't know anything anymore. It frightens me, this quiet spot. I notice my chest as it jumps and falls, like the engine of the jeep, wanting to jump-start again. It's so very rare that I feel them both, and that I feel them so clearly and so simultaneously. The joy and the terror of having traveled too far.

I sense it from both of us. We've had enough now, we simply can't wait to get out of here. My wish is granted sooner than I might have anticipated. We jump back into the jeep, and after just a few turns in the wilderness the ocean suddenly reveals, in the distance, the red-tiled roofs of a village. Charlotteville. It still is a long stretch before we get there, but the ride is different now. We have left the unknown. Soon the first signs of civilization begin to appear: cows tied on long ropes to trees, electricity poles, ramshackle houses abandoned long ago, and then the grass on the road disappears, and I see faces of children running toward us as we emerge from the woods.

The moment we reach the asphalt road that lines Charlotteville Bay the jeep collapses. A back tire has gone flat. Tony and I manage to push ahead through the jungle, but this is something neither of us knows how to do—change a tire. Two husky young men push the car for us to a nearby gas station. I walk to the edge of the beach and survey the bay of Charlotteville. There's another stillness about, different from the stillness of the jungle, lazier and calmer, but it's a stillness nevertheless. The sun sizzles high above us; the water sparkles in a sleepy emerald green. Charlotteville makes Lambeau look like a hub of activity. Tony ambles into the empty space beside me, and then we both flop onto the ledge of the boulder that shields the road from the beach. We sit and wait for the jeep to be ready. Wait to recover from our collapse. Wait to return. We'll return a different way, across the mountains and down the Atlantic side of the island. I feel my chest quietly tumble, my spine unknot. I turn to Tony. He sits close to me right now, and I watch his torso heave, as if he were still steering the jeep. Sweat dribbles from his armpits, his skin trembles.

"I didn't think we'd make it," Tony says to me with a gasp of relief.

I long to hold him, long to tell him that I understand. This drive here was his declaration of love. My relief is that this is the end of the road. Because if it weren't, I know I would have to go on.

"Let me take a picture of you," I say to Tony and pull my camera out of my bag. We're standing on a plain, pebbled beach, behind a coconut grove just off the Windward Road. Heading back toward Lambeau, looking for the ruins of a fortress that we can't find.

"Oh no," he protests, and I'm surprised at the vehemence of his rejection, at the way his body instantly turns away from me, as if there actually were a place where he could hide.

"What do you mean, no? What's the big deal about taking a picture?" I feel myself working into a rage. Tony's already taken a slew of pictures of me; now I want to do the same. One thing I know: Tony's a reluctant Catholic—this is not a religious objection. Maybe Tony doesn't want to be shown off the moment I return to New York. The native I've captured. My local fuck. But I don't even think it's that. A photo would be a record of his secret life, his life with a foreign friend, his life away from his mother. It's a record of all the borders he's crossing, here in Tobago. No, Tony doesn't want a reminder of this. He doesn't want to own this secret life. And of course, in this very act, he wants to disown me and my life, wants to turn me into that same secret, make me go away while he makes himself disappear. Yes, he wants to send me back to the place where nothing matters, not our bonds, not our differences, nothing, because all must be hidden and none of it can ever be revealed. That we're two men, that he's a Trini and I'm a German, that at night we caress each other with a burning tenderness. In this moment he throws it all to the wind.

"That's just really ridiculous," I say to him, now flailing with anger. Every ounce of my self-righteousness and arrogance is kicking in.

"Well, I don't want to."

Tony is acting stubborn and determined, and so I decide to let it go, but of course I don't, and he doesn't either. We climb back into the car, sit in silence, stew in rage, a rage that seems more threatening now that it's contained by the windshield of our jeep. I flash back to the conversation we had at the Kentucky Fried Chicken in Port-of-Spain, the day I first met him. He looked so unbearably beautiful, the way he stared at me across the plastic trays. The dark pins of his eyes, the impeccably curved pearl-white teeth, and his shoulders, fidgeting and forever shifting as he spoke of the men he had been with. There was the consul from the Canadian Embassy who sent him roses and took him to Maracas beach at night. There was the travel agent who escorted him for a weekend to Barbados. Tony has only gone out with white men. Older white men. I wondered right away, of course: Is that who I was, his next older white man? Is this what he had been like with all the other men?

My first boyfriend, Paul, was a dancer from Jamaica, nineteen when I was seventeen. He was my older black man, and a man of the world—after all, Paul had had sex. The first time he kissed me, downstairs in the dressing room of the Washington Theatre Club, during a rehearsal break, he took me without asking, as if I were his for the taking, and thrust his tongue into my unsuspecting mouth. I was shocked by the force of this grab, the strength of his muscular hands, the ferocious determination of his will. His tongue dug deep into the caves of my mouth, firmly and without relenting, as if in that moment he had to conquer me completely and there would never be another time. It was wet and hard, curved at the tip, and unremitting in its pursuit. Digging, digging, down. When I opened my eyes, there we were, Paul and I, sitting on the counter in front of the long row of makeup mirrors and naked light bulbs. I stared at his mouth, a mouth that I had admired before, at a distance. It looked so very different, now that it had kissed me, the lips thicker and wider and larger, still glistening wet, trembling with desire, the entire mouth so much larger than mine, as if it were the big bad wolf that might devour me, the big bad wolf with the protruding jaw, the mole on its left cheek that promised insatiable hunger. The setting for this kiss was flawless. We sat in front of the mirrors, and our image was immediately reflected on the wall beside us. It magnified Paul's power, the mirror, threw it right back in my face. I saw the dark beauty of his black skin, the delicate burst of his budding dreads, the shaving bumps under his chin that gave him a sweet roughness, the stretch of his shoulders that seemed so very wide as they cradled my scrawny white body, his hands that pressed hard into my back. I observed it for the first time. The beauty of the clash. The close opposition of color.

I slept with Paul simply because he was the first man who seduced me. Or so I like to tell myself. But yes, making out in the front seat of my mother's orange VW, for hours at a time, in the parking lot of a part of town that my parents, I was sure, had never penetrated, I began to taste his black skin. Smell his neck, the pit of his arms, the air between his thighs. Began to lunge into that chest, so vast and taut. Press and press my tongue into his black mouth. Inhale his black longing. It was the typical homeless teenage sex, confined to the narrow walls of a car, but

it was there, within the borders of this VW, that I began the journey to the other part of town, the part where none of the
German boys I knew in D.C. had been.

Tony and I step into a Chinese restaurant in Point Fortin, and
for a moment I forget that, today, Trinidad is where I am. I
might be anywhere—a Chinese restaurant in Manhattan, in
Berlin, in Ankara, where I had my first taste of Chinese food.
This is China without frills, the dining room dingy and dark, the
tablecloths aubergine, the color that absorbs all stains. The
sweet-and-sour chicken is more sweet than sour, the rice is rice,
and the slender strings of chicken might be any kind of meat.

I'm happy when we pay and run back out. "I want to go to
Manzanilla," I say to Tony. "I want to go to where the ocean is
wild."

Tony shrugs a lackadaisical okay, and we jump into the car
and head toward the coconut groves of Manzanilla Bay. He met
me early this morning at my guesthouse in St. Augustine. I've
hopped over to Trinidad to visit him, and it's been my first long
day with Tony on his island, driving into the far southeastern
provinces, trudging to more of the places where he never goes. I
feel like we're racing into a tunnel—that's what this road
through the grove looks like, a tunnel blazing with dark, filtered
light. The wind whips through the open windows of the car,
whips our hair into a frenzy; outside on the coast the waves
whip into the front tier of the palms, and I love it, love it so completely, this ride into a whipped-up frenzy of a world. Tony and
I are both silent, but it's a silence of complicity, a silence of joy.
I start to hum, under my breath at first, then louder and louder.
I watch Tony who sits next to me, a big self-satisfied smirk on his
face. And then I go for it—unzip his pants and pull out his penis
and blow him. Tony indulges with obligatory protests; he tries to
yank away my head, but I ignore him. I hear him heave and
gasp, he instantly rises hard into my mouth. His foot is still

pressing the gas—if nothing else, we're accelerating. I feel the hot Manzanilla wind rustle my hair, and then Tony presses my head further down, becomes the willing accomplice. His chest, his stomach start to convulse, and for once it's not the bumpy road, no, it's him, completely him, and in an instant all the movements seem to speed up and converge, the movement of my mouth, the thrust of his penis, the hit of the air, the jag of the car. And he comes, both hands on the steering wheel, his chest hurtling forward, and for a second I fear he will tumble over me, fall through the windshield.

"That was really nice," Tony says when I swing back up to my seat, wipe my mouth.

"Uhuh," I say.

Where the road swings close to the bay Tony veers off, we bounce over chipped wood, and then we stop. To my right the Atlantic rolls into shore. There isn't much of a beach here; the water rolls and crashes right up to the crest where the grove starts, but it rolls from far, far back in this bay, the waves advance and topple with foam for what seems like an eternity before they tumble onto shore. The entire bay, from where I stand, looks like one vast field of rolling white crests, starting far in the distance, a sea of billows rippling, rolling, roaring toward me, waiting to crash. I strip down to my trunks and slam into the water. Tony was right: it's shallow but wild, wilder than it looked from afar. Tony joins me, we duck, and then I get tossed about, tossed into those delicious falls where I forget where I am, what I'm doing here. Tony scurries back to the place where the waves meet the shore, right beneath the whipping palms, and I run after him and press him down into the sand. Our lips lock, his arms clasp my back, the sand beneath us is supple, it gives, and then we just toss on the beach, my chest pressing into his, his legs clamping my thighs, our lips locked as if we were each other's only source of breath, as if this were all we needed to survive. We press into each other with a desperate commitment, the waves roll over us and we just stay locked. My eyes slit open for a second, I catch a glimpse of the coconuts up high, the rough trunk of the palms, swaying, tossing, and then I close my eyes again, reenter the lock, and have a flash: We're Deborah Kerr and Burt Lancaster rolling on the beach, tossing from here to eternity, and just this moment I don't care who's Deborah and who's Burt, who's Trini and who's German. I don't care. I kiss him completely, kiss his salt-tipped tongue, kiss his salt-crusted shoulder, kiss away all the ocean crud and grime, kiss him down to his soul. I open my eyes again when I feel Tony's lips go limp, his pressure fade. I find his eyes open too, scuttling about. I catch the glimpse of terror in his eyes, the terror I know so well now. We're miles from any traffic, any cars, and we're rolling well below a place where anyone might see us, but that is the terror. Always. What if we were found out? What if we were seen here, on the Manzanilla Road, a white boy and an Indian boy, making love?

That night we park his car in a quiet lane, under a willow tree. Light settles in gold over the badminton field of the University of the West Indies campus, and Tony reaches for my hand, as he so often does, across the stick shift of his car. This is the moment right before we must part, before I go back to my guesthouse and Tony goes back to his momma. When Tony touches me he doesn't lie. Ever. I know that by now. He sits quietly. I watch him as he tries to muster strength, then he turns to me and looks me straight in the eyes: "I've never been afraid of losing anything," he says with a soft tremble, "but I'm afraid of losing you." His eyes shine so impossibly black, like bursting embers as he speaks. The walls of the car lock us in our own tiny world. Today has been one of the happiest days of my life. When Tony's hand presses into mine I have no doubt. The truth is that Tony is falling in love with me. And I'm the one who is lying. I'm the one who is scared. Because deep down I know that I, too, am falling in love, and I don't have the courage.

David Tuller

Broken Romance

In the summer of 1991, bored with my job and craving adventure, I flew to Russia and became an American sex spy.

Well, that's what my friend Ksyusha and her crowd nicknamed me, anyway, because of my persistent and—to them—rather peculiar interest in discussing what they referred to as "the sexual question." I met Ksyusha that summer during my first trip to Russia, a land whose harsh allure had long intrigued me. As a reporter for the *San Francisco Chronicle*, I was part of a delegation of Americans attending an unprecedented gay and lesbian conference in Moscow and Leningrad. The event drew hundreds of Soviet citizens to the thundering heart of the empire during a season of profound political chaos; less than one month later, in the cool rain of August, Gorbachev's bumbling lieutenants would stage their comically ill-fated coup.

The ten-day gathering bristled with discussion groups, lectures, parties, film screenings, condom giveaways, and a gay rights demonstration and kiss-in within sight of the Kremlin. At a seminar on "gay and lesbian visibility," each participant had an opportunity to say a few words of introduction. Those of us from the West were used to this routine and we prattled on cheerfully about how and when we came out to our bosses and parents and how important it all was. The Russians were not well versed in the art of public self-revelation; though a woman from Siberia vowed to bring gay liberation to the country's hinterlands, the others did not seem comfortable talking openly in front of strangers.

When the circle came round to a tall, gaunt man, he deflected the attention by gesturing grandly toward a woman sitting opposite him. "I came here with Ksyusha, and I love her."

The woman scowled and waved her hand with irritation.

"I also came here with Ksyusha, and I love her, too," chimed in a man farther along the circle.

"I love Ksyusha very much—I'd even like to marry her!" proclaimed a third.

Marry her? This conference was certainly turning out to have its own unorthodox perspective. Proposals of marriage were not exactly a routine occurrence at other gay conferences I'd attended.

All heads now swiveled toward this Ksyusha, the object of adoration; she squirmed in her chair. I looked, too. At first glance, there was nothing particularly striking about her: her skin was sallow, her features plain, and her hair chopped short in androgynous simplicity. I don't remember what she said when it was her turn to speak, but after the workshop something impelled me to corner her on the curved staircase outside the hall. Her English was bad, my Russian worse, but I managed to explain that in the fall I planned to leave work and return to Moscow for a while.

Her pale eyes leaped with fierce glee. She pumped the air with her finger. "You must meet with me, I know many men!"

Sure, I wanted to meet men—tall men and hunky ones, men pining for someone to soothe the legendary anguish of their fevered Russian souls. But here, on the curving stairway, it was this oddly compelling lesbian who captivated me. She was scrawny, yes, but she moved with the sinewy grace of a dancer, and her fleshy, exuberant hands bounced constantly as she talked. As we stood there, and as I gazed at her, an unexpected longing rustled somewhere deep within me.

I met others, too, who long simmered in my memory. There

was Gennady Roshchupkin, the country's first AIDS activist—pale as ice, angry, but soft-spoken and charming. And Arkady, a former psychiatric inmate, whose eyes darted back and forth with sinister foreboding.

Arkady had a proclivity for mumbled ravings; occasionally he'd fling his arm over my shoulder, bend forward, growl something in my ear, and stare at me with dark significance. I never understood. Others had questions about Arkady, too. Depending upon the source of information, he was either KGB or CIA or pedophile or gun-toting gangster or some of those or all of them or something else again—a persuasive one-man argument for Churchill's famous dictum that Russia was "a riddle wrapped in a mystery inside an enigma."

Arkady was not the only reminder of the brooding edge that wound through the lives and psyches of Russia's citizens. During the ten days of the conference, I listened quietly as one person after another related dramatic tales of woe: imprisonment, blackmail, KGB harassment, loneliness, suicidal despair. These stories all sounded unremittingly bleak to me, but those recounting them often adopted an inexplicable matter-of-fact tone.

I was particularly struck by a thirty-six-year-old librarian from a town in the Ural Mountains hundreds of miles from Moscow. A plain, round-faced woman, she said she had waited years to meet someone who shared her attraction to members of her own sex.

"Did you ever believe that your sexual orientation was a psychological illness?" I asked.

I knew, of course, that the answer would be yes. It had taken me endless infusions of psychotherapy to overcome the conviction that I was a disturbed human being, and many of my American friends had struggled deeply with the same issue.

Surely it had been far more devastating for this poor creature, trapped and isolated in the barren Russian provinces. I readied my notepad to record her imminent outpouring of emotional distress, and adjusted my features in an expression that reflected —I hoped—gentle understanding and the wisdom of the ages.

The woman looked at me blankly, and paused. Then she dispatched me with a derisive "No!"—as if the question itself were mighty peculiar.

I felt a brief surge of panic. If I had a need to believe that Russians experienced their homosexuality in the same terms that I did—that their path of suffering and acceptance traced the contours of my own—then her sharp retort suggested a truth more complex, and perhaps more interesting, than I had anticipated.

I was also confused by the married ones, or those who had been married, or planned to marry, or simply slept from time to time with members of the opposite sex—all of whom fell outside my standard definitions of the gay and lesbian categories. This included huge numbers of the conference attendees, far more than was the case among the admittedly unscientific sampling of my acquaintances back home. While some of the Russians complained bitterly about the need to live a double life, a great many discussed their heterosexual liaisons with a nonchalance and freedom that startled me, steeped as I was in a deep distrust of bisexuality as a fraudulent pose.

I kept asking questions and paid attention. It began to dawn on me that maybe it was too facile to characterize all these cross-gender relationships as dishonest or false, too patronizing to attribute the phenomenon solely to self-deception or fear of one's own homosexuality. As the examples mounted, my preconceptions wobbled—and my anxiety levels rose. "What the hell is going on here?" I asked Marc, my roommate at the conference and a San Francisco photojournalist with a refreshingly self-deprecating manner.

Marc just laughed and shrugged his shoulders in good-natured bewilderment.

One of my most delightful encounters occurred not at the conference itself but in a drab corridor at Leningrad's Hotel Karelia. This dilapidated building on the bitter outskirts of the city was a high-rise built with that distinctive socialist flair. Like all of these concrete slabs, it gave the impression that whoever designed it—if anyone did—was either drunk or visually impaired. Walls, carpets, everything oozed gray. The tiny elevators groaned and quivered their way between floors, and our rooms gazed out onto fields spattered with garbage.

The "key ladies" were the dowdy, round women with hair piled high who sat at rickety desks on every floor of the hotel; they collected our room keys when we left for the day and handed them back when we returned. At such establishments, key ladies were a venerable institution whose ostensible function was to serve the many needs of foreign guests. It quickly became clear that their real mission was to keep a wary eye on our comings and goings—and those of any Soviet friends. Despite the changes of recent years, hotels for foreign tourists still strictly forbade all locals from entering. Tall sour men patrolled the lobbies to repel potential infiltrators, yet some managed to shimmy past these dark-suited guardians of the social order. Key ladies acted as the second line of defense in this cloak-and-dagger drama.

The key ladies at our hotel protected their positions round the clock, glancing glumly at us as we passed, occasionally barking a mild pleasantry or a caustic observation in Russian that I barely understood. Behind the desk on the tenth floor sat Lily, a lovely exception to the general surly rule. At thirty-five, Lily was younger than most of her key-lady colleagues and far more amiable. On the way back to the hotel late one evening, my friend Sam, another of the Americans, recounted a conversation he'd had earlier in the day with Lily. She asked why he was wearing a button emblazoned with the slogan *Ya goluboi* (I am gay).

"We're here attending a gay and lesbian conference in town," Sam explained.

Lily was embarrassed, but fascinated. "You mean you are all homosexual? The women, too?"

"Yes. Except you don't have to whisper."

"As a homosexual . . . do you need a man every day?"

"No, and as a heterosexual woman, do you?"

The two of them hadn't had time to finish their discussion. Sam, a dedicated queer activist with a blond mop of hair and a mischievous streak, wanted to explore the subject further. "I'm sure she's going to tell her friends about us, and I want to give her some more 'educations' before she does that," he told me wryly.

When we returned around 1:00 A.M., Lily was folding laundry. She tossed us a good-natured smile, and we began to chat. She was an instructor of English by training; she worked the night shift at the hotel to make extra cash. "But my husband hates my job because he knows there are lots of men around, and he's afraid of losing me," she confided.

Sam laughed. "Then he should love all of us."

I told Lily I'd like to hear her thoughts about the conference. Would she mind discussing them? She'd do so with pleasure, she said, sounding flattered . . . and by the way, she had more questions and would we answer those too, please? For the next three hours—until long after my eyes began to slip shut—we consumed dozens of Marlboros and gave Lily a condensed course in gay liberation. During that smoky, freewheeling exchange, she gave us in return a revealing portrait of Russian attitudes toward homosexuality.

"It is strange, of course, that you are here." Lily parceled out her words in a crisp, cool lilt. "I am surprised because I see such people as you for the first time at the hotel."

She said that she knew no gays and lesbians, that she had never talked to any before. She might have seen a few of them on the street, but she couldn't be sure. "For my mind—I don't want to offend you—but for my mind, I think your behavior is not normal," she said gently.

Sam protested. "No, it is normal—it's just not considered normal." But Lily shook her head sadly—"I think you are depriving yourself. You cannot feel that a woman is beautiful, that she is like a flower, like a fresh rose. You cannot smell her body, and you will never know it."

Lily had many ideas about the behavior patterns of gays. Did we want to be with young boys? There were laws against that in the Soviet Union, she informed us soberly. And who fulfilled the female role? Who did the cleaning and ironing? Was it that we wanted to look like women, to use lipstick and paint our nails? Or did we actually want to be women?

Many people in the United States, I told Lily, had the same questions. Yes, some men did like young boys, and some wanted to be women. "But most gay men, like me, enjoy being men. And they don't want to be with boys or with men who want to be women, but with others who like being men." I was aware that this all sounded a bit smug, but I wanted to keep the discussion simple.

Lily shifted in her chair, tapped the ashes from her cigarette. Her opinions, which would have offended me if uttered by an American, struck me now as simply naive: she believed what she'd been taught because she never had reason to believe otherwise. Yet she was genuinely curious, and her earthy charm and gracious manner disarmed me.

Lily advanced some interesting notions about the causes of homosexuality, notions that were common among other Russians I met. One was the "prison theory"—that inmates were forced by circumstances to become homosexuals because they were separated from members of the opposite sex. "But you have not been separated that way," she acknowledged, perplexed.

Another line of reasoning: that we turned to each other out of desperation at the failure of attempts with the opposite sex. She asked about our past experiences with women. Sam said that he'd had none; I told her that I hadn't had a girlfriend in many years. Marc, who had just joined the conversation, explained that he'd been miserable when he had tried to force himself to date women. "Even my parents could tell the difference once I gave that up, and accepted my being gay because they knew I was much happier."

Lily tilted her head and absorbed this information; then, she leaned forward and playfully lifted her gray skirt above the knee. The coy, delicate gesture revealed a shapely leg. "And if you see a woman without her dress . . . ?" she asked, voice soft as a pillow.

Lily fell silent; took a slow, pensive drag on her cigarette. "You see," she went on, "I cannot fully understand men who do not want a woman as a woman. I can see now you are not deviants, that I can speak with you, eat with you, I can maybe even be friends with you. But I can't understand your behavior in a sexual way."

We talked some more. Sam, Marc, and I all tried to explain that being gay was not just sex, not just lust; that it involved emotions as round and full as those that other men felt for women, that she felt for her husband. She asked questions; we answered; she probed some more. And then—in the haze of insight that sometimes precedes sheer exhaustion—she cast her arms in the air and unfurled them over her head. What we were saying, for some ineffable reason, made sense to her now.

"California, take me with you!" she exclaimed cheerfully, to no one in particular.

Then she looked directly at us. "I do see now that being gay is a feeling. That you not only have sex"—she pressed her hands together twice in short, quick motions—"but that you love a man, too"—and pointed toward her heart.

"And after talking to you, I see that you are normal." She nodded her head gravely. "And I think that our society is guilty because it doesn't allow us to have contact with each other. . . . All homosexuals and straight people *must* be able to talk together."

A wave of delight splashed over me. For I imagined that in many ways Lily embodied the challenge facing the Russian gay movement, struggling to rouse society from its long, dour ignorance. Her lack of knowledge about the gays and lesbians all around her was unfortunate; but her willingness to listen, to debate—and, ultimately, to welcome the new ideas burrowing into her mind—was an example of *perestroika* at its most potent and thrilling.

It was now 4:00 A.M. The early light from another of Leningrad's long summer days trickled in through the window, and the conversation meandered toward a close. Lily asked us our ages; when Sam, the youngest, said he was just twenty-two, she let out a wicked little whoop. "Twenty-two years old, and already a homosexual!"

I gave Lily some lipstick as a gift and asked her to pose for a photo. "I might write an article about this," I explained.

She frowned with mock sternness. "Yes, but if you use this picture, you must not make a mistake and write under it 'a Russian lesbian.'" Just before we shuffled off to bed, Sam turned and asked one last question. "Are you going to tell your husband about us?"

Lily grinned. "Of course! First thing in the morning!"

Sam, Marc, and I, and the rest of our eclectic queer delegation, had arrived in Russia at an auspicious moment. Control of events was clearly slipping from Gorbachev's grasp, and the ultimate success of his reforms was in doubt. During the past year, the Soviet leader, hesitant and fearful, had swung back and forth between the Kremlin hard-liners urging him to impose order by force and the democrats and capitalists yearning for more freedom and open markets. A month earlier, in June, his arch-rival Boris Yeltsin had swept to an overwhelming victory in elections for president of the Russian Republic, swamping the official Communist Party candidate and becoming the first leader with a popular mandate in the nation's thousand-year history.

Amid the turmoil, the easing of restrictions on public debate had smashed the suffocating rigidity of socialist ideology. Newly unfettered media explored once-taboo topics with ferocious enthusiasm, exposing the lies of Soviet history and decrying government corruption. Plays and movies subverted cherished myths of the workers' paradise. People flocked to lectures and forums on an astonishing array of controversial subjects, from the horrors of Stalinism to the country's disastrous health care system. In previous decades, members of the intelligentsia surreptitiously traded banned books in carbon copy *samizdat* editions; now they and everyone else devoured officially published works by Solzhenitsyn and others.

Amid these developing freedoms, a tiny gay and lesbian rights movement percolated noisily. If the collapse of the Berlin Wall in 1989 signaled the official end of the Iron Curtain, cracks were finally beginning to fracture what some dubbed the "iron closet."

The movement faced tremendous challenges, not the least of which was pervasive public fear of homosexuality; in a 1989 poll, a third of those questioned said that homosexuals should be "liquidated" and another 30 percent wanted them "isolated." Nevertheless, for the first time since Stalin's terror, a few "sexual dissidents," as they began to call themselves, were coming out publicly, starting gay newspapers, fighting for repeal of the sodomy law, and disseminating information about AIDS. Despite the minuscule numbers who participated in such efforts, they had formed the issue into the public consciousness and onto the political map—and they showed no signs of slowing down.

The Soviet activists had organized the summer conference jointly with the International Gay and Lesbian Human Rights Commission, a San Francisco group that functioned on a shoestring budget as a gay version of Amnesty International. Since I covered gay and lesbian issues for the Bay Area's major daily newspaper, the idea of writing about the nascent efforts of those just emerging from their underground existence appealed to me.

So, too, did the opportunity to visit the homeland of my ancestors; my father's parents had fled from the Soviet Union to America shortly after the Bolshevik Revolution—part of the vast wave of Jewish refugees during the early years of the century. My grandfather died in 1952, two years before I was born, but Grandma Rose was the great love of my early childhood. By 1991 she had been dead for twenty-five years, yet I still thought of her every day and gained strength from the memory of our time together. Traveling to Russia felt like one more way to keep her spirit alive within me.

The conference itself was wild and wonderful and weird. In Moscow and Leningrad—soon to be renamed St. Petersburg— hundreds of men and women flooded to workshops on lesbian writing and safe sex, fundraising strategies and gay spirituality. With cultures clashing right and left, the encounters between Russians and Americans were by turns dizzy and touching, ferocious and highly comic. Irina, a statuesque interpreter who was writing her graduate dissertation on some obscure theory about the use of gerunds in English, was stumped when called upon to translate slang terms like "rimming" and "butch."

Though Irina was married and had a young daughter, the conference tapped hidden facets of her own sexuality. "I'm so attracted to the men here that I now think maybe I'm a gay man in a woman's body," she confided to me, only half in jest, on the overnight train between Leningrad and Moscow.

One young man asked Laurie Coburn, a large, cheerful woman who was a member of the organization Parents and Friends of Lesbians and Gays, to find him pen-pal parents in the States—and requested that she pass along a color slide of himself lying naked (and semi-erect) on his bed. In a poignant encounter, Laurie also met with Svetlana, a prim, plump redhead with a gay son.

Silent tremors raked across Svetlana's compressed lips. Her checks flamed with fear and too much rouge. Perched carefully on the edge of her chair, she recounted how her enraged husband had threatened their son with a knife because of his sexual orientation.

The young man, who appeared to be about twenty, looked on silently as Svetlana beseeched Laurie to help him find a way to emigrate. "Maybe there is an American lesbian who might be willing to marry my son so he can leave. I'll pray every day for the people who can help him." She squeezed her hands together tightly and delicately dabbed her red-rimmed eyes.

One of the conference's most historic events was a demonstration against the country's sodomy law on the plaza in front of Moscow's Bolshoi Theater, a site chosen both because of its proximity to the Kremlin and its reputation as the city's main public cruising spot. The press corps arrived in force for this unprecedented display, which featured speeches, banners, and enthusiastic same-sex kisses. Some onlookers stared in confusion and shock; many stalked off, enraged.

I found myself profoundly moved by the willingness of the Russians to risk public exposure, a willingness that demanded far more courage than my own coming-out years before. At one point Asya, a black-eyed Siberian beauty, grabbed the microphone. She and four friends, all in their early twenties, had traveled thousands of miles to attend the conference and had told their parents they were on a sight-seeing visit to the capital. Now, in front of television cameras, Asya led the crowd in chanting, "*My ne boimsya, my ne boimsya!* (We are not afraid, we are not afraid)."

Ksyusha, the woman I met at the gay visibility workshop, turned out to be a dyke den mother to many of Moscow's gays, and the more time I spent with her the more I appreciated her appeal. She was funny and maternal and brandished her raucous sensuality like a whip. But she had a somber side, too; at times a listless dejection dimmed the glint in her eyes.

The day after the conference ended, she kept her promise to introduce me to men. It was a Saturday evening. Marc and I had moved from the hotel to the apartment of an acquaintance, and we met Ksyusha—and her all-male entourage—at Pushkin Square in the center of town, across the street from the country's first McDonald's.

I was particularly struck by a young man named Igor. His eyes were sharp as rocks, and black; his skin, smooth and perfect. He was twenty-five and beautiful and, at least initially, aloof. He scooted forward at a bristling pace; I scurried to keep up.

I couldn't understand much of what Igor said, so I concentrated hard on absorbing the waves and rhythms of his peppery speech. He spoke in rapid, bitter explosions, his voice rough as rust. What I did catch was this: he was a doctor and, yes, he was married, with a five-year-old daughter. They lived far from the city and, of course, he loved them. . . . No, his wife didn't know that he had come to Moscow to attend a gay conference.

He pronounced the word *dochka* (daughter) with a quick

downward punch, as if asserting the fact of her existence would help him to remember it. When he spoke of his wife, it was in a tone both casual and curt; he apparently accepted his marital status as a given, but didn't care to discuss it much.

"Are you returning home soon?" I asked.

"No, not for a while." Then: silence.

Our group ate dinner at a nearby cafe; the only items available were mushrooms in wine sauce and tasteless potato salad. Afterward, two of our vodka-laden companions zigzagged off in a lover's dispute, and the rest of us debated our next move. We voted to take a stroll along the Arbat, a popular tourist shopping street where vendors hawked shawls and military hats and those irritatingly ubiquitous *matryoshka* dolls that nestled snugly inside each other.

Igor and I stayed close together, and once again he began talking, talking . . . I didn't interrupt. He took my elbow and linked it in his; then held and lightly patted my hand. I slung my arm over his shoulder, ran a finger through his thick, curly hair. He glanced around anxiously.

"People, so many people!" he muttered, then leaned over and quickly licked my lip. When we passed beneath the shadow of a tall, deserted building, I pivoted, skin hot through my shirt. He gripped me, kissed me—frankly and fully—on the mouth. The trembling intensity of that slow, aching kiss arose from the knowledge that we had nowhere to go, no chance to be alone; we were both visitors to the city, staying with our respective friends in very cramped quarters.

It was midnight in Moscow. Ksyusha urged us to crash at the *dacha* (country cottage) of an older lesbian couple she knew. Igor, eyes churning with anticipation, pressed me to accept the invitation. But as we all boarded the train at Kiev Station for the fifty-minute ride, Ksyusha pulled me aside.

"There's a difficulty," she said in a conspiratorial whisper. "I told my friends that I might bring some Americans along, so you're okay. The others are old friends, so they're all right, too. But I don't really know Igor, I just met him, and my friends are going to ask who he is and why he's come. . . . That's the way Russians are. I'm sorry, David, I can't bring him."

I shrugged my shoulders, disappointed. But what could I do? It was their country, their rules. As we settled into our seats, Ksyusha beckoned to Igor, spoke to him in a corner . . . and then he was gone. Thus was my bedmate for the night—whose lust and pain and deep, dark ardor singed my heart—cast outside the tight comfort of our circle.

I never saw Igor again. Back in San Francisco, his image fluttered in my memory like a curtain in a breeze. When Marc showed me pictures he had taken of Igor, my face flushed and my chest tightened. Later, during the blackest hours of the August coup, when I feared that my newfound friends would be arrested and shipped to another archipelago of gulags, my thoughts returned to him and to the sudden rupture of our four-hour romance.

For in some telling way, my brief experience with Igor eloquently illustrated for me many of the issues confronting Russian gays and lesbians as one world collapsed and new possibilities emerged: the passionate urgency of their liaisons; the desperate lack of privacy; the ambiguous role of marriage and family; the tight friendship networks that viewed outsiders (except for an occasional Westerner) with suspicion.

I returned to Russia two months later, and again and again through the next few years. I went to bear witness to the struggle of gays and lesbians for dignity and freedom, to record the pain and richness of their lives. And, oh, what riches they had

scavenged from the shrill and petty wasteland of their Soviet existence. Almost everyone I spoke to expressed the view that the
entire country was, in metaphoric terms, one enormous labor
camp. But the more I understood the regime's fierce efforts to
control its subjects, the greater I appreciated how those whom I
met devised inspired strategies—psychological, philosophical,
physical—to escape the onslaught.

Secret places, in the city and the country and in the mind's
depths, too, were coveted, cherished, and zealously protected.
Like convicts scraping, scraping their way out of cells with rusty
spoons, citizens of the giant Soviet gulag burrowed through the
system's cracks in search of private pockets of liberation.

Some quickly lost all strength and failed. Others succumbed
to the pressures and betrayed friends and relatives. Yet many
persevered—fueled and fortified, more often than not, by vodka
or staggering flights of fantasy, by sex or emotional extravagance
or feats of artistic creation. These very acts of defiance kept
them vital, and the dark existence that they found within the
cracks and the shadows nurtured them. If it did not always
grace them with an abiding sense of peace or stability, at least
they could linger in occasional moments of pleasure and passion—moments whose elusiveness rendered them all the more
poignant.

For those whose sexuality veered from the norm, the burden
and the despair could be far greater. But so, too, could their ability to slip through the cracks into bidden worlds. Though
defined by a difference that separated them from most, they
could gain strength from the discovery of others like themselves.

Erasmo Guerra

La Plaça Reial

I lay on the top bunk in one of the smaller rooms at the crowded
and damp-smelling Pension Colon. There was no other place to
go. I had arrived in Barcelona late in the evening, and all the
other pensions I had called from the train station were full. They
said to try again tomorrow and offered no other advice. Colon
was the last place I called because the guidebook did little to
elaborate on the fact that it had cheap, dorm-style beds. It
should have been easy to find, but Las Ramblas was packed with
artists sitting with their easels along the walk, teenage pick-
pockets hanging out on the benches, tourists drinking coffee in
the sidewalk cafés. I was able to negotiate the crowd and find the
pension only with the help of an overweight, underdressed
prostitute who had been standing on the wide pedestrian avenue with nothing better to do. I expected her to ask me if I
wanted a date, or for money to buy herself a drink. She didn't,
which was good, since I'd spent my pocket change of pesetas on
the futile phone calls.

For 1,300 pesetas I got a bed for the night, one thin sheet, and
a key to a beat-up locker that reminded me of high school.
Appropriately, other than the woman at the front desk, everyone
there seemed to be a teenager. The kids (I didn't know what else
to call them—they looked so young) sat smoking in the stairwell
leading up to the rooms or slumped on the couches of the common areas or on their bunks, legs hanging, poring over maps
and reading their guidebooks for the nth time. No one anywhere looked close to twenty-six, which was my age. I was
painfully aware of it only because I'd missed every travel dis-

count by a year. I paid full price on train and bus tickets, museum and theater admissions. Even at the pension I would have paid a surcharge had I not belonged to an international hostel organization.

I lay on the bed for a while, feeling the odd heat of a late-September night, listening to the clattering noise coming from the Plaça Reial, which sat squarely outside my window, watching the other guys stumble in with their packs or return drunk from an early trip to a nearby bar. I didn't talk to any of them, even if they did look cute and intelligent; we only exchanged silent nods as we made our way from bunk to locker to the bathroom and back to our bunks. People were speaking every language but Spanish, which I half expected. I'd read or heard somewhere that to speak in Barcelona in a tongue other than Catalán was a sure way of getting ignored, but to speak in Spanish was to spit or curse the city and the people itself. Still, every one of the boys looked easygoing. My room slept ten. The other rooms were two or three times bigger, and we had to wade through them, maneuvering around the packs laid out on the floor, to get in and out.

I studied a tattered city map I'd found discarded on one of the empty bunks, locating the street for Punto BNC and Este Bar, the supposed gay hot spots according to the same guidebook that had been all-too accurate about the pension. Then I took a nap and got up sometime past midnight. I showered, changed into a fresh white shirt, my worn blue jeans, and boots, and walked up Las Ramblas to Muntaner.

I nearly turned back when I opened the door to Punto. The place was long and clean and flooded with bright lights like a school cafeteria. The music had a loud driving beat, and a wailing diva cut in sporadically with the same five words. It was a different mix of a song that I knew already. The muscle boys I recognized too. I felt as if I had been there before, as if I were in a Chelsea bar back in New York, only with the lights turned up high. But everyone still looked beautiful. I went to the bar, stood by a modelish-looking guy wearing a Dolce and Gabbana D&G T-shirt, and ordered, of all things, water. I sipped it like alcohol, even though I was stripped to a bone-dry thirst.

I made eye contact with a nose-pierced guy who reminded me of José. When he came over, I couldn't understand how I had mistaken him for José, whom the guy looked nothing like, and certainly not like anyone I would ever want to date. The guy stretched the front of his already tight shirt across his abs by pulling on it from behind his back. His ribs made a soft hollow that looked as if it had been scooped out by sucked-in air. He didn't say much. He couldn't without letting all the air fill up his belly. He winked at me and gave me his name and a free invitation to Arena, a disco a few blocks away, where he said the crowd moved to after Punto shut down for the night.

Arena turned out to be like any other dance club. The unmarked door led to an interior of dark red velvet curtains and brushed steel walls. Past the curtains lay the large cement dance floor. Monitors, hung from the high rafters, played porn videos. A back room took up the entire rear of the club, the opening as dark and asphyxiated as an overworked asshole. The place was jammed with the usual tacky drag queens and young men with severely cropped hair and pumped-out chests. The older men huddled around the black opening in the back like weather-beaten vultures with grisly necks and bald heads. I had never seen so many men over fifty in a dance club. Unfortunately, I saw more of them than I wanted. They gathered around me wherever I stopped. I was used to it; old men usually confused me for a twenty-year-old, which, coming from them, never felt like a compliment. They were more interested in my apparent youth than anything.

I escaped to the dance floor and stayed there even when the music dried up and left me swaying to a pathetic tinny beat. The whole night was quickly turning into a disaster, with all the old guys licking their sharp lips in the distance and none of the twenty- to thirty-year-olds even bothering to look at me. I couldn't even find the guy I had met at the bar. And then a frighteningly thin man who looked like a drag queen out of drag began to bump and grind his hips against me as his pretty fag-hag friend looked on. I danced with him until he started to kiss me, and then I turned away and pretended to dance with someone else. He clutched his purse and danced with someone else too, a skinny dreadlocked boy I hadn't noticed in the crowd. I kept dancing until the guy in front of me yawned in my face and strode away. That was the end for me.

On the way out, making a final round of the club, I passed the dark opening to the back room. A porn video played on one of the monitors. I was horny enough to try anything, but looking into the room and seeing nothing but a flat, shadowless hole, I knew I didn't want to go in. All the old men watching me weren't what I wanted either. A guy came up and pestered me to go in with him. He wasn't old like the other men, and he looked rather cute in the dim light, but I ignored him because he was drunk. He wanted to buy me a drink. What did I drink? he asked. I told him to get lost. He said he'd go away if I would let him fuck me.

I started walking out, past the curtains, and ran into the boy with the dreads. He had a friend with him.

Lo ves, he asked his friend, both of them looking at me. *No te dije?*

They stared, but they didn't actually stop to meet me. In fact, the friend went off toward the back room. I was too surprised at having someone talk to me, or rather about me, to say anything. And in Spanish, too. The Spanish I understood and spoke, not the Castilian whose affected lisp made me self-conscious about whether I sounded queer.

Me gusta commo bailas con las señoritas, he said to me, referring to the guy we'd both danced with, I guessed.

Gracías. Pero prefiero los chicos.

Man, I wish I could take you home, he sighed to himself.

Where do you live? I asked.

Shit, you speak English?

Yeah. I'm from the States.

You're lying, man.

No, really. I'm from New York. Hell's Kitchen.

He looked around as if someone was listening or as if he himself couldn't believe what he had heard. He took a breath, as if to begin another protest. Oh man, he groaned. I thought you were Spanish.

I thought *you* were Spanish.

With this color?

I don't know, I admitted, wanting to touch his dark skin. You speak great Spanish. I thought you were from here.

He tried to hold back a smile, which I took as his embarrassment for wanting me and admitting it and having me hear it. I offered to buy him a drink, but he said he didn't drink. I rarely drank either. I had only offered it so that he wouldn't go away. The drunk guy suddenly came around and stood near us. He must have noticed the drunk too because he led me to the dance floor, and we danced into the early morning, the drunk guy watching, the old men having disappeared into the back room. We left the club at daybreak and walked out together.

His name was David and he spent his summers in Barcelona and, for whatever reason, had decided to stay that year until winter. He had been born in the States and now lived in either of two places—with his father in New York or his mother in

London. He wasn't slick enough to make it sound glamorous. He was more of the down-and-out set, the sandal-wearing bohemian who wound up asking for money on the metro to make it back home or to the next town.

He said awful things about New York. He didn't have one good thing to say about any place other than Barcelona and Sitges, a gay beach town south of the city. Somewhere along the walk though, he stopped talking and pulled off his sweaty shirt and tied it around his waist, showing his tightly muscled chest. I thought of it only as him showing his youth, not his body, not his sensuality. In fact, other than a few times when we'd kissed on the dance floor, he seemed devoid of it. I tried not to look at him. I didn't want him to feel how all the old men usually made me feel: powerful and confused by their adoration and then disgusted by their obvious hunger. I simply walked, guessing at his age—which is what the old men did with me too. I suspected him to be twenty-one, younger maybe. I felt like an old man.

He shared an apartment east of Las Ramblas, in the opposite direction from the pension. I nearly asked him if he still wanted to take me home, but then I saw him writing down his number on a scrap of paper. I told him that I wanted to take him back to my place, to my bunk at the pension, but that it was impossible with all the other guys. At the road where we split, he asked for a kiss. I wanted to ask him why he had decided not to take me back to his place, but then I remembered how easily my mind changed at that age. I used to want them, whomever I'd meet, whomever I'd let buy me a drink, and then for one stupid reason or another, I didn't. A crowd formed down the street from another club, a straight club it seemed from the way the women coiled themselves around the necks of the men. I gave him the two-cheek *despedida* to be safe.

I want a real kiss, he complained.

I gave it to him. The sweet-sour taste of his mouth became the only consolation as, later, I tried to sleep between fits of disappointment.

I called David late enough in the afternoon the following day that I knew he couldn't help but be awake. On the phone he seemed anxious. To see me, I thought, ever the optimist. I rushed through a quick lunch in the Barri Gotic where a waiter had me drink a glass of red wine. He said he wanted to make sure I had a good time in Barcelona. I wanted to make sure of that too, so I obliged him and drank the wine down before I ran out to see David. High from the alcohol, and intoxicated by the feral smells of the city, the sight of its leprous buildings looming in a state of impending collapse, I arrived at the apartment. My body ached from the effort. I was hoping David would be fresh from a shower and we'd forget about the plans we had made and we'd fuck into the evening. I had condoms, but I didn't think I needed them. I was negative, and the gonorrhea I'd thought I had turned out to be nothing but a throat infection, and I knew he was much too young to have been exposed to anything. Traveling sometimes had that effect on me: it gave me a false sense of security, of being exempt from the real world with its real problems, of thinking that this new place had no hold on the one I'd left behind.

He showed me his room. His balcony looked over the street where we'd parted. He acted cool, not as anxious as on the phone. Moving through the dim apartment, he had about as much personal attachment and enthusiasm as a tour guide. Not even a half-hour had passed when he insisted that we leave for the bus stop that would take us to Gaudí's Parc Güell. He rushed out and kept a few paces ahead of me, talking in a slurred speech because of a lollipop in his mouth. When he finished that one, he plunged in another. And when he ran out of lollipops, he chain-smoked a pack of cigarettes. He philosophized and spouted against the colonizing Europeans, especially the French. Customs officials in Paris harassed him every time he entered the country. In London he always got tagged a troublemaker. And because of his hair, everyone assumed he smoked hash and drank a lot and listened to Caribbean music. He felt discriminated against. I tried to sympathize, but I couldn't help but hear the bass of young angst and wish for the first time that he wasn't so young.

We didn't see much of the park other than a few chipped-rock formations and a bright-tiled, curved bench. We climbed up the dry hill above it all and lay out on the warm bleached rocks, bare chested, shorts rolled up, sharing a bottle of water. He finally calmed down, lying there in the sun. He looked dark enough already, but he wanted to be charred, he said. Black. And he showed me the pale skin on the inside of his thighs. In a moment of doomed inspiration, he took off his shorts and rolled up his boxers into a baggy bikini. I wanted to tell him that getting darker would only make his current problems worse, but he seemed beyond reason. Besides, it was the first time he'd kept quiet, and Barcelona spread all around magnificently. The Mediterranean swelled in the distance, the port pulling itself along the curve of the coastline. Over to the east glowed the bright patch of the Parc de la Ciutadella and the two towers that had been built for the Olympics. To the west, red cable cars pulled themselves from the port to the dark low hill with the amusement park and other tourist attractions I had no interest in seeing. Between these points lay the city: the bottle-necked spires of the unfinished cathedral, the wide avenues of the Eixample, and the thick swath of Las Ramblas, cutting through the dark, dense buildings of the Ciutat Vella, the old town of Barcelona.

I called my friend and told him I was here with you, David said when the silence had gone on for too long. You know, the friend I was with at the club? He's a cool guy, but he's a sex addict.

What's wrong with that? I asked, remembering the former lover of mine who had seemed to think there was nothing wrong with wanting sex all the time, even from other men. We were still together then.

Well, nothing is wrong with it if you're single, but if you've got a lover, that's pretty bad. And I've seen the guy he lives with. He's like the most incredibly gorgeous guy I've ever seen in my life.

Maybe he's not all that good, I said, defending myself, making a case for my passable looks.

Man, the guy wouldn't have to do anything but lie there and look pretty.

I don't know. I make sure I ain't the only one working.

It ain't work for me.

Well I think you just found yourself a job.

He laughed at that.

Don't tell me you don't have a Spanish boyfriend? I prodded.

Nah.

You've been here, how many months?

Four or five. I dunno.

Sweat ran down his thin, compact chest, his dark nipples erect and slick. He pulled back his dreads and leaned up on his elbows. Looking at him, I couldn't figure out why he hadn't found anyone in the city.

Not even a tourist?

I try to stay away from tourists. Here today, gone tomorrow.

I need something long term. A guy that's gonna stick around, you know.

I'm a tourist.

Yeah, but I got a couple friends in New York that'll help me hunt you down if I need to.

Maybe I'll just stay here, I said, and leaned up and kissed him on the lips. Live at the pension with the hundreds of guys lying around in their underwear on bare mattresses. It's pretty hot.

Don't you get a boner in the shower or wake up with a hard-on?

Well, the showers are stalls, which sucks. No gang showers. And everyone and his Tía Cuca wakes up with a boner. That's no secret. I'm only worried that they'll catch me looking for too long.

We kissed again, and then I went down and sucked on his nipples. His skin was dark and smooth and hairless. I suddenly realized why men found youth such a commodity. The un-marked skin, the innocence of still looking the virgin. I looked up to see the rest of him. Sweat had collected in the hollow of his neck. His head hung back loose. And then I noticed a man with a camera at the top of the hill who saw me looking at him and walked away quickly. He could have been one of the old men at the club.

There's a pervert above us, I told him, getting closer to him so that our bodies touched.

Are you worried?

About?

Gettin' caught.

Yeah, I said, kissing him.

He unbuttoned my shorts slowly and rubbed my dick, which was already pressing against the front of my underwear. He folded back the waistband and took me in his hands and then his mouth. I spread my legs wide and stared up into the fragile blue sky the color of the mantle of the Virgén de Guadalupe. He tongued the inside of my thighs, my balls. I felt the velvet of his mouth over me, and he pulled at my hips to draw me in deeper. I pulled out his dick from one of the legs of his boxers. The head looked pickled, with a bright red rash. At the base, where I held it, sat a crusty scab. I felt another one under my palm. Another under my thumb. The pre-cum began to leak out onto my skin. I did nothing but watch the liquid as it caught the light, dull and cloudy.

My hand felt heavy as a stone as I pulled it away from him and wiped it against the front of my shorts. I told him that we had gone far enough. Someone would catch us and fine us for public indecency. I rattled off a hundred other reasons why we should stop, but never the one that mattered, the one precipitated by the sight of his dick. I gagged on the question that would not come. He didn't say anything either as he put his clothes back on.

The sun still burned, but I felt a chill at the base of my spine, a cold sweat suddenly dampening the crack of my ass. I didn't know what to say to him. All of my life I had been safe, safe to the point of a stifling near-celibacy that left me lonely too many nights, nights when life felt as thin as a postcard, when life felt as far removed from living as a postcard was from where it came.

Are you going to be okay? I asked.

Are you? he shot back, his lips tight against his face.

I'm okay, I answered, and attempted a smile.

Me too, I guess. A little hungry though.

You want to go get something?

How's ice cream?

We went down the hill. The dry grass and brush felt rougher and sharper against my legs than when we had first gone up. He bought a double scoop of vanilla ice cream at the park entrance since the vendor had run out of every other flavor.

On the bus back, David spent the ride looking out the window, never saying a word. I kept looking at my hand, looking at it on my lap as if it were severed, careful not to touch my lips or the corners of my eyes. I was always studying my hands and arms and ankles, and peering into my mouth, searching for lesions or sores even though I've never tested positive. I've tested every year, sometimes twice a year, ever since my first kiss at the age of twenty. Still, I've had several bouts of crabs and scabies and genital warts, and at one point during the summer before my trip, thought I'd been infected with gonorrhea from my lover, who'd contracted it from someone else. Each infection shook me to the bone because I'd been so careful about sex that I always felt everyone else was getting laid more than me, doing it with an abandon that made real life pale.

We said good-bye at the street that led back to his place and mine. He said I should call him. I said I would, knowing that I wouldn't. I didn't think I'd ever see him again, but crossing into the Plaça Reial, I heard the cold jingle of his keys in my shorts. I bolted back, pushing through the early-evening crowd on Las Ramblas and starting a run up the block. I nearly smashed into him.

He smiled at me.

I handed him the keys and said, Yeah, I found them.

I wanted to say more or do something—I don't know what— anything that would show him that it wasn't him. It was me. I was the frightened one. Life scared me and I didn't know what I had to do to change that. Seeing how calm he was, the way his skin glowed in the failing light, I felt disgusted with what I had done. He had spared me from whatever he had the night he didn't invite me to his place, had gone so far as to get naked under the bright of day where he had no hope of hiding anything. And all I had done was walk away.

Look, I started. I'm sorry.

It's okay. I'm used to it.

Maybe you should see a doctor.

I have. Doesn't help.

I'm sorry, I said again.

Stop apologizing. You don't have to be sorry for anything.

But I am. I just feel bad.

Yeah, the easiest thing to find some days is pity.

With his words, he aged some and I fell back into a kind of immaturity, trying to grasp at a vocabulary I didn't have. He scrunched up his face with an expression of defeat and turned around and walked away. I stood there and watched him leave.

Hey, he shouted. I'll be at Punto tonight. Maybe I'll see you there?

I nodded as he faded into a crowd of people. Though I rarely drank, I thought alcohol might help loosen the tightness I felt in my head and chest, a cold grip that plunged all the way down to my crotch. I turned back toward the pension. The thought of returning to a room full of post-adolescents made me feel old again. But the weight of it didn't feel so heavy anymore. Twenty, I kept thinking. I hadn't asked David his age, so I was only guessing, but at twenty, he deserved to be flawless, unscarred, free, liberated and happily engaged with love, or at least sex. At twenty, I'd had my first real kiss and instantly fell into a panic about whether I'd just kissed death itself. It wasn't right. It was no way to live.

Michael Lowenthal

Sand Niggers and a Tallboy Bud

Only once, to the best of my knowledge, have I allowed a member of the Ku Klux Klan to buy me a beer.

I had flown from New Hampshire to Detroit to Indianapolis on the way to visit friends living sixty miles farther west, in the hills near the Wabash River. My friends don't own a car, and I had exhausted my travel budget on the airfare. I resigned myself to a slow afternoon of hitchhiking.

It was a torturous July day, the temperature and humidity battling to reach 100. I walked the couple of miles from the airport to Route 36, my body already nostalgic for the artificial chill of the DC-10 that had delivered me. I crossed the intersection and set myself up on the curb in front of a busy-looking burger joint.

Ponytailed high school girls, eyelids droopy under peacock shades of mascara, roller-skated from car to car. They scribbled orders on small yellow notepads, wheeled out of view, then glided back minutes later bearing french-fry baskets and root beer in sweating cups.

The soda wasn't all that was sweating. The long pants I wore, in some vestigial homage to my mother's insistence that one should dress up when one travels, clung to my thighs like a soggy but determined leech. My chest shone pink through my soaked T-shirt. I gave up counting when the two hundred and twenty-fourth car passed me by.

So when the massive Chevy pickup rattled onto the shoulder and the driver fired two short hoots of the horn, I forgot any cautionary rules of hitching. I didn't even look through the window. Whoever it was would have to be carrying a nuclear bomb for me to turn down the ride.

I had already tossed my pack onto the floor and climbed into the high cab before I took a look at the driver. He was a thick man with reddish-blond hair that dusted his shoulders in the back. His forearms flexed as they gripped the steering wheel, hard muscle beneath skin tanned to the dark sheen of honey-roasted peanuts. His eyes hid behind mirrored sunglasses.

"Rick," he said, extending a hand until he realized his fingers dripped with grease. He retracted the hand, and nudged his elbow toward the roast chicken between us on a crumpled sheet of tin foil. "Chicken?" he offered, ripping a strip of flesh with his fingernails. I noticed what I thought was a wart on his thumb, but it turned out to be a glob of congealed fat.

"I just ate lunch," I lied. "No thanks."

"Sure? It's good stuff."

"No, really," I said. "I'm fine."

Rick punched the pickup through its gears, and in a matter of seconds the speedometer registered seventy. The sudden acceleration caused the truck to skitter between the highway's lane dividers like the reckless crayon of a child too young to color within the lines. But I wasn't all that worried, because Rick seemed fairly adept at steering with his knees. He needed his knees because while his right hand was occupied with the chicken, his left gripped a flask of peppermint schnapps. After every two or three bites of meat he swilled a long gulp of the liquor. Then, trading the bottle for the bright yellow plastic fruit tucked between his thighs, he squirted a chaser of lemon juice. He pounded through this cycle with machinelike efficiency—chickenschnappsjuice, chickenschnappsjuice, chickenschnappsjuice—pausing only to smack his lips or reveal snippets of personal history.

Rick told me he was a "rammer," local lingo for a furnace

rebuilder at the steel mill. Feeling the violent thrust of his half-ton truck beneath me, watching him stuff meat and booze down his throat, I wondered if he appreciated the triumph of irony. A rammer, indeed.

"Where you headed?" he asked after a particularly large bite of chicken.

I told him I was going to a small town called Rockville. Had he heard of it?

"Sure, Rockville. Nice, nice area out there. Not too many niggers."

I nodded overenthusiastically, the way you do when you're catching most of a conversation but not every single word. I figured the engine noise or some unfamiliar midwestern speech pattern must have distorted my perception. I rolled up the window so the wind's whistle would be diverted above my ears.

"Yeah," Rick continued, "real nice down in Rockville. Pretty farms. Lots of Klan."

Now his words rang clear as gunshots. Instinctively I took inventory: my nose, my wrists, my attire. Did some Semitic hook, some limpness, some pastel shade give away the fact that I'm Jewish and that I'm gay? The newspaper headline inked boldly in my imagination: HITCHHIKER FOUND DEAD BY ROADSIDE: KKK MEMBER ATTACKS MAN WITH FLASK OF SCHNAPPS.

But Rick drove on, smiling chummily, apparently not considering even for an instant that I could be anything but in sympathy with his views. It was then, perhaps for the first time in my life, that I felt fully the brute power of my complexion. No matter my religion or sexuality, the pale hue of my face had granted me an instant acceptance that would protect me until I *chose* to give myself away.

"Last chance," said Rick. He had opened a second foil package and slid the glistening whole chicken toward me on the vinyl seat.

"No thanks," I said, trying to mask my revulsion.

"There's nothing wrong with it," he insisted. "It's good meat."

When I declined again, citing for the second time my recent nonexistent lunch, Rick pursed his lips and said, "Suit yourself."

He sank into a hurt silence. Or maybe, I thought, an angry one. Was the chicken a test? Some sort of a secret handshake? I braced for an assault.

Something by the side of the road caught Rick's attention. He removed his mirrored shades and craned his head, ignoring the task of driving. The truck weaved as if in imitation of a SLIP-PERY WHEN WET sign.

In the parking lot of a Shoney's restaurant, a goateed Arab man stepped from an Oldsmobile. The black-and-white-checked keffiyeh flapped behind his head in the summer breeze, a banner advertisement for the out-of-place. I felt an instant kinship.

"See that?" Rick asked, jerking his chin. "One of them sand niggers. I don't like that shit. Walking around with sheets on their heads. Ask me, we should've finished them off in the Gulf War."

He sprayed a stream of lemon juice at the back of his throat, wincing against the citric sourness.

"I say the only people with sheets on their heads should be us. Know what I mean?" Rick's right eye twitched into a wink, and in that instant of insinuation I pictured white-hooded men on horseback, circling beneath the limp form of a lynching victim.

My stomach clenched against its retch reflex, as though Rick's hatefulness were a stench poisoning the air. I shifted toward the door, lungs burning with the breath of unspoken challenges. *Speak up*, my conscience goaded. *Tell him you are offended by his beliefs and his language. Not just offended; disgusted.*

These were things I believed in saying and things I was practiced at saying. I had spoken my mind to intolerant college classmates and to colleagues at work. I had taken issue with bigoted strangers sitting next to me on airplanes, argued back to fundamentalist ministers peddling their sidewalk sales of hate. But now the words jammed like pick-up sticks in my throat. This was no dorm room debate about political correctness. There were no onlookers to back me up. I was on a desolate highway in Indiana, riding next to a drunken KKK rammer with biceps as big around as bazookas.

Fearing that Rick would solicit my opinions at any moment, I settled on a compromise: I would not contradict this hulk of a man, but neither would I agree with him explicitly. I would simply say as little as possible. Although this was a cheap solution, it was a relatively safe one. At least, I convinced myself, I would retain *some* integrity. Rick might assume I supported him, but he would have no *evidence* to that effect.

As it turned out, Rick expected little response, supportive or otherwise. He was content to ramble on in his angry monologue, punctuated with the grammar of his boozy gulping. I fixed my eyes on the narrow swath of highway, ready to grab the wheel if he faltered.

The 1992 presidential election was less than four months away, and Rick was not pleased with his choices. Bill Clinton the draft dodger wanted to let faggots in the army. Bush was slightly better, but still too soft, too eager to suck up to the rest of the world. What the hell was he doing making deals with the damn Chinese?

"If I was president," Rick sermonized, "wouldn't be no foreign aid. Wouldn't be no foreigners at all allowed in here. Send all the niggers back to Africa and gather them in one country, then blow it the fuck up till we have one clean white race."

As if taking Rick's cue, the Chevy's engine exploded in a gust of backfire. The horrible sound was followed by another, quieter one, and the truck sputtered to a stop.

Rick turned the key, and the starter motor whined like a whipped dog. He punched the steering wheel with his palm. "Shit. Out of gas. I was talking so much I forgot."

He hit the steering wheel again, then the dash, leaving greasy palm prints on the imitation wood. He got out of the truck and I followed.

As I sprang from the tall cab, my body loosened with relief, as though I were leaping from a burning building into the firefighters' waiting net. This was the perfect opportunity. I could explain that my friends in Rockville were expecting me, that if I was to make my destination on time I had to keep pressing ahead. I could walk a hundred yards up the road and start thumbing for another ride.

But something stopped me. I couldn't just walk away.

Standing there on the baking pavement, listening to Rick curse and kick the Chevy's wheel wells, I thought of a story my grandfather used to tell.

My Papa Eric fled Hitler's Germany in 1939. A conservative rabbi deeply committed to his strict brand of Judaism, he was also genuinely and generously ecumenical. Having been subjected to the violent humiliations of Nazi persecution, Papa Eric's preaching of the need for tolerance was profoundly personal.

And yet he told this story: He and my grandmother secured precious visas and booked passage on the *Île de France*. Days before they were to embark, the shipping crate containing most of their possessions was stolen. Given the political dangers, they had no choice but to make the crossing. They arrived in New York with only a few suitcases.

Since much of his wardrobe had been stolen, Papa Eric ran

out of clean shirts after just a week. He dropped his bundle of dirty clothes at one of the many neighborhood laundromats run by Chinese families, making arrangements to retrieve them the next day. When he returned at the appointed time and presented his tag, the attendant merely shrugged. The order had been lost. The shirts were gone.

"Damn Chinks," Papa Eric spat before he could stop himself.

This was the moment, he always said, when he truly understood the meaning of prejudice. Not when he heard the shattering of synagogue windows on Kristallnacht. Not when he watched Nazi guards demolish the ritual shack he had constructed for the holiday of Succos. But when he himself—having just run for his life from Hitler's machine of intolerance—was so quick to condemn a Chinese laundry attendant, not for losing some shirts, but for *being Chinese.*

At first I couldn't understand why my grandfather's story had come back to me now, as I debated whether to ditch Rick or to stay and help him get his truck back on the road. The lesson I had always drawn from Papa Eric's tale was that the instinct for prejudice is all too human, embedded within every one of us; that even the most decent person can harbor hatred. But Rick wasn't like Papa Eric. He was unrepentantly intolerant. He would not have regretted using a racial slur; more likely, he would have backed it up with violence.

But on the blistering tar of Indiana Route 36, I considered for the first time the possibility of an obverse truth to my grandfather's example: that even the most *hateful* person can harbor *decency;* that generosity, too, might be a universal human instinct.

After all, when hundreds of others had passed by the sweltering burger joint in Indianapolis, Rick had stopped to pick me up and given me a forty-mile ride. He had offered to share his food. He had asked for nothing in return.

Now he needed help. Could I turn my back on him?

A savior appeared in the form of a pimple-riddled teenager in his own pickup truck, tugging a trailer crowded with lawn equipment. The boy stopped his rig in front of us and hopped out, asking what the trouble was.

Rick chewed his lip. "Out of gas," he confessed.

"No problem," said the kid. He explained that he ran a summer mowing business and was just finishing his day of cutting grass. He pointed to the trailer bed, where two five-gallon plastic jugs sloshed with liquid shadows.

Rick gave the kid ten dollars, poured a jug's worth of fuel into the Chevy's tank, and we were back on the road.

It turned out Rick was driving only a couple miles more before veering onto a different highway. I was going to have to hitch another ride after all. He pulled off at the junction and parked in front of a small liquor store. I shouldered my backpack, preparing for the mix of excitement and humiliation of standing alone on a highway asking strangers for rides. But Rick insisted I accompany him into the store.

In the numbingly air-conditioned market, he collected a new pint of schnapps and another plastic lemon, which—judging by the prominent display of tiny yellow footballs—was a common purchase in these parts. Then he instructed me to pick out something I wanted—his treat. I protested that I didn't need anything; I had a canteen of water in my pack, and in any case, he certainly didn't have to pay. But Rick was adamant. He wouldn't let me leave empty-handed.

Finally, anxious to resume my trip, I grabbed a Budweiser tallboy from the glass-doored cooler, the bottle slick with condensation. I showed it to the woman at the cash register so she could ring it up on Rick's bill.

Outside, we stood at the Chevy. The steel hood wrinkled the air with its reflected heat. The engine pinged and popped as if it, too, were eager to get back on the road. I thanked Rick for the ride; he said how glad he was to have met me. Then he raised his hand and I met it as we toasted. The schnapps bottle made a thin tinkle against the brown glass of my Bud.

I sucked a pull of the watery beer.

"Just a tallboy?" Rick chided as he climbed into the cab. "You should've gotten a quart. I'd 've bought you a quart."

James Baldwin

Equal in Paris

On the nineteenth of December, in 1949, when I had been living in Paris for a little over a year, I was arrested as a receiver of stolen goods and spent eight days in prison. My arrest came about through an American tourist whom I had met twice in New York, who had been given my name and address and told to look me up. I was then living on the top floor of a ludicrously grim hotel on the rue du Bac, one of those enormous dark, cold, and hideous establishments in which Paris abounds that seem to breathe forth, in their airless, humid, stone-cold halls, the weak light, scurrying chambermaids, and creaking stairs, an odor of gentility long long dead. The place was run by an ancient Frenchman dressed in an elegant black suit which was green with age, who cannot properly be described as bewildered or even as being in a state of shock, since he had really stopped breathing around 1910. There he sat at his desk in the weirdly lit, fantastically furnished lobby, day in and day out, greeting each one of his extremely impoverished and *louche* lodgers with a stately inclination of the head that he had no doubt been taught in some impossibly remote time was the proper way for a *propriétaire* to greet his guests. If it had not been for his daughter, an extremely hardheaded *tricoteuse*—the inclination of her head was chilling and abrupt, like the downbeat of an ax—the hotel would certainly have gone bankrupt long before. It was said that this old man had not gone farther than the door of his hotel for thirty years, which was not at all difficult to believe. He looked as though the daylight would have killed him.

I did not, of course, spend much of my time in this palace. The moment I began living in French hotels I understood the necessity of French cafés. This made it rather difficult to look me up, for as soon as I was out of bed I hopefully took notebook and fountain pen off to the upstairs room of the Flore, where I consumed rather a lot of coffee and, as evening approached, rather a lot of alcohol, but did not get much writing done. But one night, in one of the cafés of Saint Germain des Prés, I was discovered by this New Yorker and only because we found ourselves in Paris we immediately established the illusion that we had been fast friends back in the good old U.S.A. This illusion proved itself too thin to support an evening's drinking, but by that time it was too late. I had committed myself to getting him a room in my hotel the next day, for he was living in one of the nest of hotels near the Gare Saint Lazare, where, he said, the *propriétaire* was a thief, his wife a repressed nymphomaniac, the chambermaids "pigs," and the rent a crime. Americans are always talking this way about the French and so it did not occur to me that he meant what he said or that he would take into his own hands the means of avenging himself on the French Republic. It did not occur to me, either, that the means which he did take could possibly have brought about such dire results, results which were not less dire for being also comic-opera.

It came as the last of a series of disasters which had perhaps been made inevitable by the fact that I had come to Paris originally with a little over forty dollars in my pockets, nothing in the bank, and no grasp whatever of the French language. It developed, shortly, that I had no grasp of the French character either. I considered the French an ancient, intelligent, and cultured race, which indeed they are. I did not know, however, that ancient glories imply, at least in the middle of the present century, present fatigue and, quite probably, paranoia; that there is a

limit to the role of the intelligence in human affairs; and that no
people come into possession of a culture without having paid a
heavy price for it. This price they cannot, of course, assess, but it
is revealed in their personalities and in their institutions. The
very word "institutions," from my side of the ocean, where, it
seemed to me, we suffered so cruelly from the lack of them, had
a pleasant ring, as of safety and order and common sense; one
had to come into contact with these institutions in order to understand that they were also outmoded, exasperating, completely impersonal, and very often cruel. Similarly, the personality which had seemed from a distance to be so large and free had
to be dealt with before one could see that, if it was large, it was
also inflexible and, for the foreigner, full of strange, high, dusty
rooms which could not be inhabited. One had, in short, to come
into contact with an alien culture in order to understand that a
culture was not a community basket-weaving project, nor yet an
act of God; was something neither desirable nor undesirable in
itself, being inevitable, being nothing more or less than the
recorded and visible effects on a body of people of the vicissitudes with which they had been forced to deal. And their great
men are revealed as simply another of these vicissitudes, even if,
quite against their will, the brief battle of their great men with
them has left them richer.

When my American friend left his hotel to move to mine, he
took with him, out of pique, a bedsheet belonging to the hotel
and put it in his suitcase. When he arrived at my hotel I borrowed the sheet, since my own were filthy and the chambermaid
showed no sign of bringing me any clean ones, and put it on my
bed. The sheets belonging to my hotel I put out in the hall, con-
gratulating myself on having thus forced on the attention of the
Grand Hôtel du Bac the unpleasant state of its linen. Thereafter,
since, as it turned out, we kept very different hours—I got up at

noon, when, as I gathered by meeting him on the stairs one day, he was only just getting in—my new-found friend and I saw very little of each other.

On the evening of the nineteenth I was sitting thinking melancholy thoughts about Christmas and staring at the walls of my room. I imagine that I had sold something or that some-one had sent me a Christmas present, for I remember that I had a little money. In those days in Paris, though I floated, so to speak, on a sea of acquaintances, I knew almost no one. Many people were eliminated from my orbit by virtue of the fact that they had more money than I did, which placed me, in my own eyes, in the humiliating role of a free-loader; and other people were eliminated by virtue of the fact that they enjoyed their poverty, shrilly insisting that this wretched round of hotel rooms, bad food, humiliating concierges, and unpaid bills was the Great Adventure. It couldn't, however, for me, end soon enough, this Great Adventure; there was a real question in my mind as to which would end soonest, the Great Adventure or me. This meant, however, that there were many evenings when I sat in my room, knowing that I couldn't work there, and not knowing what to do, or whom to see. On this particular evening I went down and knocked on the American's door.

There were two Frenchmen standing in the room, who im-mediately introduced themselves to me as policemen; which did not worry me. I had got used to policemen in Paris bobbing up at the most improbable times and places, asking to see one's *carte d'identité.* These policemen, however, showed very little in-terest in my papers. They were looking for something else. I could not imagine what this would be and, since I knew I cer-tainly didn't have it, I scarcely followed the conversation they were having with my friend. I gathered that they were looking for some kind of gangster and since I wasn't a gangster and knew that gangsterism was not, insofar as he had one, my friend's style, I was sure that the two policemen would presently bow and say *Merci, messieurs,* and leave. For by this time, I remember very clearly, I was dying to have a drink and go to dinner.

I did not have a drink or go to dinner for many days after this, and when I did my outraged stomach promptly heaved everything up again. For now one of the policemen began to exhibit the most vivid interest in me and asked, very politely, if he might see my room. To which we mounted, making, I remember, the most civilized small talk on the way and even continuing it for some moments after we were in the room in which there was certainly nothing to be seen but the familiar poverty and disorder of that precarious group of people of whatever age, race, country, calling, or intention which Paris recognizes as *les étudiants* and sometimes, more ironically and precisely, as *les nonconformistes.* Then he moved to my bed, and in a terrible flash, not quite an instant before he lifted the bedspread, I understood what he was looking for. We looked at the sheet, on which I read, for the first time, lettered in the most brilliant scarlet I have ever seen, the name of the hotel from which it had been stolen. It was the first time the word *stolen* entered my mind. I had certainly seen the hotel monogram the day I put the sheet on the bed. It had simply meant nothing to me. In New York I had seen hotel monograms on everything from silver to soap and towels. Taking things from New York hotels was practically a custom, though, I suddenly realized, I had never known anyone to take a *sheet.* Sadly, and without a word to me, the inspector took the sheet from the bed, folded it under his arm, and we started back downstairs. I understood that I was under arrest.

And so we passed through the lobby, four of us, two of us very clearly criminal, under the eyes of the old man and his daughter, neither of whom said a word, into the streets where a light rain was falling. And I asked, in French, "But is this very serious?"

For I was thinking, it is, after all, only a sheet, not even new.

"No," said one of them. "It's not serious."

"It's nothing at all," said the other.

I took this to mean that we would receive a reprimand at the police station and be allowed to go to dinner. Later on I concluded that they were not being hypocritical or even trying to comfort us. They meant exactly what they said. It was only that they spoke another language.

In Paris everything is very slow. Also, when dealing with the bureaucracy, the man you are talking to is never the man you have to see. The man you have to see has just gone off to Belgium, or is busy with his family, or has just discovered that he is a cuckold; he will be in next Tuesday at three o'clock, or sometime in the course of the afternoon, or possibly tomorrow, or, possibly, in the next five minutes. But if he is coming in the next five minutes he will be far too busy to be able to see you today. So that I suppose I was not really astonished to learn at the commissariat that nothing could possibly be done about us before The Man arrived in the morning. But no, we could not go off and have dinner and come back in the morning. Of course he knew that we *would* come back—that was not the question. Indeed, there was no question: we would simply have to stay there for the night. We were placed in a cell which rather resembled a chicken coop. It was now about seven in the evening and I relinquished the thought of dinner and began to think of lunch.

I discouraged the chatter of my New York friend and this left me alone with my thoughts. I was beginning to be frightened and I bent all my energies, therefore, to keeping my panic under control. I began to realize that I was in a country I knew nothing about, in the hands of a people I did not understand at all.

In a similar situation in New York I would have had some idea of what to do because I would have had some idea of what to expect. I am not speaking now of legality which, like most of the poor, I had never for an instant trusted, but of the temperament of the people with whom I had to deal. I had become very accomplished in New York at guessing and, therefore, to a limited extent manipulating to my advantage the reactions of the white world. But this was not New York. None of my old weapons could serve me here. I did not know what they saw when they looked at me. I knew very well what Americans saw when they looked at me and this allowed me to play endless and sinister variations on the role which they had assigned me; since I knew that it was, for them, of the utmost importance that they never be confronted with what, in their own personalities, made this role so necessary and gratifying to them, I knew that they could never call my hand or, indeed, afford to know what I was doing; so that I moved into every crucial situation with the deadly and rather desperate advantages of bitterly accumulated perception, of pride and contempt. This is an awful sword and shield to carry through the world, and the discovery that, in the game I was playing, I did myself a violence of which the world, at its most ferocious, would scarcely have been capable, was what had driven me out of New York. It was a strange feeling, in this situation, after a year in Paris, to discover that my weapons would never again serve me as they had.

It was quite clear to me that the Frenchmen in whose hands I found myself were no better or worse than their American counterparts. Certainly their uniforms frightened me quite as much, and their impersonality, and the threat, always very keenly felt by the poor, of violence, was as present in that commissariat as it had ever been for me in any police station. And I had seen, for example, what Paris policemen could do to Arab peanut vendors. The only difference here was that I did not understand these people, did not know what techniques their cruelty took, did not know enough about their personalities to see danger coming, to ward it off, did not know on what ground to meet it. That evening in the commissariat I was not a despised black man. They would simply have laughed at me if I had behaved like one. For them, I was an American. And here it was they who had the advantage, for that word, *Américain,* gave them some idea, far from inaccurate, of what to expect from me. In order to corroborate none of their ironical expectations I said nothing and did nothing—which was not the way any Frenchman, white or black, would have reacted. The question thrusting up from the bottom of my mind was not *what* I was, but *who.* And this question, since a *what* can get by with skill but a *who* demands resources, was my first real intimation of what humility must mean.

In the morning it was still raining. Between nine and ten o'clock a black Citroën took us off to the Ile de la Cité, to the great, gray Préfecture. I realize now that the questions I put to the various policemen who escorted us were always answered in such a way as to corroborate what I wished to hear. This was not out of politeness, but simply out of indifference—or, possibly, an ironical pity—since each of the policemen knew very well that nothing would speed or halt the machine in which I had become entangled. They knew I did not know this and there was certainly no point in their telling me. In one way or another I would certainly come out at the other side—for they also knew that being found with a stolen bedsheet in one's possession was not a crime punishable by the guillotine. (They had the advantage over me there, too, for there were certainly moments later on when I was not so sure.) If I did *not* come out at the other side—well, that was just too bad. So, to my question, put while we were in the Citroën—"Will it be over today?"—I received a *"Oui, bien sûr."* He was not lying. As it turned out, the *procès-verbal* was over that day. Trying to be realistic, I dismissed, in the Citroën, all thoughts of lunch and pushed my mind ahead to dinner.

At the Préfecture we were first placed in a tiny cell, in which it was almost impossible either to sit or to lie down. After a couple of hours of this we were taken down to an office, where, for the first time, I encountered the owner of the bedsheet and where the *procès-verbal* took place. This was simply an interrogation, quite chillingly clipped and efficient (so that there was, shortly, no doubt in one's own mind that one *should* be treated as a criminal), which was recorded by a secretary. When it was over, this report was given to us to sign. One had, of course, no choice but to sign it, even though my mastery of written French was very far from certain. We were being held, according to the law in France, incommunicado, and all my angry demands to be allowed to speak to my embassy or to see a lawyer met with a stony *"Oui, oui. Plus tard."* The *procès-verbal* over, we were taken back to the cell, before which, shortly, passed the owner of the bedsheet. He said he hoped we had slept well, gave a vindictive wink, and disappeared.

By this time there was only one thing clear: that we had no way of controlling the sequence of events and could not possibly guess what this sequence would be. It seemed to me, since what I regarded as the high point—the *procès-verbal*—had been passed and since the hotel-keeper was once again in possession of his sheet, that we might reasonably expect to be released from police custody in a matter of hours. We had been detained now for what would soon be twenty-four hours, during which time I had learned only that the official charge against me was *receleur*. My mental shifting, between lunch and dinner, to say nothing of the physical lack of either of these delights, was beginning to make me dizzy. The steady chatter of my friend from New York, who was determined to keep my spirits up, made me feel murderous; I was praying that some power would release us from this freezing pile of stone before the impulse became the act. And I was beginning to wonder what was happening in that beautiful city, Paris, which lived outside these walls. I wondered how long it would take before anyone casually asked, "But where's Jimmy? He hasn't been around"—and realized, knowing the people I knew, that it would take several days.

Quite late in the afternoon we were taken from our cells; handcuffed, each to a separate officer; led through a maze of steps and corridors to the top of the building; fingerprinted; photographed. As in movies I had seen, I was placed against a wall, facing an old-fashioned camera, behind which stood one of the most completely cruel and indifferent faces I had ever seen, while someone next to me and, therefore, just outside my line of vision, read off in a voice from which all human feeling, even feeling of the most base description, had long since fled, what must be called my public characteristics—which, at that time and in that place, seemed anything but that. He might have been roaring to the hostile world secrets which I could barely, in the privacy of midnight, utter to myself. But he was only reading off my height, my features, my approximate weight, my color—that color which, in the United States, had often, odd as it may sound, been my salvation—the color of my hair, my age, my nationality. A light then flashed, the photographer and I staring at each other as though there was murder in our hearts, and then it was over. Handcuffed again, I was led downstairs to the bottom of the building, into a great enclosed shed in which had been gathered the very scrapings off the Paris streets. Old, old men, so ruined and old that life in them seemed really to prove the miracle of the quickening power of the Holy Ghost—for clearly their life was no longer their affair, it was no longer even their burden, they were simply the clay which had once been touched. And men not so old, with faces the color of lead and the consistency of oatmeal, eyes that made me think of stale *café-au-lait* spiked with arsenic, bodies which could take in food and water—any food and water—and pass it out, but which could not do anything more, except possibly, at midnight, along the riverbank where rats scurried, rape. And young men, harder and crueler than the Paris stones, older by far than I, their chronological senior by some five to seven years. And North Africans, old and young, who seemed the only living people in this place because they yet retained the grace to be bewildered. But they were not bewildered by being in this shed: they were simply bewildered because they were no longer in North Africa. There was a great hole in the center of this shed which was the common toilet. Near it, though it was impossible to get very far from it, stood an old man with white hair, eating a piece of Camembert. It was at this point, probably, that thought, for me, stopped, that physiology, if one may say so, took over. I found myself incapable of saying a word, not because I was afraid I would cry but because I was afraid I would vomit. And I did not think any longer of the city of Paris but my mind flew back to that home from which I had fled. I was sure that I would never see it any more. And it must have seemed to me that my flight from home was the cruelest trick I had ever played on myself, since it had led me here, down to a lower point than any I could ever in my life have imagined—lower, far, than anything I had seen in that Harlem which I had so hated and so loved, the escape from which had soon become the greatest direction of my life. After we had been here an hour or so a functionary came and opened the door and called out our names. And I was sure that *this* was my release. But I was handcuffed again and led out of the Préfecture into the streets—it was dark now, it was still raining—and before the steps of the Préfecture stood the great police wagon, doors facing me, wide open. The handcuffs were taken off, I entered the wagon, which was peculiarly constructed. It was divided by a narrow aisle, and on each side of the aisle was a series of narrow doors. These doors opened on a narrow cubicle, beyond which was a door which opened onto another narrow cubicle: three or four cubicles, each private, with a locking door. I was placed in one of them; I remember there was a small vent just above my head which let in a little light. The door of my cubicle was locked from the outside. I had no idea where this wagon was taking me and, as it began to move, I began to cry. I suppose I cried all the way to prison, the prison called Fresnes, which is twelve kilometers outside of Paris.

For reasons I have no way at all of understanding, prisoners whose last initial is A, B, or C are always sent to Fresnes; everybody else is sent to a prison called, rather cynically it seems to me, La Santé. I will, obviously, never be allowed to enter La Santé, but I was told by people who certainly seemed to know that it was infinitely more unbearable than Fresnes. This arouses in me, until today, a positive storm of curiosity concerning what I promptly began to think of as The Other Prison. My colleague in crime, occurring lower in the alphabet, had been sent there and I confess that the minute he was gone I missed him. I missed him because he was not French and because he was the only person in the world who knew that the story I told was true.

For, once locked in, divested of shoelaces, belt, watch, money, papers, nailfile, in a freezing cell in which both the window and the toilet were broken, with six other adventurers, the story I told of *l'affaire du drap de lit* elicited only the wildest amusement or the most suspicious disbelief. Among the people who shared my cell the first three days no one, it is true, had been arrested for anything much more serious—or, at least, not serious in my eyes. I remember that there was a boy who had stolen a knitted sweater from a *monoprix*, who would probably, it was agreed, receive a six-month sentence. There was an older man there who had been arrested for some kind of petty larceny. There were two North Africans, vivid, brutish, and beautiful, who alternated between gaiety and fury, not at the fact of their arrest but at the state of the cell. None poured as much emotional energy into the fact of their arrest as I did; they took it, as I would have liked to take it, as simply another unlucky happening in a very dirty world. For, though I had grown accustomed to thinking of myself as looking upon the world with a hard, penetrating eye, the truth was that they were far more realistic about the world than I, and more nearly right about it. The gap between us, which only a gesture I made could have bridged, grew steadily, during thirty-six hours, wider. I could not make any gesture simply because they frightened me. I was unable to accept my imprisonment as a fact, even as a temporary fact. I could not, even for a moment, accept my present companions as my companions. And they, of course, felt this and put it down, with perfect justice, to the fact that I was an American.

There was nothing to do all day long. It appeared that we would one day come to trial but no one knew when. We were awakened at seven-thirty by a rapping on what I believe is called the Judas, that small opening in the door of the cell which allows the guards to survey the prisoners. At this rapping we rose from the floor—we slept on straw pallets and each of us was covered with one thin blanket—and moved to the door of the cell. We peered through the opening into the center of the prison, which was, as I remember, three tiers high, all gray stone and gunmetal steel, precisely that prison I had seen in movies, except that, in the movies, I had not known that it was cold in prison. I had not known that when one's shoelaces and belt have been removed one is, in the strangest way, demoralized. The necessity of shuffling and the necessity of holding up one's trousers with one hand turn one into a rag doll. And the movies fail, of course, to give one any idea of what prison food is like. Along the corridor, at seven-thirty, came three men, each pushing before him a great garbage can, mounted on wheels. In the garbage can of the first was the bread—this was passed to one through the small opening in the door. In the can of the second was the coffee. In the can of the third was what was always called *la soupe*, a pallid paste of potatoes which had certainly been bubbling on the back of the prison stove long before that first, so momentous revolution. Naturally, it was cold by this time and, starving as I was, I could not eat it. I drank the coffee—which was not coffee —because it was hot, and spent the rest of the day, huddled in my blanket, munching on the bread. It was not the French bread one bought in bakeries. In the evening the same procession re-turned. At ten-thirty the lights went out. I had a recurring dream, each night, a nightmare which always involved my mother's fried chicken. At the moment I was about to eat it came the rapping at the door. Silence is really all I remember of those first three days, silence and the color gray.

I am not sure now whether it was on the third or the fourth day that I was taken to trial for the first time. The days had noth-ing, obviously, to distinguish them from one another. I remem-ber that I was very much aware that Christmas Day was ap-proaching and I wondered if I was really going to spend Christmas Day in prison. And I remember that the first trial came the day before Christmas Eve.

On the morning of the first trial I was awakened by hearing my name called. I was told, hanging in a kind of void between my mother's fried chicken and the cold prison floor, "*Vous pré-parez. Vous êtes extrait*"—which simply terrified me, since I did not know what interpretation to put on the word "*extrait*" and since my cellmates had been amusing themselves with me by telling terrible stories about the inefficiency of French prisons, an inefficiency so extreme that it had often happened that someone who was supposed to be taken out and tried found himself on the wrong line and was guillotined instead. The best way of putting my reaction to this is to say that, though I knew they were teasing me, it was simply not possible for me to totally disbelieve them. As far as I was concerned, once in the hands of the law in France, anything could happen. I shuffled along with the others who were *extrait* to the center of the prison, trying, rather, to linger in the office, which seemed the only warm spot in the whole world, and found myself again in that dreadful wagon, and was carried again to the Ile de la Cité, this time to the Palais de Justice. The entire day, except for ten minutes, was spent in one of the cells, first waiting to be tried, then waiting to be taken back to prison.

For I was not tried that day. By and by I was handcuffed and led through the halls, upstairs to the courtroom where I found my New York friend. We were placed together, both stage-whisperingly certain that this was the end of our ordeal. Nevertheless, while I waited for our case to be called, my eyes searched the courtroom, looking for a face I knew, hoping, anyway, that there was someone there who knew me, who would carry to someone outside the news that I was in trouble. But there was no one I knew there and I had had time to realize that there was probably only one man in Paris who could help me, an American patent attorney for whom I had worked as an office boy. He could have helped me because he had a quite solid position and some prestige and would have testified that, while working for him, I had handled large sums of money regularly, which made it rather unlikely that I would stoop to trafficking in bedsheets. However, he was somewhere in Paris, probably at this very moment enjoying a snack and a glass of wine and as far as the possibility of reaching him was concerned, he might as well have been on Mars. I tried to watch the proceedings and to make my mind a blank. But the proceedings were not reassuring. The boy, for example, who had stolen the sweater *did* receive a six-month sentence. It seemed to me that all the sentences meted out that day were excessive; though, again, it seemed that all the people who were sentenced that day had made, or clearly were going to make, crime their career. This seemed to be the opinion of the judge, who scarcely looked at the prisoners or listened to them; it seemed to be the opinion of the prisoners, who scarcely bothered to speak in their own behalf; it seemed to be the opinion of the lawyers, state lawyers for the most part, who were defending them. The great impulse of the courtroom seemed to be to put these people where they could not be seen—and not because they were offended at the crimes, unless, indeed, they were offended that the crimes were so petty, but because they did not wish to know that their society could be counted on to produce, probably in greater and greater numbers, a whole body of people for whom crime was the only possible career. Any society inevitably produces its criminals, but a society at once rigid and unstable can do nothing whatever to alleviate the poverty of its lowest members, cannot present to the hypothetical young man at the crucial moment that so-well-advertised right path. And the fact, perhaps, that the French are the earth's least sentimental people and must also be numbered among the most proud aggravates the plight of their lowest, youngest, and unluckiest members, for it means that the idea of rehabilitation is scarcely real to them. I confess that this attitude on their part raises in me sentiments of exasperation, admiration, and despair, revealing as it does, in both the best and the worst sense, their renowned and spectacular hard-headedness.

Finally our case was called and we rose. We gave our names. At the point that it developed that we were American the proceedings ceased, a hurried consultation took place between the judge and what I took to be several lawyers. Someone called out for an interpreter. The arresting officer had forgotten to mention our nationalities and there was, therefore, no interpreter in the court. Even if our French had been better than it was we would not have been allowed to stand trial without an interpreter. Before I clearly understood what was happening, I was handcuffed again and led out of the courtroom. The trial had been set back for the twenty-seventh of December.

I have sometimes wondered if I would ever have got out of prison if it had not been for the older man who had been arrested for the mysterious petty larceny. He was acquitted that day and when he returned to the cell—for he could not be released until morning—he found me sitting numbly on the floor, having just been prevented, by the sight of a man, all blood, being carried back to *his* cell on a stretcher, from seizing the bars and screaming until they let me out. The sight of the man on the stretcher proved, however, that screaming would not do much for me. The petty-larceny man went around asking if he could do anything in the world outside for those he was leaving behind. When he came to me I, at first, responded, "No, nothing"—for I suppose I had by now retreated into the attitude, the earliest I remember, that of my father, which was simply (since I had lost his God) that nothing could help me. And I suppose I will remember with gratitude until I die the fact that the man now insisted: *"Mais, êtes-vous sûr?"* Then it swept over me that he was going *outside* and he instantly became my first contact since the Lord alone knew how long with the outside world. At the same time, I remember, I did not really believe that he would help me. There was no reason why he should. But I gave him the phone number of my attorney friend and my own name.

So, in the middle of the next day, Christmas Eve, I shuffled downstairs again, to meet my visitor. He looked extremely well fed and sane and clean. He told me I had nothing to worry about any more. Only not even he could do anything to make the mill of justice grind any faster. He would, however, send me a lawyer of his acquaintance who would defend me on the twenty-seventh, and he would himself, along with several other people, appear as a character witness. He gave me a package of Lucky Strikes (which the turnkey took from me on the way upstairs) and said that, though it was doubtful that there would be any celebration in the prison, he would see to it that I got a fine Christmas dinner when I got out. And this, somehow, seemed very funny. I remember being astonished at the discovery that I was actually laughing. I was, too, I imagine, also rather disappointed that my hair had not turned white, that my face was clearly not going to bear any marks of tragedy, disappointed at bottom, no doubt, to realize, facing him in that room, that far worse things had happened to most people and that, indeed, to paraphrase my mother, if this was the worst thing that ever happened to me I could consider myself among the luckiest people ever to be born. He injected—my visitor—into my solitary nightmare common sense, the world, and the hint of blacker things to come.

The next day, Christmas, unable to endure my cell, and feeling that, after all, the day demanded a gesture, I asked to be allowed to go to Mass, hoping to hear some music. But I found myself, for a freezing hour and a half, locked in exactly the same kind of cubicle as in the wagon which had first brought me to prison, peering through a slot placed at the level of the eye at an old Frenchman, hatted, overcoated, muffled, and gloved, preaching in this language which I did not understand, to this row of wooden boxes, the story of Jesus Christ's love for men.

The next day, the twenty-sixth, I spent learning a peculiar kind of game, played with matchsticks, with my cellmates. For, since I no longer felt that I would stay in this cell forever, I was beginning to be able to make peace with it for a time. On the twenty-seventh I went again to trial and, as had been predicted, the case against us was dismissed. The story of the *drap de lit,* finally told, caused great merriment in the courtroom, where-upon my friend decided that the French were "great." I was chilled by their merriment, even though it was meant to warm me. It could only remind me of the laughter I had often heard at home, laughter which I had sometimes deliberately elicited. This laughter is the laughter of those who consider themselves to be at a safe remove from all the wretched, for whom the pain of the living is not real. I had heard it so often in my native land that I had resolved to find a place where I would never hear it any more. In some deep, black, stony, and liberating way, my life, in my own eyes, began during that first year in Paris, when it was borne in on me that this laughter is universal and never can be stilled.

Paul Monette

A One-Way Fare

We were on one of those relentless cruises—a week from Monte Carlo to Venice, around the boot—where they dropped anchor once a day in a picture-book harbor and sent us off by tender to maul the local tourist goods. Warning us severely that the last tender would be leaving the dock at one-thirty—for the ship was sailing at two, with or without us. There was about all this a certain schoolmarmish insistence that we'd better stick together while ashore. For to be left behind would have the truants scrambling for a Cessna to drop us at the next port of call, untold demerits scored against us for violating the team spirit.

But as Miss Brodie was wont to tell her special girls, no one ever accused Anna Pavlova of having the team spirit. It was the *corps de ballet* that had the team spirit.

When we disembarked in Capri and wandered into town, Steve was content to commandeer a café table under the plane trees and drowse the morning away over coffee, a dream in the vast cerulean of the view to the Bay of Naples. I had already had a run-in with the Ken doll who handled excursions. I'd told him I wanted to check out the ruins of Tiberius's villa, on the steep cliffs at the eastern tip of the island. He looked as if he'd much prefer to tell me where to score the best Majolica and cashmere, but coolly noted me on his clipboard and said he'd ask around.

About a half hour later he approached us under the plane trees. "Sorry, sir, we can't arrange it," he announced with a certain smugness. The emperor's villa was miles away, and the only way to reach it was by donkey on a dusty path. And all the donkeys were sick or in the fields or otherwise indisposed. As he went away pleased with himself at having foiled an insurrection among the sheep, I looked at my watch. Exactly two hours before the last tender.

"I think you better get going," declared Steve, looking up from a scribble of postcards.

"But what if I don't make it?" I retorted. "I don't know how far it is."

"Dr. Monette will make it," he assured me. Dr. Monette was his name for my literary self—or more generally, for the intellectual dabbling I was prone to, poring over maps and monographs of the classical world. To Steve, anything east of network television constituted scholarly work. Or as he would put it, wry and tender as he watched me at my desk, filling up legal pads with a novel in longhand: "Darling, nobody reads. Don't you know *that* yet?"

I zigzagged through the tourist hordes and started uphill through the lemony air of quarter-acre groves. Having no map was another sort of defiance, and anyway I soon reached a turnoff marked with a marble plaque, "Villa di Giove," with an arrow pointing up the donkey path that ran between the crumbling boundary walls of the lemon and olive growers. Too narrow for tourist buses, too rough and unpaved for mopeds. I struck a brisk pace and made my way in the noonday sun, not even any mad dogs or Englishmen for company.

After about half an hour I was still plodding east along the spine of the island, still no glimpse of the ruins on the heights. Spying a black-dressed woman feeding chickens in her back garden, I leaned over the wall and waved to get her attention. "*Scusi signora,*" I began, but hadn't got another word out before she pointed dourly up the steep path: "*Villa di Giove.*" She seemed about as impressed by my destination as Ken the excursionist had been.

But I persevered, and in twenty minutes had left the hillside farms behind and entered the imperial precincts—wilder vegetation and here and there a tall umbrella pine to shade my way. I could make out now the stone remains of ramparts at the top, and I broke into a trot worthy of any donkey to cover the last half-kilometer. Arriving breathless at the first paved terrace, surrounded of a sudden by the bases of toppled columns, weed-choked cisterns, flights of stairs that stopped midair. The sun was blazing, but the quiet was incredible, a windless day where nothing moved except the lizards who scrabbled about.

There was no guide or guidebook available at the site, only a few tin signboards that gave a rough outline of the floor plan, all the labels in Italian. But frankly I didn't care by then, rapt as I was by the wrinkle of the azure sea below. "View" is hardly adequate to describe it. I felt as if the whole Mediterranean hovered in my ken, and the mainland shore across the water seemed a vision of the whole length of Italy.

I only knew a couple of things about this man who had lived here. That he had retired to Capri permanently in the latter years of his reign, leaving the running of the Empire to his underlings; and that he had hurled his enemies from this height, a thousand feet to the rocks below. A sybarite's dream of a place, then, unless you crossed the chief. I studied the ground plan and walked among the broken rooms, imagining them painted in the red and ochre of Pompeii. But the site had been pretty well denuded, sifted by archaeologists—no precious fragment like the Belvedere torso to be found; all of that hoarded long ago by the Vatican emperors.

And yet there was a fairly wide expanse of mosaic floor, forming a sort of triumphal path toward a grove of cypresses. Not the sort of mosaic fashioned into pictures; no coiled and rearing asps, no fighting lions or other imperial insignia. Just thousands of buff gray stones, each about a half-inch square, and laid as tightly as ever after two thousand years. I crouched and ran a hand across its seamlessness, then followed the path to the cypresses which formed two stately rows on either side of the walk, leading perhaps a hundred feet to the sheerest edge of the cliff. No guardrail of any kind, just the vertiginous drop to the sea. Doubtless the place where the enemies were flung.

I cowered back from the edge, resting in the cypress shade as I tried to memorize the place. I assumed that the downhill trip would be quicker, but I'd already passed the first hour and more. The time squeeze throbbed in my belly, affording me no leisure to spend a lazy afternoon at this lookout, picnicking in the cypress shade. All I had was a couple of speeded-up minutes to commit this glimpse to memory. I turned reluctantly away, looking back over my shoulder as the vision receded, framed by the cypress alley.

Then my downcast eyes took note of the breaks in the pavement where cypress roots had burrowed beneath the mosaic, fissuring the surface till the beaten path was littered with rubble like a scatter of dice. I knelt and picked up a loose square of mosaic, noting how its structure was in fact a rectangular wedge, whose half-inch square of exposed surface concealed the depth of the stone, a full inch of foundation below. Presumably this shape made it easier to pack them tightly together to make a solid floor.

I didn't even have to think twice, swiftly pocketing the stone and casting about for another to bring back to Steve. The first law of ruins—*Never take anything away*—surely didn't apply to me and my thumbnail souvenirs. The winter rains would only wash away these patches of broken mosaic, burying them in the mud and weeds. No team of archaeologists was going to bother reconstructing a footpath. And yet I felt oddly guilty as I made my way over the terraces and started downhill, prickling with the worry that what I'd done was just a matter of degree. A latter-day Lord Elgin, who "liberated" the Parthenon friezes and sailed them home to England, just to keep them safe. Or those whole temples carted off stone by stone by the Germans, for the purposes of study. Leaving the ancient sites as bare as the plains of Troy.

Ruins get ruined, there seems no way around it. Even Rose Macaulay—in her sinfully delicious book, *Pleasure of Ruins*—announces with a certain breezy shrug that every ruin is in constant flux:

> . . . one cannot keep pace: they disintegrate, they go to earth, they are tidied up, excavated, cleared of vegetation, built over, restored . . .*

But that only makes more urgent one's imagining, projecting the self along the "ghostly streets" of what she calls "the stupendous past." She doesn't say how long one ought to stay and contemplate, to make the place one's own. But fifteen minutes hardly seemed enough, especially as I stumbled down the rock-strewn trail like a mad donkey, racing the clock to the harbor.

Of course Steve was right. I made it with moments to spare, looking dazedly off the stern of the tender as Capri floated away. And even then it felt like a dream, my time in the emperor's ruins. I have in the four years since managed to preserve the memory intact, or almost. The cliff-edge eagle's perch, the sweep of the sea below. What I have left besides that blinding abruptness is this fragment of gray stone rubble on my desk, a single piece of the jigsaw.

And of course the story of my adventure—so vivid in recollection that it convinces after all that fifteen minutes on the heights sufficed to make it mine. And yet, so perverse is the drift of memory, that at a certain point in time I had a change of em-

---

*Rose Macaulay, *Pleasure of Ruins* (New York: Thames and Hudson, 1984), page iii.

perors, giving credit for the Villa di Giove to Hadrian rather than Tiberius. That may seem like a minor glitch, though a century separates their two reigns. But it gave me leave to populate the pleasure-palace on Capri with Hadrian the aesthete, builder of libraries and founder of the Atheneum, the gathering-place for the intellects of his age. And to remember his passion for Antinoüs, the joyous comrade of his heart, who drowned in the Nile in his twentieth year. Temples went up in his memory, and a hundred sculpted portraits besides, to assuage an emperor's grief.

So it made a kind of cockeyed sense, to picture Hadrian retiring to his widow's peak on Capri, in melancholy contemplation of stolen love. It certainly fit my fantasies, with Steve about to follow Roger through the portal from which there was no return. Imagine my confusion, then, when I sat down to write this story and turned to my classical reference books. No mention of Capri in any of the entries on Hadrian. I grew so anxious, so unable to tell the tale without proof, that Winston brought me home from the library a book-length bio of Hadrian. Capri was not in the index, or anywhere else. A skim of the text kept throwing up details—that relations between the emperor and the boy went on for nine years (and remember, the boy was drowned at twenty); that in fact there were more than five hundred busts and statues of Antinoüs still extant, more than we have of Hadrian himself. Pictures of Hadrian's villa at Tivoli. The Pantheon. The obelisk on the Pincio.*

I was mistaken, that was for damned sure. And in the process had learned more than I wanted to know about the times, preferring to see them through the mists. I'd always understood that Hadrian had had a peaceful reign, no foreign wars or bar-

---

*Stewart Perone, *Hadrian* (New York: W. W. Norton, 1960). Frankly I hate to proffer the footnote, given the rank homophobia that permeates the discussion.

barous invasions. But it seems he proposed to found a pagan colony on the site of Jerusalem, compounding the mess by outlawing circumcision. The ensuing revolt was fearfully bloody, leaving the Jews bereft of a homeland.* And still I had no answer to who had built *my* villa on the cliffs. I began leaving messages, slightly crazy, for various scholars I knew; and was starting to dial Garry Wills in Illinois, sweating like a graduate student, when the name popped into my head: Tiberius.

Of course. 14–37 A.D., a hundred years before Hadrian. A misanthrope, Tiberius, whose "reign was one of terror, with spying, prosecutions, vengeance and suicides. His life has been painted in the darkest colors by Tacitus . . ."† Well, at least it began to make sense, those enemies flung from the eagle's perch. I'd always had a difficult time trying to jibe such ruthless abandon with my image of Hadrian, the aesthete queer. And I suddenly felt absolved of any lingering guilt about stealing two chips of paving stone from the Villa di Giove. A bad guy's lair.

But it's certainly made me reconsider what's real in the facts department of my travels. They are seamless to me after all, tight as a Roman mosaic, those moments of thundering clarity on various peaks and temple sites. In the end they have come to be strung on the single thread of my sensibility, a sort of pearl necklace of wonders—and not very many of which allowed me much more than the fifteen minutes I copped on Capri.

Oh, there are places I've gone back to numerous times, and always with a fervor to recapture, to drive the experience deeper —but that is something else entirely. And there have been occasions when I've found myself in the neighborhood of one of those places barely glimpsed, and so took a second shot. Santorini for one, the lip of the volcano; or the cloister of Saint

---

*Howatson, *Oxford Companion to Classical Literature*, page 258.
†Ibid., page 498.

Trophime in Arles. Second visits that were usually more in the nature of happy accidents than the keeping of a blood promise. We may make any number of silent vows to return, to relive the flash of the sublime and maybe even the glint of a lost self. But it's like Frost's oath at the fork in the wood, swearing he'll keep the road not taken for another day—

> *Yet knowing how way leads on to way,*
> *I doubted if I should ever come back.*

We are booked for a one-way passage, no return.

The older we get, the more does it all sink in. That the trail of grain we've dropped in our wake like Hansel and Gretel has been snatched and eaten by crows. A postcard arrives from one of these magic places—dashed off by a friend who may even have gone there at our insistence—and the frozen picture is suddenly more real than our own recollection. Surely the tower was on the other side, and couldn't you see the ocean from the top?

All the more reason to get your fifteen minutes right, so the place will remain indelible, no matter if the fog of memory mirror-reverses the tower. We're told that Gertrude Stein always sat with her back to the view, so everyone else would have to face her. She also says somewhere that all views pale after fifteen minutes. She may be right: that we can't take in too much sublimity at once, or that our nature is to reduce all experience to banalities, shrink the world to postcard size. Myself, I'm after a different sort of quarter-hour—a willed intensity that meets its destination halfway, at a certain romantic pitch. Not the historian's way, by any means. Or the archaeologist's, who tries so hard not to clutter the site with preconceptions; dispassion before all else. And certainly not Gertrude's way, whose life was a sort of monumental site all by itself.

But then if it takes a whole lifetime for you to get to Mont-Saint-Michel, you have already watched the tide come rocketing in at thirty miles an hour—in your head, anyway—a hundred times. The towering rock in the bay has been waiting for you as long as you have been waiting for it. The spiral climb through the medieval quarter, the looming church at the summit, a labyrinth of stairs to reach it. What's to disappoint? The wild romantic burnish you've endowed it with turns out to be the truth. In a minute you have peopled it with a flock of white-robed monks, and you seem to float in air as lightly as the Archangel himself when you gaze up at his gilded figure high at the top of the roof, seeming to spin on tiptoe, the pirouette of faith.

Who needs dispassion?

Not that it always works, by any means. In Noel Coward's *Private Lives,* when Elyot and Amanda come face to face on their separate balconies, they're on their honeymoons with different people. They talk inanely about what they've been doing since their messy divorce. Elyot stutters through the tale of his trip round the world, Amanda nervously filling in the gaps.

> AMANDA: And India, the burning Ghars, or Ghats, or whatever they are, and the Taj Mahal? How was the Taj Mahal?
> ELYOT: Unbelievable, a sort of dream.
> AMANDA: That was the moonlight, I expect; you must have seen it in the moonlight.
> ELYOT: Yes, moonlight is cruelly deceptive.
> AMANDA: And it didn't look like a biscuit box, did it? I've always felt that it might.
> ELYOT: Darling, darling, I love you so.*

There's always that chance that you've traveled across ten meridians, only to find a biscuit box. It happened to me once in

---

*Noel Coward, *Three Plays* (New York: Grove Press, 1979), page 209.

Greece, where otherwise all holy places met my expectant heart with garlands of laurel. Steve and I lay stupefied with jet lag in an Athens hotel, waiting to board the rusty tub that would take us round the Aegean. Dr. Monette decided there was time to rent a car and drive to Sounion, the cape round which all ships made their way to Athens, the headland crowned by a temple to Poseidon. We ended up in a belching Austin mini that smelled like a farmer's truck, as if the previous lessee had been a flock of chickens.

The suburbs of Athens went on and on, concrete-slabbed apartment blocks that looked like barracks. By the time we reached the sea we were at last in open country, though it was scarred by the grisly villas of the rich. I began to have that anxious gnaw that we wouldn't be back in time, the bane of so many of my expeditions.

Then we came round a bend, and there it was on the crest of a hill—a small hill, as it turned out—its eleven Doric columns honey-colored in the heat shimmer of the summer sun. We parked and walked up past a shady *taverna* to the brow of the hill, and instantly I had to rein the poetry in. Not that I was expecting another Parthenon; and the eleven columns are no less eloquent for being built to human scale. But I'd always assumed it perched on a high cliff, rather like the Villa di Giove, so its beacon fires would be visible halfway to Crete.

No such height. Really, a bare stone's throw from the water below. And the columns themselves were covered nearly top to bottom with the names and initials of previous visits, scoring into the soft stone. Not exactly tagged by the spraycan sort of graffiti, but violated all the same. Unguarded, unprotected, an easy drive for a day-tripper. *Not enough, not enough,* my heart cried out.

But I withheld from Steve the hollow of my disappointment, especially since he'd had enough after *five* minutes, and moved to take cover in the arbor of the *taverna*, nursing a Greek beer. I wouldn't let him order any food—for Christ's sake, he wanted a salad, an invitation to crypto and who knew what other microbes. It was why we traveled by ship in the first place: to exercise some control over the food, as much as to accommodate a steamer trunk of medicine. I sat with my back to the temple, surely a blasphemy against the sea god. Glancing over my shoulder, it wasn't so bad; at least you couldn't see the hieroglyphs of graffiti at this distance.

And so we wended our way back to Athens in a smut of traffic. The pang of Sounion had mostly receded within a day's sail, as we crossed the Sea of Marmara to Istanbul. But a jumble of myth still rattled around in my head for a couple of days, the ashy taste of failure. For it was at Sounion that Theseus was meant to change his ship's flag from black to white, to signal his father the king that he'd made it home alive from Crete and the Minotaur's cave. When he forgot to change the flags, grief-stricken Aegeus threw himself off the Acropolis, to be dashed on the rocks below. Of course all of this transpired in mythic time, pre-history, and who knew if I had the facts right anyway, mostly a rehash of Mary Renault. But the feeling persisted, like a low-grade fever, that I'd somehow flunked my exam in ancient history.

The curative for which is prescribed most movingly in Cavafy's cautionary poem, "Ithaka"—

> As you set out for Ithaka,
> hope your road is a long one . . .
>
> May there be many summer mornings when,
> with what pleasure, what joy,
> you enter harbors you're seeing for the first time;
> may you stop at Phoenician trading stations
> to buy fine things,
> mother of pearl and coral, amber and ebony . . .

Keep Ithaka always in your mind.
Arriving there is what you're destined for.
But don't hurry the journey at all.
Better if it lasts for years,
so you're old by the time you reach the island,
wealthy with all you've gained on the way,
not expecting Ithaka to make you rich.

Ithaka gave you the marvelous journey.
Without her you wouldn't have set out.
*She has nothing left to give you now.**

It is hardly Sounion's fault, in other words, that it doesn't quite measure up to one's lush specifications. Perhaps the disappointments have their purpose too, to balance all those blurred mirages with a laser dose of focus. And anyway, it's not the end of the journey yet. So you reset your sights and keep going.

I needn't have fretted at all, really. The next day out of Istanbul, we turned south along the coast of Asia Minor, passing the windswept site of Troy, now utterly vanished. We stopped in the channel that lay between Lesbos and the mainland, then headed inland through miles of tobacco fields to the citadel of Pergamon. I didn't know a thing about it—neither a smatter of fractured history nor the slightest image, mirage or otherwise—and so I quickly reverted to the studious schoolboy, clamoring over the ruins and checking out every cistern, every cornerstone. It was just as Cavafy foretold, the pleasure and joy of an unknown harbor.

So we circled the watery cradle of the Aegean, dolphins leaping about our bows, and nothing looked remotely like a biscuit box. The voyage even provided one of those rare second sightings, at Delos, where Roger and I had idled away an afternoon six years before. An island that's uninhabited, the birthplace of

*C.P. Cavafy, *Collected Poems*, translated by Edmund Keeley and Philip Sherrard (Princeton University Press, 1975), pages 35–36.

Apollo, and a major center of commerce in the ancient world because it served as a crossroads for ships bound east or west. We landed just after sunup—Steve and I, his mother and sister—on the very first tender launched from the ship. So there was a moment when the first group of us had it all to ourselves, an unbelievable stillness as the sun caught fire and dazzled us with a whole world of ruins.

Just inland from the harbor there's the wreck of a colossal statue to Apollo. Two boulder chunks, one still faintly tracing the shoulders and chest of the god, the other his hips and buttocks. And if you needed another reminder that *nothing gold can stay* (Frost's rueful formulation), the guidebook reproduces a drawing from 1673. Apollo still had his head then, and the pelvis supported his thighs, almost to the knee. Too big for the plunderers to carry away, and left to the surer plunder of wind and rain. *Memento mori* for days.

But the lake of the god's birth remains, weed-choked now, more mud than water. Guarded by lions sent in tribute from Naxos, a row of heroic marble beasts sitting on their haunches, mouths agape with roaring. Disintegrating in front of your eyes, two of them legless and propped up on steel rods, and yet the guardian stance and the roaring somehow seem immutable. Though the sun god has long since departed—streaking the sky in his chariot, shedding gold in his wake—the watch of the lions remains at full attention, profound as the saints on Gothic cathedrals awaiting the Second Coming.

But enough slides of my summer vacation. You get the picture: a boy who never went further afield than a two-weeks' cottage at Hampton Beach, just across the border in New Hampshire. All the while reading too many books about faraway places with strange-sounding names. And I know exactly why I've been pulling out the scrapbooks these last weeks, because the journey has suddenly stalled. The road doesn't go any further, the bridges are all washed out, or maybe I've just gone overboard in a squall. So I gather all my memories of the places barely glimpsed, the stamps that litter my passport, and wonder if all together they prove that I went the distance.

I understand that there isn't a final exam for this. The map studded with pins is purely subjective, and in any case nowhere near the driven pace of travelers like Paul Theroux and Bruce Chatwin, who seem to live exclusively on trains and tramp steamers, or riding camelback up the sacred mountain. And needless to say, they don't stop for fifteen minutes once they get there; they stay until they've drunk it to the lees. Graham Greene in Haiti, or making the rounds of the leprosaria in the Congo. D. H. Lawrence in Italy, Joan Didion in El Salvador. Exploring the places where people live beyond the end of the road.

Of course it's no secret why my ticket has expired. Because of AIDS, the borders have narrowed further and further, till whole continents are now in the red zone. Forget Africa, or China or India, the Middle East, any place equatorial. Even when I was asymptomatic, still juggling a hundred T-cells, I crossed off half the world for being too dirty. Couldn't eat the meat or the milk or the fruit, let alone drink the water. There was something almost xenophobic in all this, overcaution that looked at the world through a glass bubble of paranoia.

As if one couldn't get just as deadly sick in one's own backyard. A doctor friend has warned me never to order water in a restaurant, or anything with ice, comparing such recklessness to dipping a cup of water from the Nile. For a year and a half I haven't touched a shred of lettuce. As soon as I heard the only safe way was to put the leaves in a sinkfull of water with a tablespoon of bleach, I went off salads entirely. Odd, because I always thought of myself as rather intrepid.

Not anymore. What amazes me now about the memory of Capri is that stride up the rocky path, especially the final burst to the summit. That's the real Dr. Monette, prepped for so many years by his daily trot on a treadmill, never out of breath for a minute, no matter how steep the trail. Now it's all come down to this swollen leg of mine, too much exertion reducing me to a hobble by day's end. Even with the addition of a stretch surgical stocking, refined last week with a garter belt that girdles my waist and clamps the stocking in place. Till I am something of a cross between an atherosclerotic old lady and a genderfuck chorus boy in a kickline. Winston calls the orthopedic shop—staffed as it is by a trio of sturdy Eastern European women—Frederick's of Poland.

We still hope the new chemo is going to work, shrinking the KS lesions in the lymph system so that the dammed blood will circulate again, flushing the swamp of edema. And I mustn't complain too much, because I've made it to the next breakthrough—a chemo regimen that has no debilitating side effects. After four doses it has flattened out and faded most of my surface lesions to mere gray smudges, but it hasn't yet drained the swamp. That tenacious "leg thing" again, so far eluding all the tricks of oncology, leaving a whole division of us limping about.

This may be the best we can do with it, sighs Dr. Thommes, pressing his thumb to the swell above the knee, leaving a dent in the flesh. *Just keep it from getting worse.*

These strange plateaus of dying, where you bargain away your dancing days as long as it doesn't get worse. If that sounds like rank self-pity, it's not intentional. I've watched this swelling go up and down for nearly a year with a certain abstractedness, testing my body mechanics, still trying to outwit the creep of complications. Staying in charge, riding my illness as if I was breaking a horse, till lately anyway. If there's one specific moment when I *got* it, all my denial suddenly in tatters, it would be last month in the Canadian Rockies.

Still on course for Ithaka, even then. A new direction—due north—and a territory unexplored, at least by the likes of me. We flew to Calgary and then headed by car for Lake Louise. We put up at the old railroad hotel at the southern end of the lake, a drop-dead view from our room of mountain peaks on either side and the glacier itself pouring slowly over the northern edge. It was the runoff that had created the opalescent green of the water in the valley. Picture-perfect.

And for some reason I had neglected to factor in my limitations. Though I could stroll along the shore for a quarter-mile or so, hiking was out of the question. But that was the way I'd always done it before—trailing up out of the valley in hiking boots, bound for the high country. In Yosemite with Roger, straight to the top of Bridal Veil by switchback. Or the Lake District, the high green hills above Grasmere, no one else at the top. The hiking having the salutary effect of letting the mind go blank; or if lost in thought, with none of the petty clutter of the quotidian.

So what was I supposed to do now, give all that up for a lawn chair and a lap robe? Waiting for a nice cup of bouillon, to be served by one of these ridiculous waiters in Swiss costume. The big event of the day being the blowing of a ten-foot Alpine horn on the near shore, "God Save the Queen" barely distinguishable from "Amazing Grace."

O Canada. Winston and I both did our damnedest not to let it separate us, trying to keep me from feeling left behind. He who had the force and energy to climb these peaks to the sky, but mostly chose to stay by me. We pretended it didn't much matter, the view from the top. And made the return trip by way of Banff National Park, the road through the vast old-growth forest quickened by elk and bighorn sheep grazing the verges without fear. We were a zoo to them, I suppose. There certainly wasn't any doubt who was caged and who was free. Home again after six days' northern passage, we finished the Canada roll of film on the front porch, mugging in our tuxedos because we were on our way to a benefit. It was those prints that couldn't lie, that seemed to show the first faint trace of the skull beneath my skin, no matter how wide I grinned. Not that I wasn't grateful for the journey, energized even, but this was the trip that would always bear an asterisk, proof that I couldn't leave AIDS behind. I remember the exact evening in '84 when César announced, *I've traveled enough*—a man whose life map was a veritable pincushion of countries traversed and holy sites. Whose only destination out-of-town from there on in—besides Death, that is—would be our house, a quick shuttle hop from San Francisco. I remember promising Roger we would get to Paris again somehow, even after he'd lost his sight and mostly lay curled asleep, Puck on the floor beside him as if they were having a sleeping contest.

Did I believe that promise? I suppose I didn't. More than anything it served as a goad to memory and happier days. Besides, I saved my deepest passion of disbelief for the opposite scenario, that our traveling days together were over—that we had no way anymore *to change our ideas,* as the French would put it. Grounded.

I was beginning to dread that I'd have to venture alone along the next leg of the journey, but not prepared to concede the point. For the lie to my intrepidness was this above all: that it wasn't any fun to be anywhere without someone to share it. Hardly the sort of attitude that will see you solo through the jungle or up past fourteen thousand feet. I'd certainly done my share of that sort of thing in my closeted days, sitting hugging my knees as I took in the view from the High Corniche, or the coral chambers visible far out to sea from a hilltop in the Bahamas—lonely, lonely, lonely. No escape and no vacation.

Somehow it all got intertwined with being in love. It surely was no coincidence that traveling changed from the dutiful checklist of masterpieces, confided to my journal to somehow make it last; changed the day I met Roger, like everything else. After that it didn't signify anymore what the destination was.

Paris through his eyes, England through mine, and then we were in uncharted waters, sailing along in our sub-sub-compact —the deal being that the one not driving was navigator and guide. Maps so cumbersome they needed a charthouse to be laid flat, flapping about till neither of us could see the road ahead. Or reading aloud the deathless prose of the Green Guide so we'd know what to look for when we arrived.

Once, on a delirious ride through fields of lavender and the dusty green of olive groves, I read to Roger from Ford Madox Ford, his love song to Provence:

> It is no doubt that illusion [of the permanence of London] that made my first sight of Provence the most memorable sensation of my life and that makes my every renewal of contact with those hills where grows the first olive tree of the South almost as memorable. It is as if one wakened from a dream of immortality to the realization of what is earthly permanence.*

Or the sudden detour into Wales to check out the ruins of Tintern Abbey. I bought us a pocket Wordsworth before we left Bath, and Roger in his mild voice recited the great poem of return:

LINES

COMPOSED A FEW MILES ABOVE TINTERN ABBEY,

ON REVISITING THE BANKS OF THE WYE DURING A TOUR,

JULY 13, 1798

We crossed the mouth of the Severn just after Bristol—its tall industrial chimneys clouding a sulfurous sky—and entered Wales. Immediately the landscape changed, electric green and pastoral, as if we had crossed the border into a reverie.

When we reached the Abbey itself, there were no other cars and no guard in the kiosk. I hadn't realized how lofty the ruins

---

*Ford Madox Ford, *Provence* (New York: Ecco Press, 1979), page 88. A reissue of Ford's text, first published in 1935.

would be. Though all the stained glass had been ripped from its windows when the abbeys were routed, the tall Gothic windows were filled instead with the green of the hills surrounding. The roof and its beams were gone, long burned away, a conflagration that took the wood paneling off the walls, along with the choir stalls and the altar. But the bare stone of the great nave was otherwise unbroken, buffered by graceful side aisles. And someone had had the aesthetic sense to mow the grass that had overrun the floor paving, so that you walked through the soaring ruins on a carpet of velvet lawn.

It was such a perfect realization of the poet's faith, the Divine-in-nature—a pagan temple now, given over to the earth, monument to the ecstatic urge of life:

> ... *something far more deeply interfused,*
> *Whose dwelling is the light of setting suns,*
> *And the round ocean and the living air,*
> *And the blue sky, and in the mind of man . . .**

Roger and I wandered around with our heads tilted skyward, tracing the noble arches and gables against the cloudless blue. I must've stopped at a windowsill to jot a note in my journal—still trying to freeze these spots of time, maybe even outdo the poet himself. Such vaunting self-assurance in those days. I finished mid-sentence, hitting the wall of clichés perhaps, but mostly trying to catch up with Rog. Behind the church proper were the briefer remains of the dormitories and kitchens and stables, easier for the anti-papist vigilantes to pull down and obliterate. You could just make out traces of a cloister, with a well in the center.

I don't remember what sparked it, but suddenly I was in a panic that I'd lost Roger. I called his name in the green stillness, then started racing about—the camera like a millstone round

*William Wordsworth, *Selected Poems and Prefaces,* ed. Jack Stillinger (Boston: Houghton Mifflin, 1965), page 110.

my neck, my journal as dead as Latin. In seconds I had him tumbling down a well, or crushed by a falling gargoyle. No other tourists, still no guards, and the fear of being alone more overwhelming even than the worry. I kept crying out, through a choke of sobs, the green river valley and the godless church as alien as the moon. *Please, please, don't let him be hurt.*

And then he emerged calm as you please from the restrooms by the kiosk, his smile fading as he walked toward me, seeing the wrench of relief in my tear-streaked face. Of course I felt a fool by then, but he gently soothed my residual hysterics, promising over and over that he was fine. I still don't know where it came from, some long-forgotten memory of being separated from my parents in a crowd. But eight years after Tintern Abbey—when Roger was running the gauntlet of tests at UCLA, on the brink of his diagnosis—the rattle of the same terror overtook me like an old wound leaking pus. Except this time it went on and on, unrelieved, for the whole twenty months of his illness. And I often think that Tintern Abbey was by way of an AIDS rehearsal, a premonition of mortality that I had no words for yet.

The incident doesn't appear in the postcards we sent, nor anywhere in the travelogue we regaled our friends with. Tintern Abbey still stood in its emerald vale—stands there yet consecrated to Pan and a host of nymphs and satyrs. The "something far more deeply interfused" lies in its green reassurance that nature stands apart from the sully of human fret and bother. In other words, the canker in the rose was all mine, baggage I brought with me. What I would lose if Roger disappeared was the reason to go in the first place.

This is a problem inherent in mixing up the journey with being in love, but it's the price you pay for being a certain breed of romantic. The "earthly permanence" slaps you in the face, mocking your little span of seasons, your fleeting embraces.

So it ought to come as no surprise that the world is vastly

bigger than all your travels, but it does. Maybe it's like reading. Starting as far back as my twenties, when my nose was always in a book, I recall the particular shiver of melancholy, realizing I wasn't going to get through the whole of Henry James. Or Dickens or Proust or Tolstoy. There just wasn't time. Even at a clip of a hundred pages a day, a vivid sense of my own limits. But I shrugged it off, assuming that was one of the boons of getting old. A rocking chair on a white picket veranda, dozing your way through *The Wings of the Dove*.

And then to be startled to find that life has become more interesting than books. Besides, you get by perfectly fine on the ones you *did* read. Even as the details start to go, you can talk with practically anyone on sheer enthusiasm alone, from *Persuasion* to *David Copperfield*. In the end it becomes enough to say how marvelous something is, how true and close to the bone. After all, the people you're talking with have mostly put off from the shore of books themselves, paddling through the shoals of life with barely a thriller on the nightstand.

Is that how traveling goes, once you realize you're not going to make it to Benares (those burning ghats) and Machu Picchu? Do you just fall back on where you've been, embroidering your stories till everyone you know has heard them twice over? Or do you prove you've gone the distance by becoming a small authority on the 7th Arondissement, or all the bronzes of Florence? Making up in sophistication for what you lack in mileage. Well, whatever works to dull the longing for what you've missed.

And anyway, you've eavesdropped enough in cafés to hear a lifetime of witless remarks by people who scarcely notice where they've been, just a string of hotels and bad meals and the shopping terribly disappointing. Like the man who approached the moral philosopher Sidney Smith* and rapped his walking stick

*1771–1845, founder of the *Edinburgh Review*.

on the pavement. "You see this stick, sir?" the gentleman boasted. "This stick has been around the world."

"Indeed," replied Smith. "And yet, still only a stick."

Sometimes what catches your fancy is the oddest detail, yet it leaves a deep notch on your walking stick. In Crete in '84, Roger and I took a solitary tour of the wrecked Minoan palaces from the Bronze Age. Four altogether, I think, and all destroyed at once, circa 1400 B.C. The palace of Knossos being the most impressive, excavated and partially restored by Arthur Evans— throne room intact and the dolphin frescoes swimming in a stairwell. So many rooms and corridors that one story has it that Knossos itself was the Labyrinth of myth. And all obliterated, so the theory went, when the great volcano blew in Santorini ninety miles away, causing a tidal wave that reached Crete within six minutes, wiping out the whole Minoan civilization. Stupendous past indeed.

Contemporary scholars have questioned the drama in all of this, convinced that the decline of the palace culture was slower, a matter of centuries. True though that may prove to be, I find I prefer the *feeling* truth of tidal wave and wipeout. But then, don't come to me for the facts.

Some miles inland is the palace of Phaestos, high above the Mesara Plain, and exquisitely unrestored. We had that one all to ourselves as well—pure luck of the draw in the Ithaka business. Up the great stone staircase into a maze, most of it leveled to the bare foundations. And in the rubble of a storeroom, according to the pidgin English of the guidebook, had been found the so-called Phaestos Disk. The sole surviving evidence that the Minoans had a written tongue as far back as the Second Millennium B.C. (but still no clue what it said).

Later that day in the Heraklion Museum, our eyes glazed over by rooms full of potsherds, we came to the dusty case where the Phaestos Disk, the thing itself, was on display. About the diameter of a Frisbee, the clay perhaps two inches thick, and the whole surface deeply incised with pictographic signs laid out in concentric circles. There were learned guesses as to what it might say, but none held water. No one knew whether it was meant to be read from the center outward like ripples, or spiraling in from the rim.

All I know is that it possessed me, holding me fixed as Roger moved on to the snake-goddess fetishes. For a little while there I actually convinced myself I could crack it. Without the slightest training in hieroglyphics, this layman who could scarcely keep Hadrian and Tiberius straight thought he could best the experts. Spellbound, getting nowhere, I must've stood there fifteen minutes waiting for a brainstorm. And then I left it with that same look over my shoulder, regret/desire, with which I'd walked away from the brink in Capri. Knowing how way led on to way; knowing I'd never be back.

The feeling returned full force a couple of years later, when a friend who'd studied Greek at Oxford told me about his tutor. An ancient dusty man with patches, wreathed in pipe smoke, whiskers in his ears, and fluent in an astonishing range of dead tongues. He happened to mention one day that he was working harder than he ever had, trying to translate all that was left of some nameless forgotten language, a slew of clay tablets somewhere between Sumerian and Aramaic. For decades he'd tried to pass it on, but it was too hard for even the best of his students. Apparently you had to know everything else to get that far.

The truly lost, the undeciphered, constitute a kind of backlash as you gather in the world, destination by destination. I never expected in my lifetime to watch a country disappear—and then the bloodshed exploded in Yugoslavia. But wait. What about our day in Dubrovnik—Steve and I—the pristine medieval port, pride of the Adriatic? Clocktower and lion fountain, steep cobbled alleys radiating off the square, old women watering their windowboxes, or leaning on the sills and smiling like cats dozing in the sun.

Do the places you've visited still exist in your head if they're reduced to smithereens? Are they anything more than postcards after all, doomed to go to the grave with you? People sigh over Beirut, the Paris of the Middle East, a distant look of confusion in their eyes, bereft of words. Or the old Tibet of the monks, the vision of Lhasa riding the clouds, the palpable Zen of desire-lessness. Before China began the genocide.

Now we hear that the Muslim fundamentalists in Egypt want to rid the place of all Dynastic monuments, from the Pyramids and Sphinx to Karnak and Abu Simbel. Graven images and, sin of sin, built before Mohammed. Or the leveling of the temples in Cambodia, of *everything* in Cambodia, a whole country committing suicide till the ground was sown with salt. There is no end to this, of course. The world is coming apart at the seams, and traveling at all becomes more rarefied every year, increasingly a fixed route to places certified intact and free of terrorists.

Elitist almost by definition, a sort of Orient Express in spirit if not in fact—brass-fitted and bottled snowmelt and turndown service at night. The planet as theme park, Disneyized. McDonald's at the intersection of Boulevards St. Germain and St. Michel, across from the ruins of the Cluny Abbey, itself built on the ruins of a Roman bath.

My cousin Harry came back from Orlando in a cosmopolitan rapture: "First night we had dinner in France, next night in Italy, then England . . ."

And his wife piped up, "Don't forget Japan.

This is not the same, itinerary-wise, as Marlene Dietrich standing on the rail platform, face like alabaster in the night, declaring: "It took more than one man to change my name to Shanghai Lily."

The sure sign of a travel snob: *been there, done that.* The world-weary affectation, preferably in profile and white dinner jacket. It's not till much later, the end of the line, that you realize what a wandering quest it's been, willed or not.

And when life brings the journey to a halt—by incapacitation, or the fares grown too stiff, or maybe just sheer exhaustion—it doesn't matter whether you're my cousin Harry or Shanghai Lily. No extra points for mileage covered or trekking the inaccessible. The bags go up in the attic, you let your passport lapse. You can actually feel the loss of motion. Then you look out the window and realize here's your Ithaka: home at last. Cavafy again, the final stanza:

> And if you find her poor, Ithaka won't have fooled you.
> Wise as you will have become, so full of experience,
> you'll have understood by then what these Ithakas mean.*

Not that I've come to a full stop, not quite yet. Two weeks after Canada we were on our way up the coast to Big Sur, the place I've returned to most, the one that never disappoints. Not fifteen minutes but days and days over the course of two decades, till I could trace every mountain slope and rocky point blindfolded. But if Canada broke the denial that AIDS could be left behind, the Big Sur trip took it further—a conscious flight from the war zone, hobbling like mad, bandages trailing like streamers. An old friend had died of AIDS the week before—and then a week after, one of my doctors. Both were diagnosed at the same time I was. We'd been on the very same tightrope without a net, like the Flying Wallendas, and now I was teetering all alone. I went to Big Sur to convalesce a failing spirit, but knowing full well it would be no cure.

Still, the first two days were a breath of air. By dint of prosthetics—Polish stocking and garter belt—I managed the full two

*Cavafy, *Poems*, page 36.

miles to Molera Beach, where I sat propped on a driftwood log with Winston at the mouth of the Big Sur River. Neither of us haunted by good-byes or the last look over the shoulder. The wildness didn't mock us or embrace us. It simply let us be. But by the third day there was business that wouldn't wait—matters of the will, the charitable trust, the selling of the house in a mummified market. Death and Taxes. Necessary though it may have been, it left us shaken and out of sorts, squashed by details. We hiked back to Molera the next day, more somber, more distant. The landscape withholding entry into the full sublime— the hawk's slow circle, the pound of the sea, the place where the deer lay down their bones.

This last a sanctuary that Robinson Jeffers stumbled on while hiking one day, a dappled glade with a clear stream running through, the ground littered with rotting bones and antlers —where the old and wounded came to die.

> *I wish my bones were with theirs . . .*
> *. . . why should I wait ten years yet, having lived sixty-seven,*
> *ten years more or less,*
> *Before I crawl out on a ledge of rock and die, snapping,*
> *like a wolf*
> *Who has lost his mate?—I am bound by my own thirty-year-old*
> *decision: who drinks the wine*
> *Should take the dregs; even in the bitter lees and sediment*
> *New discovery may lie. The deer in that beautiful place*
> *lay down their bones: I must wear mine.**

It's more than a bleak refusal to kill himself. It's that trapped detachment that goes with being human and dying alone. As if I were looking at Molera Beach, the place that has always stopped my heart, from behind a wall of glass. As if I were looking at the memory of it and not the thing itself, all the while wearing my bones like a straitjacket.

---

*Robinson Jeffers, *Selected Poems* (New York: Vintage Books, 1965), pages 100–101.

Next day we recovered our equilibrium at Tor House in Carmel, the house that Jeffers built with his own hands, boulder by boulder from the shore below. A site I hadn't visited in ten years, and then with Roger. So: one of those rare second chances. A shipshape house like a captain's quarters, with the bed by the window that Jeffers had chosen to die in from the beginning. (Otherwise used as the guest room, its true purpose withheld from the guests for politeness.) Out in the garden, the house-dog's grave: *Haig, an English bulldog.*

But more impressive than anything else, the tower at the foot of the garden—Una's tower, built for his wife as a private retreat. A tower out of a Viking saga, or from the Irish cliffs of Moher. Not thirty feet high but grander than any watchtower, and built forever, its sea-smooth boulders more massive than even the house stone. With a secret stair inside, besides the main one spiraling up the outer wall to Una's dayroom. A unicorn's lair, with a narrow double window looking out over the bay—where Jeffers swore he saw a merman once, in the turbulent winter tide, breaching the white-capped swell for a moment's look at man's estate, then diving down again.

And the final climb to the parapet, with only a swaying chain for a railing, a hawk's perch where the wind blows through you. Mythic in a word, but a myth whose gods were profoundly mortal, a man and a woman in love. No mixup here: Winston and I had found our way to a monument that was in feeling equal to the twining of our two hearts. A place of inexpressible human permanence. You come away with the understanding that Jeffers's work is twofold—the poems and the tower—like the source of two rivers.

Then coming back to L.A., and still so restless. Some part of me long since finished voyaging, yet compelled by a near atavistic urge to be a moving target, to make Death have to run and catch me. The crisis of it came upon me unawares, unbidden.

Winston had made plans, months before, to attend the annual gathering in the wild of a group of radical faeries. Nine days at the start of August, and the only time in the year when we were apart. I had no right to ask him to forgo it, in part because I wasn't sick in bed, but more because it was something he'd still have when I was gone.

This isn't to say I wasn't terrified to be left to my own devices —a late relapse of the Tintern Abbey panic and its progeny, the helpless waiting for Roger and Steve to die. Except in my case now the waiting was for me. There was nothing for it but to stay in motion.

So I asked Victor, who'd fled to Europe with me after Steve died (sniffling our way through cathedrals), and again last summer to Big Sur when Winston was off in the woods. Left it to Victor, my last best friend, to check out the availability of Alaska, a cruise along the so-called "Route of the Glaciers." Only to find that every ship was booked to the gills. For Alaska was suddenly terribly in, the prudent alternative to IRA bombs in London, tour buses strafed in Cairo, the hijacked Mediterranean.

We had to settle for a waiting list, then a cabin the size of solitary confinement in the bowels of the *M/S Sagafjord.* But you won't be spending time in your room, the travel mavens assured me. *Oh yes I will,* I thought, *nearly all of it in fact. My* role model being Simone Signoret in *Ship of Fools,* overripe with her own mortality, who didn't quite speak anyone else's language, returning home to certain imprisonment. No question about it, I needed the cabin more than the ship.

Then at the last moment there was a cancellation on the Officers' Deck at the top of the ship: somebody must've punched his ticket early, keeling over into his Samsonite even as he packed his woolens. We left for Vancouver on the 28th of July, Winston having packed me for every eventuality, practically sewing my name in my socks. With a vast pharmacopoeia of medicine in tow, an igloo just for the IV bags, steeled for a grilling at the border. Mr. Monette, could you tell us why you're traveling with forty syringes?

But Victor and I squeaked through without a hitch, and in any case I had a letter from my doctor listing all my meds though omitting to mention AIDS. This medical report had been required by Cunard regulations, to be turned over to the ship's doctor on embarkation. We were still surveying our cabin, with its own private terrace above the lifeboats, bags not yet delivered, when the doctor himself appeared. A Swede who seemed to sport a permanent curl of distaste beneath his weedy mustache, who pointedly avoided shaking my hand. He'd clearly been clued in about the "A" word, and was most concerned that our ship's insurance would cover evacuation by chopper.

"These little ports we visit," he said amiably, "they've never heard of these drugs you're taking. They're not equipped for . . ." Words failed him, but not that curl of distaste.

So he left us to our lepers' quarters. Never having caught *Ship of Fools,* apparently, or he would have had Oskar Werner for *his* role model. With his steely blue eyes and stiff-spine air of melancholy, who ended up in a shipboard liaison with the Countess (Signoret) because they shared a sense of last chances, the common tongue of irreversible fate. I did not expect our Doctor Strindberg to be slipping into our cabin for a little mid-ocean action.

But at all events, that is how it happens that I am still on the road to Ithaka, having long since learned what Ithakas mean. A landscape more staggering every day: hundreds of miles of forest right to the water's edge, lighthouses blinking time, range on range of snowy crags. And the glaciers themselves—forbidding, unyielding, cracking like rifle fire, calving icebergs into the floe-strewn bays. Not to take anything away from such exaltedness, but the main characteristic of Alaska—at least to us in

Cabin 14—is the blankness. Rather like that blankness of a day's hike, nothing else in your head, nature over mind—desirelessness, with or without the Zen.

Thus we abjure all shore excursions, lacking the team spirit, and in eight days have managed to meet not one of our fellow passengers. I have seen one eagle perched in a treetop, and the barest wave of a humpback's tail as it dove back under. No mermen of course, but these are not times that lend themselves to heroic sightings. I feel no abiding curiosity about the people or their history, having had my fill of Manifest Destiny and the tribes that have perished beneath its wheels. At least I won't get the facts wrong. No, the blankness will do just fine.

The rest is the force of memory, with its tricks and illusions, but all my own till my lights start winking out. My various fifteen-minute epiphanies have been in the nature of chance encounters, revealing things I didn't know I was searching for. Strung together, they provide a kind of window into what endures, even as it melts or shakes to bits in a quake or falls to Huns and marauders. That is how *I* see it anyway, the trail of a single traveler. Certainly no one is going to follow my peculiar progress as if it's a useful guidebook from A to B, let alone Z. My fact-free cultural map is harmless enough, no threat to the vast theoretics of ethnographers and linguists, art scholars, all those patient diggers.

My own map is freely drawn in sand, and the tide is coming in. I am unencumbered of any grand thesis, mostly ignorant of antithesis, but achieving a private synthesis all the same, though I can't really put it in words. No tablets left behind to be deciphered. Only this: the cost of a one-way fare is life.

Not that my random journey is going to help me die any easier, except insofar as I don't feel cheated, not of the world out there anyway. My hoard of destinations suffices to let me imagine the rest. Srinagar, Cuzco, Persepolis: name it and something flickers, like and not like somewhere in your head, a paradox yes, but devoutly wished.

And I will not give up a scrap of it without a fight. For years I used to save postcards, dozens of them from everywhere, because they did a better job of freezing time than my poor blind-spotted camera. Eventually they filled the secretary in my bedroom, a jumble of disorder, potsherds from a myriad of civilizations. Last year I started to use them for notecards, filling three or four at a time and tucking them into envelopes, my only real correspondence anymore.

I don't usually choose my views with any forethought: someone will get the Piero frescoes in Arezzo or a silversword cactus from Haleakala, House of the Sun). I linger a little before parting with anything Greek, however, directing these more pointedly to friends who might get a flicker of their own. I understand I am spending my loose change, scattering it to the four winds, but careful not to lighten my ballast so much that I will float away.

No, I am only sending out announcements of my last stand. When I will be taken kicking and screaming from this phenomenal world, intractable to the last, ferocious in surrender:

> With all my might
> My door shall be barred,
> I shall put up a fight,
> I shall take it hard,
>
> With his hand on my mouth
> He shall drag me forth,
> Shrieking to the south
> And clutching at the north.*

*Edna St. Vincent Millay, *Collected Poems* (New York: Harper and Row, 1956), pages 206–207. Lines from "Moriturus."

Big talk, but what do I know? I may go yet like Jeffers in the bed by the window,

> When the patient daemon behind the screen
> of searock and sky
> Thumps with his staff, and calls thrice:
> "Come, Jeffers."*

About three months ago the consummate traveler, Freya Stark, died at the age of one hundred. "The first Westerner to journey through many regions of the Middle East,"† voluminous writer and scholar and wit. Spoke Turkish and Arabic before she hit puberty. Sometimes rode for weeks by camel and donkey. Fierce anti-fascist, and hardly a country she didn't write about.

In her ninety-third year, a reporter asked her about that final port of call. She was busily on her way to Spain, but stopped to give it some thought, for Death was doubtless the ultimate foreign country. "I feel about it," she said at last, "as about the first ball, or the first meet of hounds, anxious as to whether one will get it right, and timid and inexperienced—all the feelings of youth."‡

Exactly. When no amount of intrepidness will see you through, nor the globe in your study that fairly bristles with pins. You are suddenly in the clutch of a new adolescence, watching your helpless body change before your eyes, hating every blemish, waiting with dread to see where you will next put your foot in it. The no-way trip. Be glad, I suppose, if your morphine dreams at the end are a slide show of your voyages, superimposed on the shining faces of all your beloved companions who've matched their steps with yours. No telling, since

---

*Robinson Jeffers, *Poems,* page 54.
†"Dame Freya Stark, Travel Writer, Is Dead at 100," *New York Times,* 11 May 1993.
‡Ibid.

that final Northwest Passage is all one-way. Postcards not available; or else they get lost in the mail.

Meanwhile, incredibly, there are miles to cover yet. Just now we are cruising the Kenai Fjords, a starfall of scattered islands worthy of *The Odyssey*, the lairs of giants and the call of Circe, the flashing sun on the water leaving us muzzy as the Lotos-Eaters. Tomorrow we land in Anchorage. Long past journey's end, however you look at it. But the road isn't done till it's done, and so you go on till Death catches up. Soon enough. But you wouldn't have missed these islands, surely, even if they're the last. Oh, especially if they're the last.

Contributors

LUCY JANE BLEDSOE is the author of the novel *Working Parts,* winner of the 1998 American Library Association Gay/Lesbian/Bisexual Award for Literature, and of *Sweat: Stories and a Novella,* a Lambda Literary Award Finalist. Her work has appeared in *Fiction International, New York Newday, Ms. Magazine, Aethlon, Northwest Literary Forum,* and in many anthologies.

FELICE PICANO's first book was a finalist for the 1975 PEN/Hemingway Award. Since then he's published sixteen books and has won the 1984 Poetry Society of American Chapbook Award, a 1985 PEN Syndicated Fiction Award, the 1995 Ferro-Grumley Award for Best Gay Novel, and the 1996 Gay Times of England Award. His newest volume of memoirs, *A House on the Ocean, A House on the Bay,* is a Lambda Literary Award Finalist.

JAMES BALDWIN (1924–1987) is the highly acclaimed author of many novels, including *Go Tell It on the Mountain, Giovanni's Room, Another Country,* and *If Beale Street Could Talk,* and many collections of non-fiction, including *Notes of a Native Son, Nobody Knows My Name, The Fire Next Time,* and *The Price of the Ticket.*

BRIAN BOULDREY is author of *The Genius of Desire* and editor of *Wrestling with the Angel* and the *Best American Gay Fiction* series. He is associate editor of literature for the *San Francisco Bay Guardian.* His fiction and essays have appeared in *TriQuarterly, Harvard Review, modern words, Flesh and the Word, James White Review,* and *Zyzzyva.*

HANNS EBENSTEN has arranged and conducted tours, cruises, and expeditions to remote and unusually interesting places for more than forty years. His book *Volleyball with the Cuna Indians* was published by Viking Press in 1993 and he is a regular contributor to the *Society for Hellenic Travel Review, Archaeology,* the *Advocate, Our World,* and other travel publications. When not climbing mountains, crossing deserts, and hacking his way through tropical rain forests, he lives in Key West, Florida.

PHILIP GAMBONE is the author of *The Language We Use Up Here* (Dutton) and the forthcoming *Something Inside So Strong: Conversations with Gay Fiction Writers* (University of Wisconsin Press). He teaches creative and expository writing at the Harvard Extension School. His book reviews appear frequently in the *New York Times*.

ERASMO GUERRA grew up in the Rio Grande Valley of South Texas. His work has been published in the anthology *New Worlds: Young Latino Writers* and in the *James White Review*. He lives in New York City and eagerly awaits his next big trip.

ANDREW HOLLERAN is the author of two novels, *Dancer from the Dance* and *The Beauty of Men,* and an essay collection, *Ground Zero*. He lives in north Florida and is working on a collection of short stories to be published in 1999. His next trip will be to the Salmon River in Idaho.

CARY ALAN JOHNSON is a Brooklyn-based author and activist. He has worked and traveled throughout Africa and was field officer for the United Nations High Commissioner for Refugees in Congo during the Rwanda/Burundi civil conflicts.

ADAM KLEIN is the author of *The Medicine Burns* (High Risk, 1995), and with Thomas Avena, the artist monograph, *Jerome: After the Pageant* (Bastard Books, 1996). His stories have appeared in *Men on Men 5* and *Best American Gay Fiction 1996* (Little, Brown). A novel, *Tiny Ladies,* will be published next year.

MICHAEL LOWENTHAL is the author of a novel, *The Same Embrace* (Dutton), as well as stories and essays in the *Kenyon Review,* the *Crescent Review,* the *New York Times Magazine,* and more than a dozen anthologies, including *Best American Gay Fiction* and *Men on Men 5.* He is the editor of many books, most recently *Gay Men at the Millennium* and *Flesh and the Word 4.* A 1990 graduate of Dartmouth College, he now lives in Boston.

RONDO MIECZKOWSKI's poetry and prose has received grants from PEN USA West, the City of Los Angeles, and the Massachusetts Artists Foundation. He is editor of *Sundays at Seven: Choice Words from A Different Lights' Gay Writers Series* and the author of the gay romantic comedy *Leather Jacket Love Story,* released by Goldeco Pictures in 1998.

PAUL MONETTE (1945–1995), a National Book Award recipient, is the author of the memoirs *Borrowed Time: An AIDS Memoir* and *Becoming a Man: Half a Life Story*, as well as the novels *Afterlife, Halfway Home, Taking Care of Mrs. Carroll, The Gold Diggers, The Long Shot*, and *Lightfall*. His essays are collected in *Last Watch of the Night*.

MICHAEL NAVA has written a series of mysteries featuring a gay criminal defense lawyer named Henry Rios, for which he has won five Lambda Literary Awards. The most recent book in the series is *The Burning Plain*. The essay presented here is from a memoir in progress called *The World of Born*.

ACHIM NOWAK is a native of Germany who now lives in Manhattan. "Jungle Fever" is an excerpt from *Graham Greene Is Dead*, a forthcoming memoir. Excerpts from this book have appeared in the anthology *Men on Men 6* and the *James White Review*. Recognition for his work includes a PEN Syndicated Fiction Award, as well as fellowships from the NEA Inter-Arts program and the New York Foundation for the Arts. Achim Nowak is also a founding member of Three Hots and a Cot, a collective of queer writers in New York.

JOE ORTON (1933–1967), a playwright, is author of *Entertaining Mr. Sloane*, which won the London Critics' "Variety" Award, and of *Loot*, which won the Evening Standard Drama Award, among other plays.

DARIECK SCOTT is the author of *Traitor to the Race*. His work has appeared in the anthologies *Shade, Ancestral House, Flesh and the Word 4*. He is currently a Ph.D. candidate in Modern Thought and Literature at Stanford University.

DAVID TULLER is the author of *Cracks in the Iron Closet* and a former *San Francisco Chronicle* reporter. His work has appeared in the *New York Times*, the *Nation*, the *Advocate*, and other publications. He is one of the founders of the National Lesbian and Gay Journalists Association. Tuller lives in San Francisco.

EDMUND WHITE, recipient of a Guggenheim Fellowship and the Award for Literature from the National Academy of Arts and Letters, was made a Chevalier de l'Ordre des Arts et Lettres in 1993. For *Genet: A Biography* (1993), he was awarded the National Book Critics Circle Award and the Lambda Literary Award. His other books include *Forgetting Elena, Nocturnes for the King of Naples, States of Desire: Travels in Gay America, A Boy's Own Story, Caracole, The Beautiful Room Is Empty*, and most recently, *The Farewell Symphony*.